Love, Disappointment and Other Joys of Life

Love, Disappointment and Other Joys of Life

Helen Lyne

Love, Disappointment and Other Joys of Life

In memory of my father Allan Lyne

Love, Disappointment and Other Joys of Life
ISBN 978 1 76109 114 8
Copyright © Helen Lyne 2021
Cover image: Mary Wandler from iStock

First published 2021 by
GINNINDERRA PRESS
PO Box 3461 Port Adelaide 5015
www.ginninderrapress.com.au

Contents

A Gentleman and a Scholar

It was the first day of the school year. Christine tried to still her shaking hands. Although approaching retirement, she always felt apprehensive before meeting a new class. She supposed it must be like stage fright for an actor. She wasn't too ambitious. She just wanted her students to manipulate language well and appreciate the authors they were studying.

Striding towards the classroom, she asked herself questions that toppled the self-confidence she'd built up over the holidays.

Am I getting too old?

Will I still be able to communicate with them?

Will they start by hating Shakespeare and end up hating him even more?

Will they laugh at my jokes?

Will they even recognise when I'm making a joke?

Outside the classroom which thumped with raucous male voices, she paused and admonished herself.

Look firm, organised and full of energy.

Don't let them think you're a fluffy teacher who wants to be their friend.

Go in swinging. (I can use clichés if I like, but only to myself.)

The streaming of English classes according to students' subject choices meant that her Year 11 class had nineteen boys and six girls. They'd all chosen physics, chemistry and another science and the highest level of maths. They'd probably do their maths homework every night just for the joy of it. English would be their lowest priority.

A decision had to be made in the next few seconds. How would she make her entrance – come in unobtrusively and wait for silence, or burst in and take command? Both techniques were part of her repertoire. The first was her natural style. She opted for that.

She strolled into the classroom, skirted a group of boys grieving in trumpet tones about having to walk out of this morning's epic surf, put her books on the teacher's desk and stood beside it, a pencil clasped loosely in her hands. She thought of the pencil as a symbol of her authority – a fantasy no student could possibly imagine. Silence fell in pockets until 'Bloody English – bor-ring!' from a sneering male voice tumbled into a void.

Everyone found a seat, all the girls together near the front. Christine let the silence stretch out. She had no more than a few seconds to decide what she'd say first. Would she do her blood and sex speech? If she didn't get it right, it could alienate some and offend others. If she did it well, she'd hook in most of them from the beginning. When one of the girls flicked her eyes at her neighbour, Christine knew she had no more time.

Keeping her voice low so the students had to strain to hear, she began. 'English is compulsory and Shakespeare's compulsory too. From what I've just heard, at least one of you isn't too happy about that.'

There were a few grudging smiles, but most waited warily for what was to come.

'Why do teachers inflict Shakespeare on students? Many think it's because he uses beautiful poetic language. *I* think it's because he knows about love and sex, violent jealousy and head-kicking ambition. He knows that families are breeding places for resentment and hatred.'

The girl in front of her stopped twirling a strand of hair around her finger. Had Christine hit a sensitive spot? She hoped so.

'He knows that men lust after women and some women are cock-teasers.'

There were several intakes of breath. She was launched now and gambling that no one would quote her to a parent who'd complain to the principal.

'His characters get drunk and wipe themselves out. They commit murder and treason. In battle, the mighty warrior, Macbeth, unseam'd his enemy "from the nave to the chaps".'

Faces went blank.

'Can you imagine the physical strength and sharpness of sword required to skewer a man through his navel and slice upwards though his sternum, jaw and skull? Can you see the spurt of blood and spray of teeth after the sword is swung in a sideways curve and the head, with eyes wide open, is lopped off and falls into the steaming pile of its own intestines?'

She raised her clasped hands above her head to illustrate the sword's upward movement. Without her intending it, her pencil flew in an arc and bounced onto the linoleum floor tiles. The prolonged clattering could have made her words sound ludicrous. Instead, it intensified the dramatic atmosphere she was trying to create.

All six girls were grimacing. A couple of boys sniggered.

Christine resumed. 'Shakespeare's audiences loved that sort of thing. We'll be discussing themes like morality in leadership and why horror is so attractive. As for Juliet, she was thirteen years old. Some adults think passionate love isn't possible at that age. If they read Shakespeare with sensitivity, they'd remember their youth. He certainly makes me remember mine.'

Now warmed to her topic, Christine scanned the room to identify the student whom she wanted to target, someone who was already sending signals of challenge, someone with whom she must establish contact in order to make the class worthwhile, both for him and for the others throughout the year. There he was, inevitably in the back row. His eyes were lowered. She couldn't tell if he was listening. He was slumped in his chair, hands in pockets, legs sprawled in front of him, no tie, acne, hair gelled into spikes – oozing indifference.

Fortunately today the words flowed easily. Except for the boy in the back row, the students were listening to her with full attention. Some were leaning forward. One boy had his mouth open. Confident her timing was right, Christine switched from the sensational to the mundane. She explained the activity for the rest of the lesson and gave homework. A boy groaned at the word homework.

Christine stared at him over the top of her glasses and said, 'No one else is protesting. You're obviously the only person in this class who dislikes homework.'

There were half-smiles at the small joke. The boy at the back shifted from a backwards slump to a forwards slump. He put his elbow on the desk and propped the side of his head on his fist. His desk was bare of paper and pen.

Christine borrowed a pencil from one of the girls and called the roll. When she called out a name, the student either said 'Here' or put up his hand. The boy at the back raised his forefinger. She was lucky to see the gesture at all.

When the bell rang, Christine quelled the rising hubbub. 'The bell is a signal for me to end the lesson. It's not a signal for you to stampede out the prison gates. I insist on some courtesies. At the end of every lesson, I say goodbye to my students and I expect them to say goodbye to me. My younger classes stand up and say goodbye in unison. I like to say goodbye to my older students individually. It takes just a couple more minutes and I don't expect there to be a scrum by the door.'

As the students filed past her, she remembered some of their names. She asked the others to give her a tag to help her remember.

The gelled spikes shuffled in the queue with hunched shoulders and eyes staring over her head. His non-uniform jeans were so low on his hips that she saw the top of his underpants. Although she remembered his name from the roll call, Christine debated.

Will I address him by name?

Will I ask him for a tag?

What will make the bigger impact?

As he passed her, she said, 'Goodbye, Brad.'

He raised his chin slightly. It could have been an acknowledgement or he could have been checking the crowd milling outside in the corridor. Suddenly he turned, made a sharp arm movement like an uppercut and jabbed her pencil in front of her face.

Removing it from his loose grip, she was glad she hadn't flinched. 'Thank you, Brad.'

He looked appraisingly down at her uplifted face and then joined three other boys who were waiting for him. One of them she knew to be the top maths student in the school.

He'd taken the initiative! *He'd* made contact! Joyfully she accepted the challenge. His behaviour today was stereotypical of a rebellious adolescent. What she had in mind, the words and the concept, would make him shudder, but she'd keep the cliché to herself. From this moment on, she'd work towards turning him into a gentleman and a scholar. If she succeeded, he'd be armed with the best weapons possible to be a rebel warrior. He'd skewer his opponents with courtesy and linguistic ingenuity. Maybe – and she refused to quash this fantasy – even a bit of poetry!

An Artist and His Models

I do things on impulse. Sometimes I regret them. I can't say yet if I'll regret inviting this couple to dinner. They moved into the apartment across the hall last weekend.

During the canapés, the girl, Lily, chats about the similarities and differences between my place and theirs. Having exhausted that topic, she looks at the photo on the piano and asks, 'Is that your husband?'

'Yes. He died some years ago.'

'Oh, I'm so sorry.'

The boy, Patrick, looks at me and says nothing. I call him a boy. That's patronising. He must be about twenty-three.

Lily asks, 'And you have a cat?'

In the photo, Dennis is holding our little grey moggy.

'Not any more. Misty died of old age earlier this year and I'm not sure if I'll get another one.'

'Oh dear.'

Two deaths within minutes of walking through her new neighbour's door – she's momentarily mute! She pulls herself together. 'I have a Norwegian forest cat. Have you ever seen one?' She chatters about the species and Fluff's endearing habits.

I try to read Patrick's expression. He watches her as if he's listening with his eyes.

After I put the main course on the table, Patrick holds my chair and then pushes it under me. It's a ceremonious, old-fashioned gesture for a young man. Lily chirps relentlessly through the meal. Long before we tackle dessert, I've tuned out and am happily observing them as a couple.

Her prettiness comes from vivacity and youth. She flicks a glance at Patrick every now and then, but mostly behaves as if she's gossiping with a girlfriend. Her T-shirt clings to her full breasts in a way that would disturb a young man. Whether she's looking at him or not, he keeps his eyes focused on hers. At the same time, however, he's attentive to me, passing bread and topping up my wine.

His thick black hair frames a pale face. His eyes are large and almost black. When I was young, I would have loved to have a man watch me with such intensity. Lily seems oblivious to both his gaze and his attentiveness. He passes whatever she needs the second she starts looking for something on the table. During the dessert, he relaxes a little. Occasionally, he smiles at me as if we're complicit in appreciating Lily's brightness.

'Oh, and Jean,' she suddenly exclaims with total disregard for whatever it was she's just been talking about. 'Isn't that a pretty picture?'

'My granddaughter, Evelyn, painted it.'

'Oh, that's so nice.'

I accept the niceness as referring to my having a granddaughter. The painting is a blur of roses or camellias (I can't tell which and don't dare ask) and muddy daisies. The gloomy flowers clash with the bold acrylics in the other paintings in the room.

When Patrick speaks, I'm startled.

'You like the postmoderns?'

'Some.'

He opens his mouth to continue, but Lily interrupts.

'Oh, Jean. I haven't told you. Patrick's an artist too. He's in a gallery, aren't you, Patrick? You should see them. He doesn't do flowers, not till I asked him to do some for me and he did them in watercolour. They're so pretty. They hang over our bed. You must come and see them.'

From his smile, I guess Patrick is endorsing the invitation, perhaps not to their bedroom but to the gallery. That's a lot to read into a smile, but I find myself paying more attention to his silence than to her prattle.

When I offer coffee, he says, 'Lily doesn't drink coffee. Thank you, Jean. What a sensational meal! Fabulous lemon tart! You went to a lot of trouble.'

I did go to trouble. I love cooking. I'm chuffed at the compliments.

Over the next few days, I don't see either of them. I'm curious but don't want to be a nosy old woman whom young people avoid.

On Saturday morning, there's a knock on my door. Patrick is standing there holding a bottle of red wine.

'Hi, Jean. This is for you. It's a bribe.'

He smiles and, old fool that I am, my heart flutters. I'm happy not to have lost my susceptibility to male charm.

'I'm going to ask you a favour.'

I'm ready to do just about anything.

'If you're not going out later on, I wonder if you'd feed the cat. We're going to a party in the Blue Mountains and we'll be away overnight. Lily worries when the cat's routine's upset.'

He grins and I take that to mean 'but I don't give a shit'. He wouldn't use that word to me. Not yet.

At five o'clock promptly, I use the key Patrick's given me and enter the apartment. The cat does figure eights around my feet as I walk straight along the bare passageway to the kitchen. His dinner is in the fridge in a bowl marked 'Fluff'.

As he eats, I lean against the sink. The kitchen is exactly like mine before I had the renovations done – brown plywood cupboards, linoleum tiles of indeterminate colour, brown wooden venetians. Nothing indicates that anyone cooks or is interested in food. There is, however, a shiny, formidable-looking coffee-making machine.

The doors off the passageway are all closed. I'm tempted to snoop, to look at the flowers in the bedroom, but don't. The one beautiful thing I see is the cat. He's three times the size of my little Misty, magnificent and sleek, with a leonine ruff around his neck. Fluff! What a silly name! I'm sure Patrick didn't call him that.

'Have you finished, Emperor?'

The bowl is clean. The cat sits beside it, licking his paw and washing his face. Fluff, Emperor – he doesn't care – as long as someone feeds him.

Over the next few months, we get into a routine, Patrick and I. He brings wine and once or twice a week I feed Emperor. Lily never asks and never thanks me when we meet in the hallway.

One day I say to Patrick, 'Don't buy any more of that tuna soaked in prawn juice. Emperor doesn't like it.'

'You mean Fluff, don't you?' His mouth isn't smiling, but his eyes are.

'Yes. Sorry. He's so beautiful and regal.'

The next time Patrick knocks on the door, he hands me a small sheet of soft cardboard and there he is, Emperor: magnificence in three purple strokes.

'Oh, Patrick! I love it!' I hope he doesn't think I'm gushing. I look at the small flourish under the tip of the tail. 'I'm so pleased you've signed it. Thank you.'

My granddaughter, Evelyn, pops in after uni that afternoon. Seeing Emperor on the piano, she does a double take. 'OMG, Gran! A Patrick Gill! Where did you find that?'

'The young man across the hall did it for me.'

She positively squeaks. 'What? He lives here!'

'No. Across the hall.'

'He's the one – you're feeding his cat and you didn't tell me!'

'He's well known, is he?'

'Well known!'

She waves her hand in helpless illustration of the enormousness of my ignorance and collapses on the sofa, mouth agape. When words tumble out, I discover that Patrick Gill is the hottest thing in the current young art scene.

'Will you introduce me to him? Can I come with you when you feed the cat? When will that be? What's he like? Have you seen what he's working on? Does he have a studio in the apartment?'

'No, you can't come with me and he has a girlfriend.'

Evelyn raises her chin. 'I'm interested in his art.'

'And I was Rubens' mistress.'

She flounces towards the front door, swings around and bounces back to give me a smacking kiss. She says, 'I bet you would've been if you'd been alive then.' She dashes out, slamming the door behind her.

I hear the lift come and go several times. I look through the peep-hole and she's standing there, hoping, no doubt, that Patrick will materialise.

I google his name. He has several works in a gallery in Manly. On the drive there, I think of Evelyn's murky paintings. Each time she does one, I hang it in my living room among the postmoderns that she loathes. Her enthusiasm for Patrick may have more to do with the smouldering young man pictured on his website than with his art.

The gallery has allocated a whole wall to Patrick's two paintings. Just as well. Their colours cannibalise whatever else is there. Menacing purples, inferno reds, ferocious greens and flame yellows send me reeling backwards and then, from a distance, morph into landscapes with writhing mountains, snarling rivers and contorted trees. I can't look at them for long. I do some shopping and come back. They're disturbing. I love them.

After Christmas, when Lily and I are waiting for the lift one day, I see she's pregnant. I ask when the baby's due.

'The end of March. Mummy and Daddy will be coming down to help me.'

'Where do they live?'

'Ipswich. They're thrilled, of course. They don't like Patrick but Daddy's going to have to be nice to him. You'll have to meet them. I've told them all about you and how you look after Fluff.'

Fluff? For a moment I don't know what she's talking about.

'Mummy says I'll have to get rid of him. It's dangerous having a cat around a baby.'

I don't like the sound of Mummy and Daddy.

The next time Patrick brings a bottle of red, his face is drawn, his normal luminous pallor a pasty grey.

'Sorry, Jean. We're going to Ipswich for the weekend. Could you do both Saturday and Sunday please?'

'With pleasure. Why don't you bring Emperor over here? Then he'll have some company.'

'That'd be great!'

His face lights up.

'I wonder…actually. I've just had an idea. Um, you wouldn't like to keep him, would you?'

I'm so surprised my mouth forms a silent O.

'Sorry. Sorry. You've been so kind as it is, but…'

'Won't you come in and have a coffee?'

He glances at the door of his own apartment and answers with forceful fervour. 'Yes, please.'

I grind the beans and ram them into my espresso pot.

Patrick leans against the kitchen cupboard, arms crossed. 'That coffee smells so good. I haven't had one at home for weeks. Lily can't stand it.'

I take a guess and say, 'We can have it on the balcony and you can have a cigarette if you like.'

He looks at me with wide-eyed wonder. 'You smoke?'

'I used to, but I don't mind the smell.'

'I'd love a smoke, but I've left the makings at a mate's place. Lily can't stand tobacco either. Doesn't seem to mind paint and turps.'

'I don't have any makings, but I always keep a pack for emergencies.'

We move to the balcony. I'm delighted to see Patrick relax and prop his feet on the edge of a plant pot.

'What about it, Jean? It would be a tremendous favour. I know you like him. He's Lily's cat but she's lost interest in him since she's having the baby. I've grown fond of him. He's a great model. I could pop over and do a sketch every now and then. Add to the one on the wall.'

'And have a coffee and a cigarette.'

'And have a coffee and a cigarette. So you'll take him?'

'As a boarder until you get something permanent sorted out. I travel too often to have a cat.'

'Fair enough.'

He grins and I know I've just signed the adoption papers. Our conversation about Emperor's diet and idiosyncrasies is interrupted by a voice at my front door. Evelyn is popping in to see me. Patrick stands to shake hands. He's polite. She gushes. I'm horrified. She sounds as vapid as Lily. Does Patrick have the same effect on every young woman? He heads for the front door. As I open it for him, he winks. I feel like giggling. At this moment, the only difference between Evelyn and me is forty years.

In the first week of March, I'm having coffee on my balcony when an old Commodore pulls up in the street. The couple who emerge can be no other than Mummy and Daddy. Mummy carries a shiny pink plastic bag with kittens cavorting over it. Later that afternoon, I meet kittens, Lily and Mummy and Daddy at the lift. Lily introduces me as the cat lady who's adopted Fluff.

Mummy simpers, 'Helloooo.'

Daddy reaches past his stomach to crush my hand. He's surprised when I crush back. (Playing piano in a jazz band maintains useful strength when a bully shakes my hand.)

I set out for the corner shop and kittens and co. drive off in the Commodore.

I don't see Patrick for about a week. Emperor appropriates the sofa during the day and my bed at night. Evelyn's visits change from haphazard popping in once a fortnight to every second day. One evening when she's stayed until almost midnight, I snap off the reality show she's not watching, put her mobile and car keys in her hand and accompany her to the lift. She's breathless with expectation. When the lift arrives, she wistfully scrutinises its emptiness. Finally she steps in and takes a long time searching for the button for the ground floor.

For no particular reason, I glance towards Emperor's former apartment and see the door's slightly ajar. Impulse urges me to knock. The door swings open. A light flicks on in the passageway and Patrick appears.

'Hi, Jean. Come in.'

'I'm sorry I woke you.'

'You didn't wake me. I'm working.'

'I won't interrupt but the front door was open.'

'Really? I probably didn't shut it properly. Don't like closed doors. People should be free to come and go.' He waves me into the apartment and then into his studio.

Canvases and easels lean against a wall; brushes, rags, jars and other paraphernalia are neatly arranged on floor-to-ceiling shelves. The painting he must be working on faces away from me. A painting with a black slash across it is propped against a green plastic garbage bin.

Patrick gestures towards a wine rack and bar fridge under the window. 'Glass of wine?'

'Yes, please.'

'Shiraz okay?'

'Fine.'

'I have some cheeses. Just bought today. Lily doesn't like the smell.' He takes a goat's cheese, a slab of blue and a crumbly cheddar out of the fridge and puts them on a wooden board spattered with dried paint.

All the furniture, including the upright chair he invites me to sit on, is utilitarian; the orderliness is soothing. The only jarring note is the black slash. I peer at the painting. Patrick swings it onto an easel. It's a nude of Lily. She's breathing! If I touched her arm, it would be warm. Her breasts and belly glow with tenderness. Shockingly, her eyes are as lifeless as the black slash.

'Lily's father did that. Burst in while I was working and grabbed the brush out of my hand.'

I gasp.

'Told me he wouldn't have his daughter put on display for arty-farty

snobs to snigger at. Said if ever I came near her or his grandchild, he'll
have me arrested. Dunno what for. He'll think of something.'

'What did Lily say?'

'Nothing.'

'Nothing?'

'He told her to get in the car and she went. Seemed quite happy
about it.'

He swings the portrait off the easel and puts it on the floor facing
the green garbage bin.

Unable to identify what he's feeling, I prod gently, 'And now?'

'She'll be back when I'm more famous and making more money
than I do now.'

I detect neither regret about her departure nor eagerness for her return. And now I understand the intensity of his gaze when they came
to dinner. There'd been no love involved. He was studying how to paint
her. I gesture with my wine glass to the painting he's working on.

'Come and have a look.'

It's another portrait, a much older woman with wrinkles quilting
her face. As with Lily, the skin is alive. I'm drawn to the eyes. One moment they smile at me sardonically, the next they flash with a curious
kind of passion.

His voice comes over my shoulder. I'm surprised by the uncertain
tone. 'You don't recognise her?'

I feel breathless. 'The eyes startle me.'

'Why?'

'There's so much depth in them.'

'You've never looked at yourself in the mirror?'

'I've not seen that.'

He's silent for so long, I need to break the tension. 'Your portraits
are so different from the landscapes in the gallery.'

'I paint what I see.'

I turn my head. His face is next to mine. Oh, that I were forty years
younger! I've always liked dangerous men. I also have a sense of self-

preservation and didn't marry one. The dangerous man standing next to me wants everything: models, a patron, fame, money and a hand to stroke his ego and his sex. I've been his model, albeit unknowingly. When I tell him that the double bass player in my jazz group happens to be the owner of Gallery X in Paddington, I've no doubt he'll brush aside the forty- year gap. Vanity will prevent me from letting him. Nevertheless, I think I'll make Patrick my first. It takes talent to identify talent. I like the idea of being recognised as a patron who promotes exciting young artists. I'll try to prevent it but Evelyn will probably throw herself at him as a model. I'll pat her heaving shoulders when he replaces her with the next model or when Lily returns.

He won't replace me.

He rolls a cigarette and dims the lights. The ruby softness of the shiraz illuminates our conversation about his future and my place in it.

An Unwanted Guest

Whenever I dream, I'm aware I'm dreaming. I know when I'm having a nightmare. Four weeks ago, I dreamed I was in a small boat on Sydney Harbour. The sun was shining, wavelets splashed cheerfully against the side of the boat and sails floated in the distance. I didn't know if my boat had oars or a motor. It began to rock. I leant over the side and saw a large black shape swimming beside me. The shape deliberately bumped the side of the boat with its flank. Although it did it only once, the thumping echoed around the boat for a long time.

I woke up, my heart racing. I was covered in perspiration. It's rare at my age to perspire. Was I having a heart attack? They say you feel pain with a heart attack. I felt no pain.

Faintly I heard, 'Miss Richardson.'

Could that be right? Maybe I was still dreaming.

Again, 'Miss Richardson.'

No one calls me that any more, not my GP, not my audiologist nor any of the other medical people who look after me.

'Miss Richardson.' Thump. 'Miss Richardson.' Thump.

Dim light framed the blind. Moonlight? Dawn? Normally, I sleep through the whole night. That's one of the advantages of being hard of hearing. Noise doesn't usually wake me.

I threw back the bedclothes, shrugged on my dressing gown and went to the window. I didn't want to draw attention to myself by raising the blind, but the gap between the blind and the window frame is about four centimetres wide. It's the right angle for me to look down onto the porch below. I could see the top of a woman's head and her bare shoulders. She was young. She must have been freezing. It was July, a Friday night. When I go to the Opera House on a Friday or Saturday, I see all the young women wearing skimpy dresses and very high heels for their night out. This one must have had high heels. She wasn't steady on her feet. She made a fist and thumped on the door.

'Miss Richardson.'

It had to be an ex-student. From time to time, a woman with several children in tow stops me on the street and says, 'Oh, Miss Richardson. I'm Jodi, from the class of '99. You haven't changed at all!'

I'm tempted to say, 'So at the age of fifty, I already looked seventy?'

I didn't turn on any lights. I've lived in this house so long I can feel my way around. I went down the stairs, careful to miss the one that slopes and creaks. The tall clock in the hall said two-forty. I looked at the woman through the peephole in the front door. The house was built long before peepholes were invented, but I've made a few improvements. The face, although contorted by distress and the curved glass, was vaguely familiar. I couldn't find the name. It would come.

When I unlocked the door, it swung open so quickly I jerked back to avoid being hit. The woman must have been leaning on it. She stumbled inside and steadied herself with one hand on the wall. She swayed and shivered. Her face, shoulders and legs looked blue, the effect of the moonlight on her bare and freezing skin. She had on a short flared skirt, a bustier top and stiletto-heeled shoes. No handbag. She clutched her phone.

I closed the door and switched on the hall light, Taking one of my coats off the stand, I draped it around her shoulders.

She gave me a smile made ghastly by her extreme pallor and dark smeared lipstick. 'Thanks, Miss Richardson. I knew you'd help.'

'This way, Geraldine.' (The name had indeed come.) 'Let's get you warm.'

'Bathroom,' she gasped.

I moved to her side and took her arm to guide her. She was taller than me and heavier. The thought flashed through my mind that if she fell, she'd bring me down with her. She was young enough for a fall not to have serious consequences. I'd have broken bones. As she took a step,

I noticed blood on the inside of her thigh and calf. Had her period come unexpectedly or had something terrible happened?'

'Would you like me to call a doctor?'

'Nah.' The tone was a brush-off.

I wondered about calling the police. She smelt of something. It wasn't marijuana. I'd smelt that often enough on my students. With the cocktail mixtures young people drink nowadays, it could have been alcohol. I doubted it. If I called the police, she might be in trouble. Or perhaps she was a victim. I'd wait until I knew more.

She spent a long time in the bathroom. I had time to go upstairs, put in my hearing aids and get Dad's pyjamas and dressing gown out of the wardrobe in his old room. None of my clothes would fit her and his would be warm. I made up the sofa bed in the living room. I was about to knock on the bathroom door when she opened it and stood swaying. Her pallid face showed she'd made an almost successful effort to remove her make-up and she'd cleaned her leg. She held her phone against her chest.

'Here, put these on,' I said. 'They'll be nice and warm. The sofa bed's comfortable. There's a bottle of water on the small table beside it.'

She stripped and stepped away from her shoes and two items of clothing. She didn't have any underwear. Again I wondered what had happened to her. She pulled on the pyjamas and wrapped the dressing gown around her, not once letting go of her phone. I walked beside her to the sofa and lifted the sheet and blankets.

She flopped onto her back. 'Thanks, Miss Richardson.' And she was asleep.

I went upstairs, grabbing the banister to haul myself over the creaky step. If Geraldine had been raped, shouldn't I call the police? Too late now. She'd been in the bathroom. Somehow I suspected that her underwear hadn't been ripped off. She hadn't worn any. No handbag? The girls I've seen dressed up in the city have either a tiny jewelled purse or just their phone.

I got into bed, too agitated to sleep. Geraldine must be about twenty-five, twenty-six years old. She was in my last Year 12 class. That was eight years ago. I don't remember exactly what I wrote on her first semester report, but it must have been something like 'Geraldine is an intelligent student who shows a deep understanding of the texts during class discussions. If she did more than the minimum amount of work that she's doing now, she's capable of earning excellent results.' In other words: brains but no effort.

The report prompted her father to make an appointment to see me. He hadn't come to parent-teacher night. He said, 'Missed it? Didn' know it was on. Gerry's gotta tell me this stuff. Can't keep track. Work all hours. She knows that. Hafta – with her mum gone. An' there's her baby sis. Eight she is.' He took the carefully folded report out of his pocket and pushed it towards me. 'Didja see what the others wrote?'

Mine was the most positive of all the comments. He sat crumpled on the other side of my table. He wore jeans and a blue and green flannelette shirt. His hands were rough and grimy with the kind of dirt that can't be removed with shower gel.

I had insisted that Geraldine be present, but regretted it straight away. She sat as far from him as possible while technically still being at the table. During the whole ordeal, she didn't look at him once. I was used to teenagers being embarrassed by their parents. Geraldine appeared to be ashamed. I felt sorry for him and for her too, even if she was being a nasty little snob. I didn't know what he meant by her mother being gone. Had she died? Or had she left him with the two girls?

So many questions then and now. Why had Geraldine come to me tonight? Was it the convenience of the bus stop? My students knew where I lived. My house is on a stop on the direct route between the city and the school. They often saw me get off the bus, cross the footpath and open the front gate.

What about tomorrow? I'd cook a decent breakfast. She could have one of Dad's jumpers. I hadn't been able to give all his clothes away after he died. Maybe his tracksuit pants wouldn't be too big.

I woke up with a start. The sun was shining around the edges of the blind. If I didn't get up and into the shower straight away, I'd be late for my bridge club. And then I remembered. I had a guest.

I flung on my dressing gown and went downstairs and into the lounge room. Geraldine wasn't there. The bedclothes looked as if she'd just jumped out of them. I went to the bathroom. Empty. In the kitchen, my phone charger was on the table. I keep it in the dresser drawer. Perhaps I'd forgotten to put it away. I'm inclined to forget small things nowadays. Otherwise, she must have opened drawers. The possibility that she might have been snooping gave me a funny feeling. I wouldn't have minded if she'd taken food. Nothing in the fridge or the pantry had been touched.

I searched the whole house. She'd gone. Good! Remembering the politeness she used to show in the classroom, I knew she had manners then. She'd apparently forgotten them. I had a few harsh thoughts while I folded the bedclothes she'd scrambled out of. Dad's pyjamas had been tossed onto the brass guard in front of the fireplace.

I didn't mention Geraldine's visit at bridge. I'd stopped talking about my students not long after I retired. I used to talk about the amusing things they did, their cleverness and their successes at university and in their careers. One day I saw two women roll their eyes when I started another student story and that was the last one I ever told. Goodness knows what the bridge players would make of Geraldine. They'd probably not approve of my letting her stay the night. I didn't want to be lectured about what I could or should have done.

I had a quick shower, got dressed, skipped breakfast and picked up my keys from the hall table. They felt light. I went through them. Garage, shed, car, letter box, back door – they were there. The front door key was missing. I felt the hair rise on my scalp. Had Geraldine asked, I might have given her a key. No, I probably wouldn't have. I don't know. It would have depended on how she'd asked. But now, I didn't want her coming back.

Fortunately, the house is old. Although I never use them, there are sliding bolts at the top and bottom of the front door. I slid them into place. When I turned to pick up some loose change for coffee from the brass bowl on the hall table, it appeared not to be as full as yesterday. Maybe I was misremembering that too. I left the house through the kitchen, making sure I locked the door behind me.

I didn't linger after bridge. I was anxious to get home, to repossess my house, so to speak. I opened the kitchen door and froze. On the table there was a half-eaten pizza in a takeaway box. I closed the door softly behind me. I didn't lock it. How many people were in the house? Maybe only one, but how would I know? Luckily, I was wearing soft soled shoes. I peeped into all the rooms on the ground floor and checked the front door. The bolts were still in place. The brass bowl on the hall table was empty. In the lounge room, I looked at the poker beside the fireplace and hesitated. I'd never hit anyone in my life. Wasn't I being a bit melodramatic?

I crept up the stairs, missing the creaky step. All the doors along the hallway were closed. There was a light under one of them. Dad's room. I stood outside it and knocked lightly. How ludicrous! Here I was, in my own house, knocking at the door of my dead father's room, behaving with good manners towards an unwanted guest! There was no answer. I waited and knocked more loudly. I was trembling, more from mounting anger than from fear. I turned the handle slowly and eased the door open. The blind was up and the sun was streaming in. Dressed in a grey tracksuit, Geraldine sat cross-legged on the bed. Her grubby runners rhythmically tapped the white counterpane. With her phone in her lap and buds in her ears, she was unaware of my intrusion. *My intrusion!*

I hung onto the door and shouted, 'How did you get in?'

Startled, she turned to look at me. She removed one bud and held it as if intending to put it back immediately.

'How did you get in?'

'The window was open. I climbed the tree.'

We stared at one another.

I broke the silence. 'Are you okay? You were bleeding yesterday.'

'A bit of blood. No big deal.' She continued staring at me and since I said nothing – I couldn't think of anything to say – reinserted the bud and closed her eyes.

I looked around Dad's room. Nothing appeared to have been moved. I backed out and went to my room at the other end of the hall. The window was open a couple of centimetres. This old house needs fresh air. I open the windows in Dad's room and mine from time to time, but the other bedrooms remain closed and smell mouldy. No wonder she picked his room to sit in. Desecration!

I plopped onto the window seat and tried to think what to do. After Dad died, I'd felt uneasy in the house by myself and had bars installed on the downstairs windows. I hadn't bothered with upstairs. The euca-lypt outside Dad's room was spindly then. Even now, I'm surprised it held her weight.

Staring at Geraldine from the doorway, I'd been tempted to ask how long she intended to stay. I'd resisted, partly because I feared an answer like 'for ever' and partly because it was a rational question. The situation wasn't rational. Should I get in touch with her father? She'd paid no at-tention to him when she was seventeen or eighteen, so why would she now? Maybe I could contact the secretary at the school and persuade her to give me the phone numbers of Geraldine's friends. I'd have to explain why I wanted them. It would sound unbelievable. I hardly be-lieved it myself.

But what friends? In my class, Geraldine sat by herself. I never saw her in a group giggling with the intimate silliness that teenage girls rel-ish. She was a loner. Like me. That somehow made the situation more sinister, and at the same time gave me a little confidence that I could cope. What if I called the authorities? But which ones? The welfare sys-tem? The police? Geraldine hadn't threatened me. My fear had more to do with imaginings than with anything she'd said or done. Taking a key and pilfering a few dollars were hardly crimes. Besides, I'd allowed her into my home. I'd get her out as kindly as I could.

A sparkle on the dressing table caught my eye. A ray of sun was hitting Dad's wedding ring. Maybe I should hide it and the few pieces of jewellery he'd given me. Would Geraldine steal something of value? If so, I'd definitely call the police. It struck me that I wouldn't really mind losing the jewellery. I never wore it; the memories were too heavy. I left it where it was.

We settled into a routine of sorts. I didn't bolt the doors. If Geraldine was determined to enter the house, I didn't want her climbing in or breaking a window. She came and went at all hours. Sometimes she stayed out all night. Once, she stayed away for two nights and I began to hope. If she wasn't home – my home, not hers – if she wasn't back by the time I went to bed, I didn't take out my hearing aids. I lay awake listening for her. If we crossed paths, I'd say, 'Hello, Geraldine.' She'd say 'Hi' if she noticed me and wasn't concentrating on whatever was coming through the buds in her ears. She didn't touch my food. I threw out lots of greasy boxes from the local pizza shop. I was thankful she used the house only as a place to sleep and eat takeaway.

I went to bridge as usual. Nobody expected me to chat. Since I'd stopped talking about my students' achievements, I'd concentrated on my game and improved it. It was funny – people now jostled to be my partner! During my talkative days, I'd hinted that my students' excellent HSC results and subsequent successes were due to me. Indeed, some of them were. I didn't talk about the failures, of course. I'm expert at quashing bad memories.

Geraldine – I'd failed her. She kept taking days off in the middle of Year 12. On the occasions she was in class, she was horribly pale and had a greasy sheen on her face. If I stood beside her desk, I could smell her bad breath. I kept nagging her to hand in work.

One morning when I got off the bus, she emerged from behind the bus shelter and, without any preamble, asked me for money. She mumbled something about a doctor and medication. She looked cold although the day was warm and she was wearing her bulky Year 12 jersey.

Ignoring my misgivings, I took a fifty-dollar note out of my purse.

Geraldine clutched it and stared at me speculatively. 'Can I come and stay at your place tonight?'

Was there no other adult she could turn to? There was plenty of room. Suddenly she looked as young as she was. Hope bloomed on her pinched face. She continued to stare at me.

I faltered. Have a student in my house? Dad was sick. I couldn't look after two sick people. It was out of the question. I gave her what was left in my purse and said, 'Why don't you stay with a friend?'

Hope leached out of her face. 'Thanks, Miss Richardson,' she said in a bleak voice.

She ducked behind the bus shelter. I trudged towards my classroom.

She never returned to school. Staffroom gossip was evenly divided. One half said she'd been dealing drugs and had been expelled. The other half said she was pregnant. I doubt she'd have asked to stay with me if she'd been dealing.

I struggled to force her request and hopeful face out of my mind. Dad's illness and retiring a year earlier than I intended – that helped.

Her words haunt me again. I can't bear to think what my money helped pay for. Where did she spend that night? Thinking of the possibilities makes me nauseous.

The other day, I went into Dad's room when she was out. The bed hadn't been made or changed since she arrived. A drawer in the chest was open and a tracksuit was missing. A supermarket carry bag contained the flared skirt and bustier and some make-up. There were no other personal possessions. There were no pills or anything to indicate what put her into a weird state on Friday and Saturday nights.

Contradictory emotions battered me: pity for the young woman who seemed homeless and alone, guilt for my failure to help the stricken, motherless girl she'd been, and anger at being used. The fact that she barely acknowledged my existence was both a relief and an affront. Was I being a coward or was I trying belatedly to make amends?

For a while, I slumped into a passive stupor, waiting for something to spur me into action.

Something woke me two nights ago. A draught maybe. Lying on my side, facing the bedroom door, I watched it glide open. Greyness surrounded a black shape. I closed my eyes to slits and deepened my breathing. Geraldine tiptoed over the thick carpet. I closed my eyes completely. On her first night, I'd thought of bringing the poker from the lounge room and putting it under my pillow. I'd spurned the idea as fanciful. How foolish of me! There's a brass lamp on the bedside table. I wouldn't have the speed and strength to surprise her. I smelt coffee mixed with whatever substance she uses.

I almost jumped when she whispered close to my ear, 'Miss Richardson, are you awake?'

I snuffled and made a slopping noise with my tongue and concentrated on breathing deeply.

The act was either convincing or she didn't care. She moved to the other side of the bed. I heard a scraping sound. The zip of my handbag. I heard another zip – my purse. Inwardly, I smiled. It had thirty dollars in cash. My credit card was in the rice canister in the kitchen.

My flesh crawled as I heard her moving behind me. Would she get angry on finding so little cash? Since I didn't think she was rational, I was constantly nervous about the possibility of violence. More scraping sounds. She'd closed the two zips. Did she think I wouldn't notice the missing money? The smell came close. I felt her breath near my ear.

'Thanks, Miss Richardson,' she whispered.

How dare she! Had I been even twenty years younger, I'd have grabbed the brass lamp and swung it. Weighed down by bedclothes, fifteen kilos lighter and more than forty years older than she, I knew there'd be swift and painful retaliation. The greyness diminished and disappeared as the door closed.

I shot up in bed, my heart thumping. I unplugged the brass lamp and, holding it to my chest – a ridiculous sight if anyone had been there to see – tiptoed to the door. The key was in the lock. Overcoming my trembling, I turned it as quietly as possible. I didn't think Geraldine was on the other side of the door. She was probably in Dad's room. I didn't feel entirely safe, but safer with the door locked. There's no tree or drainpipe or anything to climb outside my window.

Still clutching the lamp, I looked at the time on my phone. Four o'clock. I'd wait until she left the house. That could be many hours. I realised I was shivering and couldn't decide whether it was from cold, fear or anger. I placed the lamp on the floor, pulled my woolly dressing gown around me and curled up on the window seat facing the gap between the blind and the window frame.

I fell asleep, but was lucky. I awoke just in time to see Geraldine go down the front path. She gave a little wave to someone in the street. Groaning from the stiffness in my knees, I knelt on the floor and raised the blind a little to see who it was. Well, well – the young man who worked in the pizza place down the road!

She flung open the front gate, bounced up to him, stood on tiptoe and gave him a peck near his lips. He started to curve his arms around her, but she twirled away and danced towards the corner. He sprinted to catch up with her. I heaved myself to my feet and stubbed my bare toe on the lamp. Fury shook me.

That's it! No more! She's not alone. She has someone to look after her. No more intrusion into my life, no more contempt for me or my possessions. I stormed through the house locking every window and bolting both the kitchen and the front doors. I lit a small fire in the fireplace and burnt the only two items in her supermarket bag, the flared skirt and bustier. I sprayed the lounge room ferociously until pine air freshener dominated the stink of burning clothes. I vacuumed and tidied Dad's room and stripped and remade the bed.

I stayed at home all day. There was no need to go out. It wasn't a bridge day. I carried my mobile in a pouch around my neck in case she returned and tried to get in. If she did, I'd call the police. I'm an elderly woman living alone. She's robust and using some substance that's probably illegal. They'd see I needed protecting. I went to bed at what had formerly been my normal time. Tense and wide awake, I alternately listened to the radio and read a page-turner.

I became aware of some rustling outside. I put my book down, switched off the lamp and turned up my hearing aids. I hadn't been mistaken. Something was rustling in the tree outside Dad's room. Too big to be a possum. I got out of bed, but didn't dare peep through the gap between the blind and the window frame. I stood beside the window with my back to the wall. The rustling intensified. Not even two possums having a fight would make that much noise. Suddenly there was a crack, a swooshing sound, a thud and then silence. I looked through the gap. Because of the angle, all I could see on the path was a pair of legs in tracksuit pants, the feet in runners. This time, the tree hadn't borne her weight. What would she do when she got up? She didn't. I began to hear cries. They persisted. She must be injured. I went down the stairs and looked through the peephole in the front door. Wrong angle. I couldn't see anything. The cries stopped. Maybe she'd got up and left. Maybe she was prowling around the house.

I went back upstairs at what for me was a run. I looked down. The legs were still there. Ambulance. There was an emergency number on my mobile. I'd never used it. I shuddered. I'd have to go with her. There was no one else. Yes there was! The man from the pizza shop, Emilio. I didn't know his last name or how to get in touch with him. Her father? She was Geraldine Smith. How would I ever find his number? In a sort of mental paralysis, I sat on the edge of my bed. I heard a siren. The neighbour must have heard the cries and called an ambulance. She noticed noise. She often complained about the volume of my radio and television. The siren came close and then faded into the distance.

I lay down on my bed. I took out my hearing aids and turned on the radio. It was after three o'clock. The first joggers would come past at five.

Once again, I had the dream of being in a little boat on Sydney Harbour. The water sparkled, the sun shone and something was thumping against the boat. I wasn't afraid. It wasn't a shark. It was a dolphin.

I woke and the thumping persisted through the morning news on the radio. Daylight surrounded the blind.

'Miss Richardson! Miss Richardson!' The faint voice was male.

I got out of bed, raised the blind and looked down. A police car was parked out the front. My neighbour was hovering near it. Two policemen were at the front door. One stepped back and looked up at the windows on the first floor. He saw me and waved me down.

The police have gone. I'm trembling. I'm sitting in my kitchen with my neighbour. This is the first time she's been inside the house. The police thought we were friends. One asked her to make me a cup of tea because I was so upset. I hate tea. There's some left over from before Dad died. It tastes of nothing. The police seemed convinced I couldn't have heard anything. They'd had to shout over the radio until I went upstairs and turned it off and put in my hearing aids. That's when the neighbour had slipped in to snoop.

I want her to go, but I don't. When she leaves, the terror will rise. Geraldine's still out there. She'll be back. I'll have to keep the house locked up and stay alert. I'm sorry the tree didn't hold the dead man's weight. I'd been relying on him to lure Geraldine away from me. The dead man, Emilio.

The police said it was probably an attempted robbery. I didn't say it was more likely an attempt to see Geraldine. Silence is a good policy. The police saw me today – distraught, frail, elderly. I'll choose what I say when Geraldine returns and I have to call them. On the other hand (and this is a bit optimistic), she might stay away. She mightn't have had any feelings for Emilio at all. Maybe she'll find someone else to prey on.

When things have settled down one way or another, I'll sell the house. Bad memories ooze out of every wall. Three climbers: Geraldine, Emilio, Dad. Dad's foot slid off the creaky, sloping step and he fell. He shouldn't have tried to climb the stairs. He was weak from the chemo. I'd set up the sofa bed in the living room. He kept badgering me to bring down his wedding ring and I kept forgetting. I suppose that was what he was after. He never explained. That night too, I'd taken out my hearing aids and turned on the radio.

35

Anzac Assembly

Isn't it funny how you can be friends with someone for years and not really know them? I feel that about my friend, Leah.

She and I have taught at the same school for almost twenty years. She teaches maths and I teach English. Our kids have grown up together and two years ago her son, Cameron, and my daughter, Jodie, became what our students would call 'an item'. Leah and I were delighted. We fantasised about a wedding. Oh, I don't mean a wedding wasn't going to happen. It's just we imagined it the way we, not our children, wanted it: hordes of relatives, pageboys, flower girls and champagne in the Botanical Gardens. Recently, however, there've been ructions. Jodie met another boy and she and Cameron have been fighting. He still comes to our house almost every night and if she isn't there, he stays and talks to me. Today's Anzac memorial assembly has put a new light on what he's been saying.

Leah came up to me in a flap a fortnight ago. The deputy had asked her to give the key address. 'Why me?' she wailed. 'Just because I brought some memorabilia for the display in the library, she wants me to talk about how war affected my family. I don't know what to say. I never talk to students about my family. In front of the whole school — I'll be terrified. She should have asked one of the history teachers.'

'Did you say that to her?'

'Yes, but she's made up her mind.'

At nine o'clock this morning, the students boiled into the hall. Any interruption to normal lessons is a good deal. Teachers patrolled the aisles, glaring at the whisperers and fidgeters. I had organised readings of extracts from soldiers' diaries and letters, so I was sitting with the principal and deputy on the stage and could hear and see everything.

After the readings, the deputy announced the keynote speaker. A wave of murmuring swelled along the rows of students. Leah doesn't have a high profile. The murmur would have been appreciative for the PE teacher who plays for Hakoah or the art teacher who rides a BMW motorbike. This murmur signified anticipated boredom. The teachers paced and glared.

Leah walked slowly to the microphone and, with shaking hands, spread her notes on the lectern. 'When I was a child…' her voice quavered.

Come on, Leah, I thought. You can do it. They shut up when you talk about surds and theorems. This is more interesting. They'll listen if you challenge them to.

As if she heard me, Leah squared her shoulders, raised her head, waited for silence and spoke in a firm voice.

'When I was a child, my father used to march every Anzac Day. By the time the rest of the family woke up, he was long gone to the dawn service at the Cenotaph. He used to take my youngest brother, Danny. Mum, my brothers, sister, and I would catch the train into the city and join the crowd waiting for the march. Children were pushed in front of the adults so we always had a good position. I loved the horses, the brass bands, the bagpipes and the smart way the men marched swinging their arms, their medals swaying on their chests. I liked it that my father had a long row of medals. "Gongs" he called them. I'm talking about the 1950s. The war had finished only ten years earlier. The men were mostly in their thirties. They strode out vigorously as if they were still in uniform. The old men from the First World War marched too and got a lot of applause. In those days, only the ex-servicemen participated. The march didn't include family members. Occasionally, a man would carry a small child on his shoulders but that was unusual. My father was a larrikin…'

She looked at the row of Year 12 boys sitting at the back of the assembly. '….a bit like some of the young men in my HSC class.'

The boys smirked and slumped lower in their seats.

'He loved an audience,' she continued cheerfully. 'That's why he always took my brother with him. Danny rode laughing on his shoulders and waved at the crowd. Dad held Danny's leg with one hand, waved with the other and shouted things like "G'day", "How ya going?", "Great day for a march" – even if it was raining. People shouted "G'day" back. Keeping in step with his mates, his gongs swinging against Danny's shoe, Dad would yell, "One on the shoulders and four more at home. Still doing my bit for the country!"'

A murmur of amusement surged towards the stage and the lone figure at the microphone.

'Mum would squeal, "Here they come" when the banner of Dad's battalion came into view. We waved our flags and yelled, "Hello, Dad", and he'd grin and shout, "Hello, love! Hello, kids!" He'd turn to the men on either side of him and point us out. "That's the missus and kids. Aren't they bonzer?"'

Leah paused and looked at the assembled students. They sat still, intent now on hearing the story.

'You've probably never heard anyone use the word bonzer, have you? You know what it means. Dad would gesture to Danny with his thumb. "Look at this little bloke! He's what Australia's all about." The men marching beside him grinned. They were used to my father. The people in the crowd turned and looked at us. Some smiled and said, "Hello, kids." Sometimes they cheered. I was so proud he was my father. After the march, my mother would take a large packet of liquorice all-sorts out of her handbag. We knew they were there. This was the bribe to make us all stay together while she dived into the crowd to get Danny. She'd come back dragging him by the hand. He tugged against her, howling because she wouldn't let him go to the pub with Dad and his mates.'

A boy in the back row gave a snort of laughter. The others joined in. Leah stood with her head up and her hands hanging loosely by her side until they nudged each other into silence.

'By the time Mum got us home, we were whining and squabbling and she was giving slaps all round. Parents did that in those days.'

The back row made disapproving tsk sounds. A teacher hovered menacingly. Leah smiled and a boy who'd snorted gave her the thumbs up.

'We were tired and over-excited by the early morning train ride, the crowds, waving our flags, patting the police horses, cheering Dad and his mates, sunburn and too many liquorice all-sorts. Mum was pleased when we had television after 1956. As a treat, we watched the march on the evening news.'

Year 7 students in the front rows looked perplexed at this idea of a treat.

'My father never got home until after we were all in bed. I always woke up when he banged the screen door. He'd give my mother a smacking kiss and say something silly like, "How's my beautiful girl?" She'd giggle and shush him and make him Vegemite toast. He'd sing one of the popular songs from the war. He had a voice a bit like Neil Diamond.'

A murmur of mild derision rippled through the rows.

Leah shrugged in sympathy. 'Mum would say, "Shh. The kids are asleep." But he'd keep singing. Listening to them and smelling the toast, I used think they were behaving like children. I always make Vegemite toast for my two sons on Anzac Day. My oldest son is twenty-four. He hates Vegemite but he eats it for me, and his crusts too, on Anzac Day.'

Goose bumps popped up on my arms when I heard her refer to Cameron.

'Dad seldom spoke to us kids about the war. What little he said, we heard over and over again. He'd enlisted in the infantry because that was the fastest way to get into action. He hadn't wanted to miss out. He had no time for the men who hadn't enlisted and was sorry for those who were rejected. Did you know the army rejected men with flat feet?'

Some Year 7 mouths dropped open.

'His battalion was sent to Queensland to train. Dad didn't have much time for the high-ranking officers. "Brass" he called them. He thought the NCOs, the sergeants, should be running the war. In

Queensland, the men drilled with wooden rifles. There weren't enough real ones. From the Queensland rainforests, they were sent to the north African desert. Some had never fired a gun. My father was proud of being a Rat of Tobruk and always spoke respectfully of Rommel, the German commander. Dad thought he was a real soldier. The Brass in their wisdom, as Dad put it, sent his battalion from floundering through sand in the desert to wading through mud in the New Guinea jungle. He spoke with great affection of the Fuzzy-Wuzzy Angels. That name isn't politically correct now, but it's what the Australian soldiers called the local people who acted as guides and carried the wounded. Dad respected their strength and endurance. He couldn't get over the equipment the Americans had in New Guinea. He said there wasn't much you could say for Australian army bully beef, but it was a bloody marvel how the Yanks had ice cream.

'My dad was an ordinary Aussie bloke. He never complained about the illnesses he contracted during the war. Every now and then, he'd stay in bed for a few days sweating and shivering. Mum told us he picked up malaria in New Guinea. He was proud of having fought for Australia. When my little brother, Danny, signed up and went to Vietnam, Dad was proud of him for defending Australia too. Danny was excited about going into action overseas like his father.

'I dread Anzac Day. Some people say the march glorifies war. Some say it honours the dead. I don't know. I'm too emotionally involved to think either way. I spend the day remembering Dad and Danny, what fun they were, how much they enjoyed life. Dad died when he was sixty-one. The doctors – "quacks" he called them – said his system was weakened by parasites picked up in during the war and frequent bouts of malaria. Danny died a year after returning from Vietnam.'

Leah turned over the last page of her notes with a shaking hand.

'My eldest son will wear his grandfather's medals at the march tomorrow. I shall not go to the march, nor will I watch it on TV.'

Her voice was low, but her words ravaged the silence. 'All those young men wearing dead men's medals.'

She stopped, her head bowed. Many students bowed their heads too.

'That's how war affected my family. Thank you for listening.'

The silence continued for what seemed a long time, but probably no more than thirty seconds. Then the back row of boys stood up, raised their arms in salute and applauded with hands hardened not by drilling with wooden rifles, but by hefting surfboards and cricket bats. The students in front of them sent wave after wave of applause crashing over the lone woman at the microphone.

I knew Leah's father had fought in World War Two and Danny in Vietnam, but not the rest. Cameron's been telling me how exciting the army looks in the current recruitment ads on TV. He thinks Jodie will feel bad if he turns up one evening in uniform. He has an interview today. I've been calling him but his mobile's switched off so I've left the same message several times.

'Call your mother immediately and tell her what you're doing. If you don't, I will.'

A Red Rose

There was an excited buzz in the crowd that was unusual after a funeral. The coffin and white wreath had been trundled out of the sandstone church and slid into the hearse. A red rose had been conspicuous on top of the white flowers throughout the service. Now it was gone and to Emily the coffin looked drab.

She shuffled with her parents in the long queue of people waiting to pay their respects to the widow. On the other side of the hearse, the queue in front of the son was shorter.

Emily's mother, Liz, whispered loudly enough to ensure she'd be heard by everyone around them, 'Donna looks devastated.'

That's not how Emily would have described her. As the focus of attention, the widow was receiving words in praise of her husband as if they were about her. Resplendent in black, from her wide-brimmed hat and veil to her patent leather shoes, Donna was playing her role with a dignity that Emily thought bordered on relish.

Liz flicked a look at the shorter queue and said, 'It's such a pity Peter and his girlfriend broke up just before Jack died. She could at least have come to the funeral.'

Emily was momentarily nonplussed. What girlfriend? Peter had a lot of women friends, but… Then Emily remembered. Her mother had never met Pat. Yes, his departure had been precipitate and cruel and now, with Jack's sudden death, Peter was the one looking devastated. When would her mother, and Donna too, stop pretending there was ever going to be a girlfriend?

'And,' her mother continued, 'I've never understood why you and Peter didn't get together. Your father and I would be grandparents by now.'

Emily's scalp itched immediately and harsh words flooded her mouth. She turned her head and gazed at the camellia bushes in the driveway of the house next to the church. She was angry at herself for being angry with her mother. Here she was nudging forty and reacting like a teenager!

'And some people have no taste.' Liz was referring to the red rose.

There'd been mutterings in the church.

'Who put it there?'

'How dare they!'

'The funeral people should've stopped them.'

'Why didn't someone remove it?'

'How upsetting for Donna! As if the heart attack wasn't enough!'

'Probably one of Peter's friends.'

With only one couple ahead of them in the queue, Liz sniffed. 'At least someone had the decency to get rid of it before it went in the hearse.'

Donna cut short Liz's teary condolences in her eagerness to trumpet to the black-robed minister, 'And here's someone else that Jack successfully mentored. This is Doctor Emily Barton, lecturer in English Literature at Sydney University.'

Emily wrapped a smile around her face while Donna recounted her oft-repeated version of the mentorship, ending as always with 'And that prize marked the beginning of Doctor Barton's academic success.'

With a few polite words about the appropriateness of the eulogy, Emily left her parents standing beside the nodding minister and joined Peter's queue in time to hear him being asked, 'Do you know who put the rose there?'

'No. An admirer, I suppose. He had many.'

Peter glanced along the queue and when he saw Emily, he gave a small nod. Taking after his father, he was both intuitive and intelligent. How much did he guess?

She'd arrived early, bringing her briefcase as well as a handbag. She was going to a faculty meeting after the funeral. Inside the briefcase, a clear plastic cylinder protected a long-stemmed red rose. Her intention had been to pop the rose among the masses of flowers heaped in front of the altar. Suddenly realising she was alone in the church and on an impulse she hadn't yet explained to herself, she whisked the rose out of its cylinder and laid it on top of the white wreath on the coffin. Hearing people's voices at the main entrance, she didn't have time to remove it, even if she'd wanted to.

In a turmoil of emotions, she sat with her parents in the middle of the church and watched people take their places. The pews filled quickly. Conversations were muted like the light coming through the tall, narrow stained-glass windows. She recognised family members and Peter's friends. Jack's journalist colleagues stood at the back and along the sides of the church. Some of them were well known from the television news.

Her eyes kept turning to the red rose. Bad taste? A flash of melodrama? A moment of madness? She didn't regret it. The minister launched into a sermon-cum-eulogy. She kept her face impassive as her thoughts wandered.

'You're not doing Schoolies, and that's that,' her mother had said.

Emily had been irritated by Liz's imperiousness, but also relieved. Her Year 12 classmates babbled with excitement about the parties they'd have on the Gold Coast after the HSC exams. They repeated salacious stories about several girls in last year's class. Emily didn't want to be one of the female nerds so plied with alcohol and pills that she didn't know the name of the panting body that ended her virginity. Now, if asked where she was going for Schoolies, she would further elevate her nerdy image by confessing that her parents were forcing her to go to their friends' holiday house at Nelson Bay. Fortunately, Peter was a nerd too, so she looked forward to arguing with him about poetry and trying to beat him at chess.

Jack and Donna's holiday house was set on a rise just high enough for people on the veranda to see the ocean over the tops of wind-stunted trees. When Emily and Peter were children and if Jack happened to be spending the weekend at the house, he drank endless cups of coffee on the veranda and taught them to play chess. Once, for no apparent reason, they all looked up simultaneously and saw the shiny grey curves of a couple of dolphins frolicking near the shore.

Parking in the driveway of the beach house after Emily had finished her exams, Liz marvelled, as always, on how many bedrooms there were. 'Enough for Peter and Jack and Donna to have one each and we can have one each too!'

Emily helped unpack the car and then set up her laptop on the veranda. She watched her father and Peter, transformed into giant stick insects by multiple rods and other fishing paraphernalia, descend the sandy path towards the beach. Jack followed soon after, the top of his wetsuit still dangling around his waist. His board swished against the low foliage on the sides of the path. She opened her emails to see if she'd received any rejections today. No emails at all. Good!

In the kitchen, Donna and Liz chatted over cups of tea, oblivious to the probability that Emily could hear them through the open windows.

'It suits me having separate rooms,' Donna said. 'Been through the change. Not interested any more. Jack's happy in his own room with all his books and his computer.'

Liz sympathised. 'That's what all marriages come to, don't they? So boring. Always the same. Still, wouldn't it be great if our two get together? They've been pals since they were tots. Emily would cringe to hear me say it, but she'd look so lovely in white. I keep telling her, "You're only eighteen, sweetheart. You should be wearing bright colours, not black."'

Emily closed the lid of her laptop, slipped off the veranda and fled towards the beach. Plain and bespectacled, immersed in medieval English poetry and existential French literature, how could she, Emily, possibly fulfil her mother's dream and trip down the aisle frothed up in a white meringue?

There was a shuffling and a flicking of paper. Emily emerged from her sunlit dream into the dimness of the church. The minister had finished the eulogy and people were looking at their order of ceremony sheets. Her mother blew her nose and wiped her eyes.

'Am I being cynical,' Emily wondered, 'in thinking Mum's crying because that's what you do at funerals?' Liz had always been civil to Jack's face, but behind his back she accused him of using his job as an excuse to avoid the responsibilities of being a husband and father.

The minister announced a short musical interlude, an excerpt from Verdi's *Requiem*, one of Jack's favourite pieces. Emily was surprised. She didn't know Jack had liked classical music. She didn't know what sort of music he did like. Maybe this was the sort of thing Donna thought appropriate for a funeral. The men standing along the sides of the church shifted their feet. The ones nearest her looked irritated, probably desperate to open their phones.

What would Jack have thought of the droning minister, the women patting tears off their make-up, and all his mates togged up in suits? 'A right palaver' – that's what he'd say. She stopped herself from smiling. It was one of his favourite expressions. The first time she'd heard him say it, she'd been very young. Grade 2, maybe. She'd asked, 'What's a palaver?'

'A dog's breakfast dressed up in a dinner suit.'

She waited, looking up at him. He squatted down so they were at the same eye level and explained the word's meaning, correct usage and origin. He loved and respected words. He'd been her first true English teacher.

The evening meal of the first night at Nelson Bay featured the fish caught that afternoon by Emily's father and Peter. Talk centred on the week's menu and activities. The older people kept away from dangerous subjects, like the current affairs and world events that constituted Jack's working life. Emily and Peter would have enjoyed listening to some of his stories about the shenanigans in Canberra. Their mothers would have vigorously defended the politicians they liked.

The meal was almost over when Liz attacked the topic of Emily's future. 'An Arts degree doesn't lead to any kind of decent career, Emily. I don't know why you put it on your uni application. You should have put Law. Your teachers say you'll get the marks to be accepted. Anyway, this'll be the last summer holidays you'll have time to fiddle with those stories of yours.'

'Stories?' Jack asked.

Emily opened her mouth to forestall her mother, but Liz was used to talking over her.

'Yes, she spends hours locked in her room, hunched in front of her computer. Terrible for her posture. She says she's writing stories but she won't let her father or me read them. She sends them off to competitions and publishers and nothing ever happens. You're a writer, Jack. Couldn't you give her some advice? See what she's doing wrong?'

Emily was both embarrassed and amused. Her mother liked saying, but never in Jack's presence, that journalism wasn't proper writing, not like literature.

Jack scribbled his email address on a paper serviette and slid it over to her. 'Send me one, if you like.' His tone was casual and he was smiling.

Emily nodded. She guessed that if she didn't send anything, he'd let the matter drop. After dinner, she made a few edits to the story she was about to enter in a competition and attached it to an email. Her finger hovered over the send key. She'd never written a story like this one before. It had stretched her imagination. What the heck! She pressed send. Jack's criticism would be forthright but kind.

The next morning, the men set off for the beach and Donna and Liz drove into Nelson Bay to try the tea and scones in a new café. Emily set up her laptop on the veranda and started a new story. She'd done a few hundred words when she heard the swish of Jack's surfboard against the low bushes and he emerged from the sandy path.

He bounced up the four steps onto the veranda, leant his board against the railing and turned his back to her. His grey wetsuit glistened. 'Hey, Emily. Give us a hand with the zip, will you?'

She took hold of the strap attached to the zip and pulled it to down to his waist.

'Thanks. How about a coffee? Can you make one while I have a shower? Then we can have a word about your story.'

Much to their mothers' disapproval, both Peter and Emily had picked up Jack's coffee drinking habit and Emily manipulated the elaborate machine with ease. She put their steaming mugs on the veranda table and sat on the bench facing the sea. She was apprehensive about what Jack would say. A few minutes later, dressed in board shorts and a new-looking white T-shirt, he joined her. His hair was slicked down. She realised its fairness probably obscured any grey he might be starting to have. The smell of soap, coffee and salt air mingled pleasantly.

Jack laughed. 'That's some scene you wrote: middle-aged mum having sex with the young teacher in the kindergarten classroom! Very funny.'

Emily felt herself going red. Maybe it was funny because it sounded as if she didn't know what she was talking about.

'The story's got everything: strong storyline, good characterisation, good build-up of tensions and – the big plus – humour. What's the competition you're sending it to?'

She told him.

'Don't fiddle with it. Send it off the way it is. It's great.'

They sat side by side looking at the ocean swells and the sea gulls soaring on the wind currents. Emily felt fizzy with elation. She wasn't wasting her time after all. The first comments she'd received about any of her stories had come from a professional writer and they'd been positive. The rejections she'd received shrivelled to less importance.

She was aware of him turning towards her.

'If I kissed you, would you tell me to get lost?'

She was so astonished her mouth popped open. She shut it hastily and looked at him. Her breathing quickened. He leaned towards her. She smelt the coffee on his breath. When his tongue touched hers, a tingle shot through her body and her toes curled.

He moved back from her. 'Would you like to take this further?'

She didn't know if the thumping in her ears was her heart beating or the waves breaking on shore. A breeze played on her skin. She moved slightly and their bare knees touched. He held out his hand. She put her hand in it. With his arm around her, he guided her through the house and into his bedroom. She'd never been inside it before. It was a little steamy from the shower and smelt of leather and soap. She kept her eyes on his face but was aware of books on floor-to-ceiling shelves. Soft light filtered through the shade blinds.

He took her shoulders and kissed the corner of her mouth, along her jaw and down her neck. Releasing her, he reached back, grabbed a handful of his T-shirt and pulled it forward over his head. She couldn't resist running her hand over his chest and shoulders. The muscles were hard and the skin was soft. He slipped out of his shorts and sat on the edge of the bed, drawing her between his knees. He slid his hands under her T-shirt and she raised her arms to make it easy for him pull it off. He undid her bra and she leant forward to shake the straps off her shoulders. It fell to the floor. Slowly he lowered her shorts and panties. They too fell to the floor and she edged them aside with her foot. She stood naked in front of him and watched his eyes as he looked at her. When she had to take a gasp of air, she realised she'd been holding her breath.

He looked up at her face and said, 'You're beautiful.'

Happy warmth suffused her. He stood up and half lifted her onto the bed. She lay on her back and he hovered over her, kissing and licking until she was wet and trembling all over.

'You like that, do you?'

'Pretty much.' She laughed and wriggled in anticipation of whatever was going to happen next.

He sat back on his heels and caressed her cheek with the knuckle of his forefinger. 'Before we go any further, you need to know – I've had the snip.' His finger stopped moving. 'A vasectomy.'

Her body blazing, Emily hardly registered the implication of what he was saying.

He continued, 'And I need to know, are you intact? I mean, are…'

She put her fingers on his mouth. She hadn't had any experience but she didn't want him to think she was ignorant and didn't know the meaning of the word. She turned her head to one side so he wouldn't see how embarrassed she was. 'I use tampons,' she whispered.

He sat still and she turned her head back. He smiled and ran his finger from her lips, down her neck, over her breast and stiffened nipple, down the length of her body to her hip bone. He straddled her and with slow tenderness caressed her pubic hair with his penis.

The music had stopped and the people in the pews were getting to their feet. The minister read the final prayers and blessings. Everyone faced the central aisle and two dark-suited undertakers propelled the coffin on its waist-high metal trolley towards the sunlit entrance. A tiny breeze created by the propulsion fluttered the petals of the white flowers and the red rose. Emily made no connection between the man she'd known and what was inside the coffin.

The smell of sweat, his and hers, mingled as they lay entwined and let their breathing slow. He held her for what seemed like a long time and when he moved his body away from hers, the cool air brought goose bumps to the part of her skin that had been touching his.

'We'd better move before the others come back,' he said. He brushed her mouth with his and rolled off the bed as if to set the example.

She pulled her clothes on and at the door turned and gave him a shy little wave. It was a silly gesture, but she knew he wouldn't laugh at her.

That afternoon, he left for Canberra. His phone was full of messages. A scandal the press had known about for weeks was about to break. Jack didn't return to the holiday house that summer and Emily was pleased. The glow from the experience stayed with her. She wandered along the beach and swam and did nothing, savouring the memory of having been found beautiful. She knew this would be the only time with Jack. That pleased her too.

The next time the two families met, he congratulated her on winning the competition with the story he'd found so funny.

'You see what happens when Jack helps you,' her mother said.

'I didn't help at all. The story didn't need a thing doing to it.'

Donna and Liz smiled. They knew better.

Emily and Jack never spoke of or referred to their afternoon together. She read his articles and he congratulated her on her academic successes as both of them would have done anyway.

Emily slid along the pew behind her parents and they joined the crowd following the coffin out of the church. She didn't notice when the rose had disappeared. Irked by the whole palaver, she was anxious to get away and, after promising Peter she'd call him, she joined the departing convoy of journalists' cars.

How lucky she'd been that her first experience had been a good one! No subsequent lover had been as skilled. None had been so deliberate in ensuring that everything he did gave pleasure to both of them. She didn't think the less of them for that. With each of the others, there'd been a relationship that had added complications to the love-making.

A few weeks after the funeral, Peter invited her to the holiday house. There was just the two of them. They went fishing, cooked their catch on the barbecue and ate it at the opposite end of the veranda from the sandy path that was now concrete. They drank lots of wine and played chess. The dolphins were moving north and every day glistening grey curves leapt out of the water. The first time they saw them, Emily let the tears flow down her face and wet the front of her shirt.

Peter took her hand and rubbed the back of it with his thumb. He said, 'He was never around, but I miss him.'

'I do too.' Emily didn't say it aloud. She missed knowing he was alive and somewhere in the world.

Guilt

Simon Edwards jerked awake. The phone was shrilling. The figures on the digital clock gleamed. Two thirty-seven a.m. The police again. He yawned and held the sides of the pillow over his ears until the shrilling stopped. While silence expanded into every corner of the room, he lay staring at the ceiling visualising, rather than seeing, the elaborate plaster rose in the middle. He couldn't linger for long. The phone would ring again. Habit had perfected his timing. He sat up, swung his legs over the side of the bed and picked up the handset on the first shrill.

'Edwards? It's Peterson from Manly. Mrs Edwards rang. You'd better get over there.' Something soft in the voice communicated sympathy.

'Thanks, sergeant. Quiet night?'

'For a Friday, yes.'

Simon hung up and, with his elbows on his spread knees, ground the heels of his hands into his eyes. Would he take a shower and get dressed on the off chance he'd be away a long time or just pull on some trackies? Whatever he chose would be wrong. He sighed, dragged some clean trackies out of the oak chest, shook a cigarette out of its pack, snatched his keys from the hall table and braced himself for the cold outside.

He no longer bothered parking in the garage. It took too much effort to open the wooden gates, and sometimes the call was more urgent than this one appeared to be. He filled the car with exhaled smoke and pulled away from the curb without looking in the rear-view mirror or using the indicator. He switched on the headlights at the corner. The car knew which way to turn.

Six minutes later, he entered the visitors' car park and lit another cigarette with the butt of the last one. Why did he get a cramp in his chest every time he came to this place? It was the best he could find. It should be. It gobbled up three-quarters of his salary. No wonder Melanie had left him. He couldn't afford kids. If his mother would let him sell the vast old house he was rattling around in, there'd be enough money to move her into a better nursing home and buy Melanie and himself a small house in an outer suburb. He shook his head as if to empty it of guilt. She'd struggled to care for him after his father left. Now it was his turn. He shouldn't begrudge her. It must have been hard for her to come home from a tedious job to a fractious five-year-old when all her Mosman friends spent their days shopping, waxing their legs and having lunch.

He rubbed his head as Melanie's words echoed there.

'Oh, for goodness sake, Simon! Other women had much worse to contend with. She had only one child. And the house. Your father's leaving was tough but she wasn't destitute.'

Melanie didn't know what a difficult child he'd been – dyslexic, getting into fights from the age of five and doing everything badly at school. One of the counsellors his mother had dragged him to talked about 'continuing grief for a departed father'. His mother had wailed, 'What about me?'

He heaved himself out of the car, ground the cigarette into dust in deference to the no smoking sign and pressed the night button. The woman on duty smiled and waved through the glass as she came down the hallway to unlock the door.

'Hello, Simon. Did your mother call the police again? I'm sorry. You really should remove the phone. At night, at least.'

'Hello, Fiona. Yes, you guessed it. I don't like to remove the phone. Do you remember the hysterics the one time we did take it away?'

'We need to be firm, Simon.'

'And she charmed old Jameson into lending her his mobile.'

'We can deal with Mr Jameson. This can't continue.'

Those had been Melanie's words too. 'This can't continue, Simon.

I'm thirty-eight. How much longer before you decide you want a family? Your mother's not going to get any better. The only things wrong with her are normal for her age. If you're going to wait until she dies, it'll be too late for me.'

Simon nodded vaguely at Fiona, headed for his mother's room and knocked on the door.

'Who is it?' The voice quavered.

'Simon, Mother.'

'Come in.' The voice had jettisoned its tremolo. 'You took your time. Sergeant Peterson said he'd call you straight away.'

'He did, Mother.'

Simon looked at the upright form sitting in the chair by the window. The floor lamp shone softly on rosy cheeks and brilliant white hair that had been blow dried yesterday afternoon. 'Why didn't you ring for the nurse?'

'You don't think, do you, Simon? I'm by the window. The buzzer is by the bed.'

'The staff must have put you to bed at your usual time. You got to the window by yourself. You can get back to bed by yourself.'

'Don't scold me, Simon.' The voice had a catch in it. 'You don't know what it's like to ache in every bone. Just wait until you're eighty-one.'

Yes, and who'll be there to look after me, Simon wondered.

'So, Mother, you want help getting back to bed? I'll ring for Fiona.'

'No, darling. You do it.'

'I've told you I won't any more. These people are professionals. That's why you came here, to have proper help at all times.'

'That's why you said I had to come here, Simon. You looked after me so much better when we were together in our home. Now you're abandoning me, just like your father did.'

Simon reached for the buzzer.

'Please, darling. Just this once. Since you're here anyway. You know how much it would please your poor old mother.' The voice had reverted to quavering.

Simon pressed the buzzer.

'Ungrateful boy!'

He resisted the temptation to cancel the call. That went along with the decision he'd made recently not to spend all his non-working, non-sleeping time visiting his mother.

'And another thing,' he said. 'You mustn't call the police again. They've got work to do.'

'They're always perfectly polite. They're the only ones I can count on to respond immediately.'

Fiona knocked and entered briskly. 'Now, Mrs Edwards. What's the matter? Let's get you back to bed. Do you want to go to the bathroom first?'

'I'll wait outside and come back to say goodnight.' Simon left the room with what he felt was an undignified scuttle.

The falsetto pierced his ears. 'Don't touch me there. It hurts.'

He slumped against the wall, staring at the tree skeleton stencilled by moonlight onto the window at the end of the corridor. Perhaps he could ask Peterson to visit his mother and tell her formally not to phone the station any more. No, that was the coward's way. Melanie had never said he was cowardly when dealing with his mother, but she'd made him feel it. The best way to solve the phone problem would be to re-move it at night and let the tantrums happen. He could threaten to re-move it altogether. Was that bullying? He sighed. A coward and a bully – terrific! His mouth tasted sour from too many cigarettes. He'd taken up smoking again when Melanie left. It didn't matter then how bad it was for him. Where was the line between bullying and firmness? At least Melanie never accused him of bullying. What a weakling she must have thought he was! He cringed in retrospective embarrassment.

Fiona came into the corridor with the phone in her hand. 'All tucked up. No need to go back. She's fallen asleep. She tired herself out sitting up.'

Simon felt relief sluice over him. He didn't have to go back for a prolonged goodnight.

'Thanks, Fiona.' Impulsively, he gave her a peck on the cheek and recoiled at the wistfulness he saw fill her eyes. 'Bye,' he said gruffly, turned away and immediately forgot about her.

He bounded to the exit, sprang down the steps and lit a cigarette as he strode towards the car. That's it, he thought. Bullying or cowardice, whatever you call it – no more phone at night.

Although the calls from the police hadn't made Melanie leave, they'd precipitated her going. The first one came one Sunday morning when they were in bed at her place. His mobile kept ringing at short intervals. Finally, defeated by deflation, he answered with a sharp, 'What?'

The caller, in a bland voice, identified himself as Sergeant Peterson from Manly Police Station. 'Your mother called us. She's distressed and doesn't know where you are. Officers Cairns and McGill are with her now. She's fine. Can you come home?'

'I'll be there in ten minutes.'

Peterson later gave Simon a less robust version of what one of the officers had told him. 'When we rang the bell, the old girl opened the front door right away. All tarted up she was. High heels, hair sprayed on – the lot. She ordered us to come in. "My son, Little Lord Up-his-Bum," she said, speaking down to us plebs, "my son is missing. I'm concerned for his safety." You'd think he was five years old. I asked for his mobile number. She claimed she didn't have it. We spotted it in big print along with his work number on the fridge. When you phoned 'im, the poor bastard must've been at it! You should've seen him come charging in! Heart attack material.'

After the phone call from Sergeant Peterson, Simon had rolled onto his back beside Melanie and said, 'Sorry. I have to go. She's called the police.'

'This is a new game, dragging them in. She's clever.'

'Stop. Let's not argue about her again.'

His mother was the only topic they'd ever argued about. No more arguments now – they weren't a couple any more. Melanie was seeing some bloke from her office. She'd probably marry him soon and have kids. Not that she'd love him the way she used to say she loved Simon. Shit! Cowardice, bullying and now self-delusion. What a bloody mess he was! In that case, he might as well go for broke. Later this morning, in business hours, not this three a.m. malarkey, he'd contact the management and tell them to take away the phone at night. Let the old witch squawk.

After lighting a cigarette, Simon realised he still had one burning. He flicked the first away and as his eyes followed its arc, he noticed a black cat slinking along the paling fence. Never before had he referred to his mother as a witch. He inhaled gulps of pleasure with the smoke. The old witch, the old witch, the old witch. His mother wouldn't mind the 'witch' so much as the 'old'. She loved asking people to guess her age and purred when they told her a few years less than they probably thought.

He leant against the car. Would he give up smoking again if Melanie came back? *If* she came back. Why should she? To a mother-bedevilled weakling with a foul breath and a softening, middle-aged gut. Bullying, cowardly, self-delusional and now self-pitying – what a prize!

Shivering under the funeral company's umbrella, Simon couldn't wait for the whole event to be over. He didn't care about the rain, or the cold or the mud sticking to his new shoes or even Melanie standing on the other side of that bloody oblong hole. All he wanted was a cigarette. He fingered the pack in his pocket. It wasn't wet, although the matches were damp. Who could he ask for a light? His mother's friends probably remembered smoking the same way they remembered sex, a long-past and messy so-called pleasure. The friends nearer his age tolerated his smoking as a temporary manifestation of grief. Maybe the funeral people – they understood the basic needs of the living.

He stared at Melanie. Once, she'd been a basic need. Yesterday, she'd dropped words of comfort into the phone. Today, he didn't need words of comfort, pats on the hand or kisses on the cheek from kind cold lips.

He needed to be leaning against a bar with a wide screen in the corner, drinking a beer and watching muscle-bound thugs careening after a ball.

The last two weeks had been a cross between a horror movie by Charlie Chaplin and a comedy by Alfred Hitchcock. Hysterics, threats of a hunger strike, threats to disinherit him, quavering sweetness and promises of huge sums of money he didn't know existed were punctuated with accurately thrown shoes.

Fiona confiscated all missiles after a shoe hit a cleaner. She caressed Simon with soothing words. 'You don't have to visit your mother after work every day. Her favourite pastime is inventing the best nasty thing to say to you when you arrive. She doesn't need the phone at night. The buzzer is on her bed. We've spoken to Sergeant Peterson. He'll call us, not you, if she uses Mr Jameson's mobile or a new carer's phone again. She's not going to overdose. We dispense her pills. She sends all her meals back but she's not starving. Mr Jameson is supplying chocolates and cakes. His daughter tells me she's astonished her father has suddenly developed a sweet tooth at the age of ninety-one. Mr Jameson's daughter's beside herself. He says he'll buy a waterfront mansion in Kirribilli if your mother marries him.'

Simon was grateful, touched, amused and wary. Fiona was a nice lady, but desperation lurked in her eyes. Bloody women! One had left, one made his life a misery and one was signalling that he was her last prospect!

A week ago, Fiona had called. 'You asked me to let you know when things had calmed down. Your mother has slept through the last two nights. There've been no hysterics. That doesn't mean things aren't brewing,' (Fiona was sounding more and more like Melanie) 'but if you want to visit, today might be as good a time as any.'

'Darling, there you are,' his mother simpered when he entered her room. 'I knew you'd come today. How are you, my sweet?' The voice hardened. 'I've made up my mind. I can't stand this prison any more. Either you let me out or I'll kill myself like your father.'

'What do you mean "like my father"?'

'Like your father.'

'You told me he died.'

'He killed himself. He died. It's the same thing. That's what I'll do.'

'No. It's not the same thing at all.'

'Simon, you're not listening to me.'

'You never told me he committed suicide.'

'It happened years ago. It's not important now.'

'Yes, it is. To me. When did you find out?'

'Oh, I don't know. When the police called me. So what?'

'So what? So what? You've known since I was five years old and you never told me.'

'I don't know why you're carrying on. I'm here. I'm the one who's suffering now.'

'Why?'

'My dear boy, don't be obtuse. It's obvious, isn't it? I'm locked in this prison.'

'No. Why did he commit suicide?'

'Oh, I don't know.'

'You must have some idea. Try to remember.'

'Oh, I think he'd got into one of his black Irish moods.'

'You mean depression.'

'Do I? Is that what they call it now? Well, I'm depressed. I'm in a black mood now.'

'Mother, you have no idea what a black mood is.'

Simon spun away from the bed and strode to the door. 'I'll put it this way. You have a choice. Leave the home if you want. Take responsibility for yourself. Or, you can stay here, benefit from the excellent care and go out to lunch with me every Sunday. It's up to you. Actually, I don't give a toss what you decide.'

His mother opened her mouth and raised a threatening finger.

He cut her off. 'You left me in ignorance for forty-one years. That's something I'm going to have to think about and come to terms with.'

He opened the door and shut it quietly behind him. He walked past the nurses' station, past Fiona's desk, ignoring her 'Is everything all right?' and out the sliding doors.

In the car, he lit a cigarette. The truth at last. He crossed his hands over the steering wheel and rested his head on them. Smoke curled up to the car's ceiling. The butt sizzled when it burnt down to his wet fingers.

Four nights ago, Fiona called. 'An ambulance is on the way. Your mother fell and hit her head in the bathroom.'

She never regained consciousness. Her death, Simon concluded, was not suicide; it was stubborn foolishness. She'd decided to take a shower after dinner without telling anyone or buzzing for assistance.

Now, at the funeral, Fiona exuded emotional support and Melanie sympathy. Simon gazed past both of them. The rain eased to a dribble and the minister droned on. Simon closed the umbrella and squinted. A ray of sun shot through the clouds, expanded and ripped them apart. Suddenly, he knew. Tendrils of warmth unfurled through his body. He didn't want Melanie's sympathy or her child. He didn't want Fiona's emotional support or her desperation.

It was as if he'd suddenly dropped two heavy suitcases. Guilt had gone. He didn't know what he was going to do this afternoon, or tomorrow, or next week. It didn't matter. He was free. He tossed his cigarettes on top of the dreary pink flowers on the coffin, grinned at minister and mourners and squelched cheerfully through the mud to his car.

At the exit from the cemetery he hesitated. Left? Right? Straight ahead? The way straight ahead was clear. He chose that.

The Exam Supervisor, the Accountant, his PA and the Wild Young Man

Eight rows, fifteen candidates in each row – all that youthful energy compressed into fingers and squeezed through the points of plastic pens. I pace. I count: left-handers, boys with earrings, girls with nose studs. I try to guess who will leave the exam first: the boy who writes a little and then gazes into space or the one who's been writing furiously and is now cracking his finger joints. I feel the breeze from whirling brains. This is English, the first of the HSC exams. I'm rostered for nine more – a lot of time to pace, to keep alert, to think of Africa.

I wear flat, soft-soled shoes. There are two criteria for this job: possession of sensible shoes and a minimum age of sixty-five. I don't feel sixty-five. I have three-inch high heels at home! Inch – the word identifies my age.

I'm glad to get away from the house. Life's been a bit strained since William retired at the end of the last financial year. By Monday 4 July, I realised he was hoping for cups of tea on call and three cooked meals a day. By 5 July, his hopes were dashed. Sometimes, however, I relent when he looks particularly wistful. Miss James, his PA of thirty years, used to make tea to accompany his homemade sandwiches. I can't think of her first name. Rosie? Rosemary? Rosalie – yes, that's it.

Only twelve minutes since the start of the exam and already a candidate has his hand up. I pad to his side. He wants to go to the toilet. Exam nerves? Probably. He can't cheat. One of the men supervisors will walk with him to the toilets, which have already been checked for graffiti.

Another hand. A girl. She waves an answer booklet at me. I smile encouragingly as I hand her a new one and she flashes me a look of gratitude with huge brown eyes that I recognise instantly. How can that be possible? I haven't seen those eyes for over forty years. I look at her name on the candidate card on her desk. Yes! The name's right. So distracted that I wouldn't notice a forest of thrashing hands, I drift away from her to the back of the hall. She must be his granddaughter. She's the right age. No doubt he'd fathered children after I left him. Possibly before. I mustn't be hasty. Jackson's a common name. Siobhan Aoife Jackson. He wasn't Irish but he'd like an Irish name for his granddaughter.

It's a two-hour exam. How better to pass the time than thinking of him? I've daydreamed about Africa all my married life. William has excellent qualities: reliability, even temper, patience, devotion to accuracy – qualities you require from an accountant. Well, he is an accountant and I do appreciate his qualities.

But Terry Jackson, oh Terry, the wild man of my youth! We hitch-hiked on any form of transport – rust bucket, dhow, bus, camel, donkey cart – and sometimes we even paid, to go from Sydney through Africa and Europe to London. We slept in caravanserais next to camel drivers who used water only to make coffee and we learnt local slang from Sudanese truck drivers who watched us instead of the road as they hooted at our pronunciation. When we were hungry and nowhere near a town from which I could telegraph my parents for money, we smoked whatever the locals generously shared with us. One time, after we hadn't eaten for thirty hours, the taste of a hand-rolled cigarette was so nauseating I suspected dried cow dung but didn't dare ask. The Sahara was savagely beautiful, the stars in the desert sky were spectacular and the sex was splendid. What more could you want at the age of twenty-two?

Terry wanted everything: endless fun and adventure, all the home brew, hash and substances that would give him a high, acknowledgement of his genius as a poet and every girl he saw when he wasn't with me. And also the ones he saw when he was with me. I quashed my jealousy. He kept coming back to me. There's something both flattering and exciting about a handsome, charming man who strays but treats you as his centre of gravity. And I didn't really mind the lack of money. At times, there was plenty. If there was a bet to be laid – on a cockfight, a camel race or on which cockroach would drown first in a puddle of beer – Terry would walk away with a fistful of dinars, pounds or lire. When we were together, I ricocheted from delirious happiness to fury at his blasé attitude towards money, to terror for our personal safety, to heart-clawing jealousy. Life was never dull.

I can't say that about William. He's steady and safe. I'm glad I married him, but sometimes, when boredom lurks, I think of what life would have been like with Terry. I had the choice. Terry mentioned marriage as we jumped off a bus crammed with travel-sick women, yelling children and silent, despairing chickens. Bou Sada, a pretty little village on the edge of the desert in Algeria, would have provided a date palm background to a ceremony witnessed by whom? I didn't let Terry get that far. He was actually despondent for a whole day.

A hand goes up near Siobhan's desk. Other supervisors head in that direction. I get there first. A request for tissues allows me to pass Siobhan as I fetch them. I take a careful look at her. She has her head bent over her writing. Maybe I'm fantasising. Maybe I was taken in by expressive brown eyes. No. She has the nose too. Classical Greek. His eyes, his nose, his surname. She must be related.

How to find out? Do I even want to find out? Best to sleep on it. I'm sure to supervise her in other exams. Today wouldn't be a good day to approach her. The first exam – I might make her nervous. She might not like the idea of being supervised by someone who knew her grandfather, especially if he's still irresponsible and wild. I won't say how well I knew him. I'll sound casual. 'You wouldn't happen by any chance to be related to Terry Jackson?' She can say yes or no. Obviously. What if she says yes? I'm not going to do anything. I'm not unhappy with my lot. I just get restless. Sometimes I'd like a bit of excitement. More than just sandwich fillings.

I remember once popping in to see William at work. Rosalie kept me waiting near her desk and bustled into his office to announce my presence. She came out all fluttery and red in the face, ushered me in without looking at me and closed the door with a reverential click.

In an attempt to wind him up, I said, 'That woman has a crush on you.'

'Has she?' His tone was totally indifferent.

I'm not one of those wives who fail to recognise her husband's affair with his PA. His tone would have been an insult to Rosalie had she heard it. William has no talent for dissimulation.

I teased him. 'Doesn't anything exciting ever happen in this office?'

'I get all the excitement I can handle from you.'

'From me? What on earth do you mean?' I was genuinely mystified.

'I look forward to seeing what you've put in my sandwiches for lunch. They're a mystery every day. And I never know what you're going to do next, like coming in and asking me for money. Has David Jones rejected your card again?' There was no irony in his tone.

'Yes, dear.'

I settled down to listen to the lecture, knowing it would be followed by more cash than I intended asking for. It was a revelation to discover that William found his sandwiches exciting. Thereafter, I made sure he had interesting and different fillings. He never mentioned them again, but at his retirement party Rosalie told me that he took no calls between twelve thirty and one. At that time, he ate my sandwiches and drank her tea.

I decide not to approach Siobhan until she's settled into an exam routine. At the end of English, I sign the sheets of candidates two rows away from her, as if fearing she'll recognise me. How irrational! Terry always made me irrational.

After the collation of the English papers, there's a two-hour break before this afternoon's exam, so I go home for lunch. It's a short walk across the park. As I come to the end of the gravel path, I see a woman sitting on a bench partly hidden by overhanging trees. Rosalie. I didn't think she lived near here. Actually, I don't know where she lives. Is this how she spends her days? She retired at the same time as William. I suppose I'm being ageist in thinking she should have left earlier. Last year, William was coming home exasperated. Rosalie was not adapting well to the new office technology and refused help from the young receptionist.

She hasn't seen me and something prompts me to avoid her. I circle through the park and enter our garden by the side gate. To William's surprise and pleasure, I offer to make sandwiches for both of us. I don't mention having seen Rosalie. If sitting in the park hoping for a glimpse of him gives her pleasure, that's no different from the way I dream about Terry.

Siobhan doesn't do any of the next eight exams for which I'm rostered. I'm panicking about the possibility of not seeing her again. The last exam on the last day is Design and Technology. My heart flips when she enters the exam room. This time, I'll sign her completion sheet.

I observe her carefully while she writes. After all, I saw her almost a month ago in the general buzz about the first exam. Perhaps I'd been mistaken. Perhaps the similarity to Terry wasn't as great as I imagined. She looks up at the ceiling fan cranking over her head and catches my eye. I turn the fan off and she gives me a lovely smile. My heart flips again. Terry smiled exactly like that whenever he lit a cigarette he'd rolled for me. I can taste now the one I smoked lounging on a sand dune, watching feluccas criss-crossing the Nile.

Design and Technology being the last exam, it's no surprise there's an exodus after the first hour. I move away from any candidate who looks about to finish. The other supervisor can sign the sheet. I watch Siobhan, who writes furiously until the last minute. She's filled extra booklets and takes time putting them in order.

I check them, sign her sheet and say casually, 'I bet you're glad that's over.'

She rolls her eyes and grins.

'You remind me very much of someone I once knew. I wonder if by any chance you'd be related.'

She looks at me expectantly.

'Terry Jackson?'

A shadow crosses her face. 'That's my grandfather's name.' She stands and edges towards the door, good manners stopping her from turning her back on me.

'He lives in Sydney?'

Her voice is flat. 'Behind our shop in Forestville.'

Oh, my gosh! Jackson's Forestville Fruit Market.

She flees. I could interpret her flight as eagerness to enjoy her first moments of post exam freedom. She'll quickly forget the grey-haired nonentity in the exam room.

I can't believe it! I sometimes shop at Jackson's. It's the next suburb from us. Avocados. William loves avocados in his sandwiches. I'll buy some for his lunch tomorrow. Lemons too, so the avocados won't go brown. I mentally add to the list as we collate the exam papers. By the time the presiding officer has signed me off, I'm trembling with impatience. The list covers a week of sandwiches and cooked dinners

I almost run across the park. Flat, soft-soled shoes are useful for other things besides padding around exam rooms! If Rosalie had been on the bench, I'd have rushed past her. I go straight to the garage and back out the car. It'll take me seven minutes to get to Jackson's. Then what? I don't think about that. I concentrate on not exceeding the speed limit.

The car park is half full. Good. I won't be conspicuous as the only customer. I put my green shopping bags in a trolley and saunter towards the aisles. The only employees in sight are two girls at the checkouts and the old man who fills the shelves. He's a bit dippy. I've seen customers ask him where things are. He doesn't answer. Head down, he mutters to himself and sometimes points vaguely. I wander up and down the aisles, scrutinising every fruit tray and not seeing any of them. I walk past the avocados and have to go back.

Fifteen minutes later and with a trolley full of vegetables, I notice a man opening the third checkout. Two women zip ahead of me. I'm happy to let them. I observe the man at the checkout: too young to be Terry. Siobhan's eyes. Terry's eyes. He must be her father and his son. What will I do? One woman ahead of me. I have to stop staring.

I turn my gaze to the old man who's collecting the empty trolleys obstructing the checkout area. I've never looked at him carefully before. White hair sticking out from a beanie, white stubble on sagging jawline, scrawny arms, skinny body wrapped in a long apron. But the nose – classical Greek, the same shape as that of the man at the checkout. It's him! My knees give way. I clutch the counter beside me. No! I don't want it to be. His right hand shakes as he reaches for each trolley. His left arm is curled against his chest. I think of long curly brown hair, muscular arms, a slim golden body diving into the sea at Hurghada. The place was a village then; it's a resort now. The man at the checkout says something, I don't know what, to attract my attention. It's my turn. I throw all the stuff onto the counter, fling cash at him, toss the bags into the trolley and hurtle to the car.

As I slow to turn into our garage, I glance towards the park. The bench is occupied. William helps me carry the shopping from the car to the kitchen.

'Are we having a dinner party?' he asks.

'Yes,' I lie. I'll think of people to invite.

He empties and smooths the paper bags. 'You've been to Jackson's. Good man, Sean Jackson.'

'You know him?'

A tomato rolls towards the edge of the table. Swooping to catch it disguises my astonishment.

'Yes. He was one of my clients. I'm glad you're giving Sean our business. He's had it tough.'

'Oh?' How much casualness can you stuff into one syllable?

'Yes. His father walked out, leaving his mother with three little kids. When Sean looked old enough, he lied about his age and did a paper run to help his mum. He delivered ours. Do you remember the skinny little kid? Always arrived right on the dot and handed me the *Herald* and the *Fin Review* as I was leaving for work. Oh good, you bought avocados.'

There've been a lot of skinny little paper boys. Which one was Sean?

'How did he end up with the fruit market?'

William methodically stacks vegetables in the crisper as he answers. 'Worked for years for the Italian family, bought them out, got married, had kids and then, some time ago, decided to go looking for his father. He told me when he got back. Oh good, and cherries too. We haven't had any since last summer.'

'Back from where?'

'Sierra Leone, would you believe?'

I certainly would but don't say so.

'His father was living in Sierra Leone?'

'Yes. He was in a bad way. He'd been a mercenary for some tinpot warlord. Was wounded and then got some disease. Sean was organising to bring him home. I'm not sure if he did. He told me all this a year or so before I retired. Rosalie said the old man died, but I don't know how she knew. She became strange after I announced my retirement. Asked me a lot of questions, sometimes quite personal, about what I intended to do, whether you and I'd be travelling, things like that. The silly woman is sitting in the park again. What do you think she's doing there?'

'I told you years ago; she has a crush on you.'

'Mm, so you did. Oh well, a cold rainy day will soon put a stop to that. What are we having for dinner?'

I have my doubts about the rainy day. Dinner? I haven't bought any meat.

'What about a vegetable lasagne?'

'Great! You haven't made one for ages.'

I go into our bedroom. Changing into my slippers gives me an excuse to get away from William. I look through the window that overlooks the park. Rosalie's still there. I feel like waving to her, but I don't. Why spoil her dreams with the reality of recognition? How much does she want to know about William? Would it interest her that he likes vegetable lasagne?

How much do I want to know about Terry? Nothing more. I don't want certainty. Death or dementia – neither suits him. Sierra Leone. I'm going to believe he's living in wild and beautiful mountains with brave men who protect villagers from marauding warlords. He writes poetry about freedom and lions.

Children's Hands

Luxor 2008

I'm scared. They're children and I used to be a teacher, but I'm still scared. Impossible to tell how many there are. Why, oh why, did I turn into this street? A moment ago, it was empty. And then suddenly one child, a little girl, bobs up in front of me. Tangled hair. Stick arms. Shapeless dress. She jabs her fingers towards her mouth. Fingernails rimmed with dirt. Hungry? Of course she is. Maybe, just this once, I should give money. Oh, but I don't have any. I haven't brought my purse. It's in the hotel. The others said I didn't need money for a little walk to the corniche. The child's eying my backpack. I needn't have brought that either. But it's got water and sunscreen. And a cellophane packet of pens. When the group first met in Cairo, the tour leader said, 'Don't give money to children. Give plastic pens.' I bought some in the hotel shop. What good's a pen if a child's hungry? Well, that's all I've got to give her.

As soon as I swing my backpack off my shoulder, a mob of boys materialises. They shove the girl away. She flits behind them. Stubborn. She saw me first. The boys' faces have flaking skin. Their eyes and teeth flash. Dust-coloured clothes. Brown hair tinged with yellow. They mill and jostle, thrusting out their open hands. They don't touch me. Will they? I could drop the backpack and run. Stupid idea! I'm too old to run. And they'd probably fight for the contents. Somebody'd get hurt.

The zip is stiff. Don't tug at it. Let them think I'm calm. For a moment, I concentrate on opening it. I hear a grunt and look up. Six inches from my face there's a pair of eyes. One is badly turned so the boy – he's not a boy, he's older, bigger – he looks sinister. I mustn't recoil. The smaller boys whine. They're saying words. I don't know what they mean, but it's definitely words. He grunts. His hand, dirt-encrusted, waves close to my chin and mouth. How well can he see?

The zip gives and I slide it open just enough to reach inside and grope for the cellophane packet. Several boys are edging behind me. I don't want to be encircled. I shuffle backwards till my shoulder blades touch the metal grating of a closed shop. The mob surges into a tight semicircle, so I'm trapped anyway. There's a smell, an intensity of dusty bodies. I gasp. I've been holding my breath.

I smile and say, 'I have pens. *Stylos, stylos.*' Thank heavens I remember the French.

The fringe of the scarf I wear in mosques is twined around the cellophane packet. I could take them both out of the backpack. I don't want to make a sudden movement. I fear they'll snatch. Not that I care about the possessions. I don't want to lose… What? Control? Dignity? The illusion of safety?

'*Stylos, stylos.*' Two boys begin a chant.

White teeth flash. Hands reach at me. The whines go up in pitch. The ragged girl hovers, jigging up and down, craning to see me. The scarf has fallen away from the cellophane. I start to withdraw my hand. The wall-eyed boy grunts more urgently. He prods the backpack with one finger. Two smaller boys pat it and pull back their hands. I make a tsk sound, shake my head and smile. They stare at me, not smiling, but not hostile either. Their hands are poised in mid-air.

I sling the backpack onto one shoulder and hold up the cellophane packet for the mob to see. How many boys are there? Fifteen? Twenty? There are twelve pens in the packet. The boys at the back push the others forward. I feel breaths on my face. Will they let me hand out the pens one by one? What will happen when they realise there aren't enough pens for everyone?

I don't like taking my eyes off the big boy, but for a second I glance over his shoulder. The street is still empty. It's Friday. Metal shutters cover the shopfronts. The guide said the shopkeepers will open them when they return from prayers. What time will that be? I'm suddenly aware of my watch. It's only plastic, but highly visible as I wave the pens about. I lower my arm. The shops near the hotel were being opened when I set out.

The driver of a caleche hassled me a block from here. He called out, 'Ferrari ride? Luxor Ferrari. Where you going?'

I couldn't bear the idea of being dragged around by a poorly shod, half-starved hack.

Last night, I saw one still attached to its caleche, scavenging in a garbage skip. Do these children eat garbage too? Chanting '*Stylo, stylo,*' they splay tentacle fingers. Have they ever held a pen? Do they go to school?

I rushed into this street to escape the hawkers.

'No hassle. Just look.'

'No pay to look.'

'Where you from? English? American? Française? Deutsch?'

'What you looking for?'

'Hey, madame, you want pashmina? Madame!'

The street descends to the corniche along the Nile. Plenty of tourists there and hustlers offering felucca rides. Yesterday, one offered sex!

I tear the cellophane carefully. I don't want to scatter the pens on the ground. There might be a scramble. Someone might be trampled. I take out a pen and put it into a hand. The whining rises in pitch. Hands undulate like the fronds of sea creatures.

The wall-eyed boy snatches a pen and grunts urgently in front of me. My heart pumps. I shove a pen into a hand that waves between two bodies. I hope it's the little girl. The swarm presses forward. Hands flutter and grasp. I stand up as straight as I can. I mustn't show I'm scared. The wall-eyed boy snatches a second pen. I feel the strength of his fingers. His straight eye glares. I thrust the last pen into the smallest hand I see.

The cellophane bag is empty. One by one, the grasping hands drop. The boys spread out. The little girl, pressed against the grating of a shop across the street, is watching me. She's clutching a pen to her chest. The big boy doesn't budge. He snarls, his upper lip uncovering beautiful even teeth. His breath smells of mould. The metal grating digs into my back. I sense, rather than see the little boys closing in again. The big boy's face blurs. Will he touch me? If so and I scream, will anyone come? Yesterday someone threw a stone at a woman in our group. I'm a woman, a foreigner and alone.

Something cracks against the metal near my head. Are they starting to throw stones? No. The small boys have vanished. Just like that. The wall-eyed boy hisses. A second crack makes him flinch. There's a third crack and a stream of Arabic. He flees.

A stout man in a white turban and long brown *gallabiyah* is hitting the grating I'm leaning against with his stick. He's shouting. At me? I don't wait to find out. I run. I actually run. Past a stinking garbage skip towards the corniche. I hear the rattle of metal. I stop, gasping for breath, and look back. The man is using his stick to hoist up the grating and open his shop. Metal jingles beside me and I jerk around. A skinny horse stands trembling between the shafts of a silver-decorated caleche.

'Luxor Ferrari?

'Yes, please. The Mercure Hotel.'

I don't ask the price. The guide said we should, but too bad. I'm safe and the driver has to earn a living.

I point to his whip. 'Please don't use that. The horse can walk.' I plop onto the leather seat.

The driver shouts and the horse lurches forward. Bare patches on its hide twitch with vermin. When I get to the hotel, I'll ask the guide to tell the driver in Arabic that I want him to use some of his huge fare to give the horse a decent feed. A futile gesture – I know! And the children? From now on, whenever I buy water from a little grocery shop, I'll fill my backpack with packets of chocolates and sweets. Pens too. My mob seemed to like them. I have no illusions about providing proper nutrition. I won't tell the others. They'll say I'm encouraging the children to beg. Too bad! My aim will be to put tiny pieces of fleeting pleasure into children's hands.

At Home With Fear

'Poor woman,' Andrew thought. 'Is she always to be plagued by puffed-up prats?'

He eyed with distaste the enraged bantam on the other side of his desk. 'You can go upstairs, Bob,' he said. 'Like I told you last week, plenty of empty rooms up there.'

'Why should I change rooms when she's the one causing the disturbance?'

'The rooms upstairs aren't big enough for her class. Yours will fit nicely.'

'The woman has no class control.'

'This is night school, Bob. We're dealing with adults.'

Andrew stood up, walked to the open door of his office and looked back expectantly. His face purple, Bob swivelled on his heel, brushed past him and stormed into the corridor. A few seconds later, Andrew heard the slam of a classroom door.

'Poor Mary,' he thought, 'copping it at home and at work.'

He remembered what he'd heard from other principals about Mary Fletcher's husband. After years of parental complaints and being shunted from one primary school to another, Frank Fletcher took voluntary redundancy when the Education Department was culling a surplus of teachers. What a contrast with Mary!

Andrew left his office. As he passed Bob's classroom, he refrained from looking in through the corridor window. Guffaws, impassioned protests and bursts of applause from a room further along drowned whatever Bob was telling his students. Andrew hastened his stride in anticipation.

When he opened the classroom door, no one noticed him. A semicircle of desks faced two desks with buzzers on them. Students were yelling encouragement, advice and supposedly correct answers at two contestants who were thumping the buzzers. Mary Fletcher, a brown cardigan sagging from her narrow shoulders, wrote each contestant's score on the whiteboard. Silence halted the commotion whenever she explained her judgement. At times, on a signal that Andrew never saw, she said phrases in French and the class repeated them after her. During the short time he stood in the doorway, he learnt how to say, 'You're wrong', 'She buzzed first' and 'He's cheating' in French.

Still unnoticed, he closed the door and returned to his office smiling. Grey-faced, grey-haired and dressed in drabness, Mary Fletcher looked as if she would flinch at shadows, but the appraisals written by her students spoke of lessons full of romance, adventure, excitement and joy.

The following Monday, Andrew was pinning a new classroom allocation to the noticeboard in the school's foyer when Mary arrived panting. As she checked the noticeboard, she mastered her breathing.

'Hello, Mary. Early as usual, just like your students. The first ones are already here.'

'Hello, Andrew. Oh dear. I wanted to put some vocabulary on the board before they arrived,' she said. 'The early ones probably want to show me their homework. They're certainly different from the students I used to teach. These ones actually demand homework.'

'Well, if you insist on being here before them, why don't you do what the other teachers do – stoke up on a big afternoon tea, leave home early and have dinner after the class?'

The gaiety of her laugh contrasted with the dreariness of her clothes. 'Oh, if it's a matter of insistence, my husband has to have his dinner on the table at six, so I can never get away before six thirty. The bus passes the end of our street and I have to run for it. Fortunately, it stops outside here, so I just have to run across the road.'

Andrew flicked a glance at Mary's shoes: sturdy lace-ups, polished to a shine. Their bulk emphasised the twig thinness of her legs.

'Actually,' Mary continued, 'tonight's lesson is about food. We're going to learn how to order a meal in a restaurant. We'll do a role play. Someone will be the waiter, and everyone else will be patrons.'

She sighed with mock exasperation. 'Maybe we'll have to have a waiter and a sommelier, a wine waiter. They're starring roles and the prima donnas will vie for them. There'll probably be a bit of uproar again. I'm so glad you've put Bob's class upstairs. He bailed me up after last week's lesson.'

'He did?' Andrew felt annoyed at Bob and protective of Mary.

She laughed again. 'Yes. I've spent a lifetime in high schools and he's a babe in nappies compared with some of the bullies I've dealt with. Adolescents are scarier than adults, don't you think? They're unpredictable, even to themselves. Anyway, if you'd like to see what the class is doing, why don't come in? You don't have to stand in the doorway. See you later perhaps.' Her smile lifted the weariness from her face and she hurried towards her classroom.

Mary loved teaching adults. Although demanding, it was less stressful than teaching adolescents and less work. What joy to have no exams to set and mark, no reports to write, no parent-teacher nights and no playground duty! Activities that worked well with adolescents also worked well with adults. Her class played games and performed role plays. As a reward for doing their homework correctly, she taught them songs. 'Le Hoogie Boogie' was a favourite. In the current class, all students except one would form a circle, roar out the words in French, putting feet, hands, heads and bums in and out and shaking them all about. At the end of every term, Andrew talked to the teachers about dropouts. Mary was always delighted when told she had the fewest.

Arriving at her classroom, she said, '*Bonjour. Comment allez-vous?* to the two students she mentally labelled 'the Mosman Mums'. While they replied with carefully correct pronunciation, she thought, 'Nothing mumsy about those two. I'm the *mémère*, the French granny-type who wears her apron under her coat to market and sniffs every piece of fruit before putting it in her basket. These two, they're *haute bourgeoisie*.'

As she gave them new expressions to practise, she observed with admiration the subtly coloured hair coiffed for coffee at Les Deux Magots, the designer jeans and the sleeves of cashmere sweaters tied carelessly over polished cotton shirts. It was up to her to ensure they could confidently order a café crème or a kir royal while their husbands attended a finance conference in Paris in a few weeks' time.

Then, as she would have with adolescents, she asked them to sit down while she wrote the lesson on the board. For the next two and a half hours, inside a classroom, cut off from the world with her students, Mary would be safe and happy.

How hopeless she'd felt when Frank insisted she retire as soon as she could access her superannuation! She had dreaded not having to contend with adolescent angst and aggression. She'd miss the students' whingeing about what a slave driver she was and sending up her accent, which showed how well they'd acquired it. She'd miss the warm feeling of security each time she entered the school gates.

The farewell school assembly was a memory she brought out like a photo album whenever she had a particularly bad day. Frank hadn't answered his invitation to attend so she'd light-heartedly left him at home and afterwards, not having been asked, told him nothing about the honours she'd received. At assembly, the principal had presented her with a rose-gold bracelet. Knowing they would sustain her in the future, she'd taken care to memorise his words.

'On this occasion, Mary – yes, I'm taking the liberty of calling you Mary in the presence of the whole school…'

A thousand-throated voice murmured approval.

'On this special occasion, it's an honour for me to give you this token of our respect, admiration and affection. No, affection isn't the right word for what the students feel. They love you. The t—'

Applause interrupted him. Mary turned her face from the principal to the back row and quelled with a look the whistles from the Year 12 boys. One of her favourite thugs had once said her glare could sterilise rabbits.

The principal continued, 'The teachers pay homage to a brilliant colleague. We did a whip around to buy you this present. When I say we, I mean everyone, teachers, students, office, library, IT and canteen staff, the maintenance team and the P & F. Thank you for your contribution to this school community. We'll miss you and wish you happiness in your retirement.'

He presented the small gift-wrapped box and bent down to kiss her on both cheeks. The students surged to their feet. They whistled, stamped and thundered their applause. The principal moved away from her so she stood alone on the stage of the auditorium, a frail little woman in a sagging dress of indefinite colour. Suddenly a single voice soared above the pandemonium. A boy in her Year 12 class, the most dangerous street fighter in the school, was singing. The applause switched off. Mary clutched her box to her chest and tears rolled down her face as the beautiful tenor sang, *Non, je ne regrette rien*. When he finished, she put her box on the podium and led the applause. Then, before the whistling started, she took a step forward so the students knew she was going to speak.

'*Merci*, Damian. A beautiful voice in a beautiful person.'

She let herself be buffeted by a thousand-throated hoot of laughter and then took another step forward.

Silence.

'I'm overwhelmed. And yes, I do have regrets. You're teenagers and I'm an old woman, but we do have one thing in common. We've spent our whole lives in school. I shall regret walking out of the school gates for the last time. Every day my students, my colleagues, all the people who say *Bonjour* to me in the corridor have given me joy. *Je vous tiens tous dans mon coeur.* I hold all of you in my heart.'

Pandemonium.

Mary wore the gold bracelet once. The next time she took it out of its box to put on, she found the clasp broken. She hid it with the few other broken treasures she still had. The most important thing had been the words.

Regularly since then, the deputy principal phoned and asked her to substitute for an absent teacher. Frank didn't mind if she worked a day here and there as long as it didn't interfere with the things he needed her to do. When she had a day's work, she fled the house like a child escaping from a cupboard where she'd been locked for punishment.

After Frank took redundancy, his interest in racing, previously restricted to placing a bet at the TAB on Saturday afternoons, now ruled his life. He followed the races all over Australia and was in constant contact with his bookie. He became obsessed with the certainty that his latest system would reverse all his losses. A year after they both retired, he was spending the whole day in his armchair in front of the television, with the radio and phone beside him. He needed Mary within earshot to bring drinks and snacks.

Once his redundancy money and superannuation lump sum were gone, they lived on her superannuation and casual pay. The need for additional income reconciled him to Mary applying for a job at the evening school. Andrew offered her two classes but Frank said one was enough.

It was wonderful having a class of her own again. Teaching, as always, made up for everything.

Mary finished writing the *Menu à prix fixe* on the board and turned round. Nate and Ernie had arrived. This odd pair had become friends: Nate, the ambitious young solicitor and seventy-eight-year-old Ernie, terrified of dementia. They vied with one another to be word perfect. Mary often said that if she awarded stars, Nate would receive gold ones for pronunciation and Ernie would receive them for accuracy and spelling. They laughed but one looked smug and the other triumphant on the few occasions she awarded the hypothetical stars the other way round.

Three other students arrived in a clump. Anne, a happily divorced science teacher, was particularly interested in grammar. Every lesson, architect couple Joe and Jenny gave an open invitation to anyone in the class who'd like to share the multi-bedroomed cottage they'd hired in the Dordogne for three weeks in July. Nate said he was thinking about it.

John Fleming had slid, with his usual morose unobtrusiveness, into the back seat next to the window. He stayed there, rigid with distain, during the games, songs and role plays. His reason for learning French was not clear. He talked vaguely of the pilgrim route: Vézelay, Rocamadour, Compostela. Mary often saw him staring straight ahead, his thoughts obviously far away. He became animated when Anne asked about grammar and, had Mary allowed it, would have argued endlessly about points of syntax well beyond the scope of the course.

Mary gauged the mood of the class. They were unsettled. They greeted one another perfunctorily and opened their notebooks in silence. Anne looked distracted. Ernie looked ill. His right hand was shaking. Joe and Jenny seemed more stressed than usual. Nate was fiddling with his mobile and tapping his foot. There'd be no games until she had them all attentive and working.

At two minutes to seven, almost everyone was present. Mary heard a tap-tap and jingling coming down the corridor. The students turned their eyes expectantly towards the door. Only John continued gazing at the knotty branches of the tree outside the window next to him.

In a jangle of bracelets, earrings, parrot colours, swirling skirts, shawls and chatter, Luce Macon erupted into the room. *'Bonjour,* Marie. Hello, everyone. I am late? No, I am not late. It is a miracle. My husband, he says it is a miracle. I come late to everything. I am late to our wedding, but I do not come late to the class of Marie. What do we learn today, Marie?'

Luce glanced at the whiteboard as she danced towards the vacant desk in the third row. 'Ah. Food. My husband, he loves my cooking – he loves everything else too – but I do not know how to spell the words. Ah, flambé. I see, with an accent.'

Mary and the class watched as Luce plopped onto her chair with a spreading of skirts and, still talking, extracted exercise book, textbook and fat purple pencil case from her red, blue and green plastic shopping bag.

'Seven children and now I learn to spell. My husbands – I have had four, all wonderful men, I am so lucky – they do not care how I spell. That is not what they want from me. *Hé*, Nate, do you not agree - when you like a woman, the spelling – bah! No importance. In Martinique, my mother she does not afford school clothes for all of us. We are seven children too. The oldest, we go to school in the morning. We come home at midday and swap clothes with the others and they go to school in the afternoon. I write…

Mary cut in. 'We're going to do a lot of writing today, Luce, and the past tense.'

'I am sorry. I talk much. Now I am silent.'

Having heard variations on the husbands, the children and the school in Martinique before, all the students except John looked indulgently amused or at least more relaxed than before Luce's arrival.

John was drumming his fingers on his desk and staring out the window. Mary saw a pulse throbbing near his jaw. Following his unblinking gaze, she thought once again of the similarity between adult and adolescent students. Extremes of weather – heat, cold, wind and rain – agitated them. Tonight, a blustery wind was thrashing the branches of a tree against the window. To focus the attention of the class and settle them down, Mary wrote the heading '*Passé Composé*' on the board and the conjugation of the verb 'to eat'.

Luce sighed. '*Hé*, Marie, we are not going to play a game? What about, I go to market? That is good for learning food words. You said we learn food today. The past tense it is so boring. I am not interested in yesterday. There are so many yummy things to eat today.'

Smiling, Mary ignored Luce and continued writing on the board. Suddenly she heard a crash, a cry and the scraping of feet. She swung around, the board marker still in her hand. A plastic chair lay upturned on the floor. In the centre of the room, John and Luce stood clamped together. He had seized a fistful of her clothing and was twisting it upwards with his left hand, lifting her almost off the ground. The veins stood out like ropes in his forearm. Her toes made circling movements on the floor. The bunching of layers of clothes under her armpits made her arms flail helplessly. Her fingers opened and closed. With his right hand, John held the tip of a narrow knife to her throat. The blade glinted in the fluorescent light.

His face contorted with fury, he hissed, 'Shut up! Shut up! Shut up!' Saliva gathered at the corners of his mouth and his forehead shone greasily.

The other students sat frozen at their desks. Ernie's seat was empty. Slowly, as she always did when she finished writing on the whiteboard, Mary put the marker on the teacher's desk. John sucked in his saliva, his Adam's apple bobbing like a faulty piston. He twisted Luce's clothes with a jerk and slid the blade up her throat, forcing her to tilt her head back. Eyes bulging, she opened her mouth wide until her jaws appeared to be locked. The only sounds were the branches scraping at the window and Luce's agonised gasps.

Her eyes on John's face, Mary took tiny steps towards the couple. 'Look at me, John. Give me the knife.' She used her normal firm classroom tone.

As she repeated the words, she moved closer. When she was about a metre from him, he shifted his head slightly in her direction. His eyes reminded her of the eyes of a tiger she had seen once during a visit to the zoo. She and the tiger had stood face to face, separated by a glass partition. While appearing to look straight at her, the animal's eyes made no connection. There was no sign in them of focus, intelligence or emotion. John's eyes had the same primeval blankness. Mary was certain that if his eyes focused, he would loosen his grip on Luce and the knife.

She kept repeating, 'Look at me, John. Give me the knife.'

She was aware of the low musicality of her voice. It had been an asset in the control of classes throughout her career. She kept her facial expression pleasant. Her hand held out, she slid close enough for John to put the knife in it if he chose. His knuckles were white against the orange of Luce's vest. The grease on his forehead congealed into drops. No one else moved or spoke.

Mary raised her outstretched hand a couple of centimetres. His eyes wavered in response. 'Give me the knife, John.'

In an explosion of energy, he shoved Luce away and hurled the knife onto a desk, where the tip stuck in the wood and the blade quivered. He shouldered past Mary and strode out of the room. Mary rushed after him. He broke into a run. Ernie and Andrew entered the corridor from the other end.

Andrew saw the tall man sprint around the corner and the small woman dive back into her classroom. He hurried after her. Students milled around Luce and Mary who clung to each another in a hug. It was impossible to tell who was comforting whom. Andrew was struck by the contrast between the two women, one scrawny and grey, the other robust and dazzling.

The students jostled and shouted over one another.

'What a madman!'

'Call the police.'

'He should be locked up.'

'Are you okay, Luce? Did he cut you?'

'He's sick in the head.'

'A maniac, that's what he is.'

'Mary, you were so brave.'

'Andrew, do you know what she did? She's a heroine.'

Mary stepped out of the hug but kept hold of Luce's hand. 'Let's not get things out of proportion,' she said. 'I am not a heroine and I was not brave.'

There was a babble of protest.

'Nonsense!'

'Don't be modest, Mary. You were great.'

'God knows what would have happened if you hadn't taken control.'

As Andrew was about to intervene, Mary raised her voice above the clamour and said, 'It's over now. Andrew, did you call the police?'

'Yes, they're coming.'

Mary said, 'Well, while we're waiting, let's have some tea and coffee. There are supplies in the staff room and there's instant hot water. Put your books away. There'll be no class tonight. Can we straighten the room and put the desks in order.'

Normally so vivacious, Luce had remained quiet throughout the hubbub following John's departure. Now she placed her hand and Mary's over her heart. Anticipating histrionics, Mary wanted to pull her hand away but Luce spoke with dignity.

'Thank you, Mary. You saved my life. You are a lady with a big, big soul. My whole heart thanks you. *Je vous remercie de tout mon cœur.*' She lowered Mary's hand as if it were a precious object.

Anne made Mary sit down at a desk and put a cup of tea in front of her. She picked it up gratefully and almost dropped it. Her hand had no strength. She plunged both hands between her thighs to warm them and stop the trembling.

Gradually, the students sat down with their drinks. One after the other, they narrated the incident as they had seen it, anxious to add a detail not mentioned by the previous people. The words 'brave', 'knife' and 'maniac' hovered in the air like speech bubbles.

Mary pushed aside her empty cup and put her clasped hands on the table. 'Please stop saying I was brave. As the teacher, I'm responsible for what happens in my classroom. I took charge. That's my job.'

People started to argue but became silent when Luce waved her hand, rattling her bangles.

'No, no, no,' she said vehemently. 'Like all of you, I do not agree with Marie, but if she does not want us to use the word "brave", we must respect that. I do not like the word "maniac". Please do not use it about John. I was much scared, but he is not well. I am sorry for him. Maybe he has a fit or he forgets his medicine.'

'Medicine my a—' Nate looked at Mary. 'My foot!'

'We don't know that,' Jenny said, 'and anyway, illness is no excuse for holding a knife to someone's throat.'

'I chatter a lot,' Luce said. 'I drive people mad. All my husbands, they say so.' She paused and smiled, inviting the others to smile with her.

Anne appealed to reason. 'We should save our stories for the police. We're starting to get carried away with lurid detail.'

Luce quelled the rise of indignation by saying, 'Who will drive Mary home? She does not have a car.'

Voices rose stridently as people vied to offer a lift. Mary was grateful when Andrew prevailed and she didn't have to choose between the students. She was also grateful to Luce for changing the course of the conversation.

She listened distractedly as the chatter quietened around her. She hoped the students didn't think she was falsely modest. She hadn't been brave. Bravery, she thought, isn't taking a knife from someone who's temporarily out of his mind. Bravery is facing things that make you shrivel inside. It's overcoming your own paralysing terror. A few minutes ago, she'd been in control of herself and had taken control of the situation. Her mind had been clear, her actions deliberate and based on rational thought. There had been an adrenalin rush and her heart had pounded. Whatever the students might call them, those reactions had nothing to do with her concept of fear.

The police took statements, Henry offered Luce a lift home and the other students dispersed. While Mary went to the bathroom, Andrew looked up her address in the computer.

In the car, Mary said, 'The police have to charge John, don't they?'

'Of course, but I'm sure the kind way both you and Luce spoke about him will be taken into consideration.'

At the red light before Mary's street, he said, 'I know this isn't a good time to discuss next term, Mary, but we have enough enrolments for two classes. Please consider taking both of them. You don't need to give me an answer now. Let's talk about it next Monday. This street here? To the right? Tell me when to stop.'

Mary shrank against the car door. 'Here, please,' she said.

He braked sharply and apologised. They were outside number 18. He was sure the computer had said 28. With a quick thank you, Mary shoved open the door and almost tumbled into the gutter. She scuttled across the footpath and opened the gate. Andrew waited to see that she got inside safely, but instead of going to the front door, she went down the side path and disappeared. He waited for a light to go on. The house remained dark. Uncertain of what to do, he drove the car past number 28, parked and turned the engine off.

Mary collapsed onto the bench in the side porch and waited for Andrew to drive away. She held her breath in case he could hear the rasp and then rebuked herself for being irrational. It seemed a long time before the car drove off. The porch protected her from the wind. Although she wrapped her cardigan, coat and scarf tightly around her, their warmth didn't stop her trembling. It would get colder and her clothes wouldn't be heavy enough for her to stay here all night. How good that would be! The owners were away for a few days. She'd collected their mail this afternoon.

The students had tossed around the word 'fear' like a crumpled paper ball. They had no concept of what it meant to her. Fear grew like sediment laid down by innumerable small acts: a sneer, a dish left to burn in the oven, a library book missing until after the due date, a television channel changed in the middle of a program, a cup of tea knocked over, a photograph removed from an album, a postcard from a past student thrown out with the newspapers, faeces left unflushed in the toilet, a broken clasp. Her stomach went into spasms. What small thing had Frank spent the evening preparing for her to come home to?

His home, not hers. She veered away from thinking about it. She didn't have to leave here yet. There were still a few minutes before her usual arrival time. Home – the students had no concept of what it meant to her. Anne had lost her home in the divorce, but she seemed cheerful about her small new unit. It was much easier to clean, she said.

The wind whistled past the porch and rustled the leaves of the bushes nearby. Mary rubbed her gloved hands together more to stop the trembling than to make them warm.

Two classes. Andrew's offer made her warm with pleasure. What if? No. She wouldn't have the strength. The students said she'd been strong. What did they know? But what if? With her superannuation, two classes and casual work – a small unit? Would there be enough money? The Mosman Mums, their husbands were in finance. Maybe they could recommend an adviser. And Nate, he was a solicitor.

She shivered, this time from a tiny upsurge of excitement.

No, she was going too far, too quickly. Frank would stop her somehow. She couldn't tell her students about the sort of things he was likely to do. They'd think she was a coward. Well, she was and she couldn't bear them to know. Anyway, Nate wasn't in family law.

There was a scuffling under the bushes outside the porch. The woman owner had mentioned a possum. She said it made her flesh crawl. Mary said a silent hello to the possum. Entering Frank's home was what made her flesh crawl.

There might be someone in family law in Nate's practice. If she was going to ask him, she'd have to do so before the end of term. He might go away. He was thinking about sharing the cottage in the Dordogne. France in summer – what a long time since she'd been there! Joe and Jenny said there were six bedrooms. What if?

Mary stood up. She didn't have to respond to Andrew's offer until next Monday. She'd have a week to think about it. She went down the side path and opened the gate quietly as if someone could hear her. She smiled at her irrationality. It's strange, she thought, the things that people are afraid of – like a possum! If people said she was brave, maybe she could be. She stepped into the street and let the gate shut with a clang. She'd phone Andrew tomorrow. Then she could speak to Nate and Joe and Jenny on Monday.

In his rear-view mirror, Andrew saw the small woman creep along the footpath, stop outside number 28 and straighten her shoulders. He'd phone her tomorrow and check that she was okay. He'd put some pressure on about the two classes.

Conversations, Commotion and Silence

The Inn Home Care woman is leaving. She's new. 'There we go,' she chirrups. 'All clean and comfy till Monday.'

I'm very old, but that's no reason to speak to me as if I'm a toddler. In one sense, I am a toddler. I'm unsteady on my feet.

'I don't work on Mondays. You'll be getting Jason.'

Thank heavens! Jason doesn't chirrup.

The woman seems to imagine that I won't need or want a shower over the weekend. Jason wouldn't make such an assumption. After several visits, he said, 'I could come every day if you like, Anne. The Inn Home people don't need to know. You can pay me directly.'

Smart boy, Jason.

'No, thank you.' I smiled. 'I can manage.'

'Okay, but don't forget to wear the emergency tag when you take a shower.'

Actually, my emergency tag, so to speak, is my second daughter-in-law, Olivia. She calls me every day. I'm waiting for today's call now. Oh, hurry up, Olivia! I'm itching to turn on the computer. The American stock market's down a thousand points, according to this morning's news. I can't wait to see what to tell my stockbroker to buy. Because my voice sounds youthful on the phone, his tone is usually flirty. It changes to respectful whenever I make a killing on shares he advised me against.

Ah, there's the phone now.

'Hello, Anne. How are you?'

'Fine, thank you, Olivia. And you?'

'Good, good. Anything you need?'

'Not a thing.'

'Take care. I'll call you tomorrow. Bye'

'Bye.'

Now that's the sort of conversation I like: short and to the point. None of the fluff, bubbles and venom which her predecessor, my first daughter-in-law, injected into our verbal skirmishes.

'We're so sorry, Anne. If we'd known poor Dad was so sick, we'd have come and seen him. His death was so sudden, such a shock to all of us!'

Not the thing to say to me at the funeral of my darling Tom. And don't call him 'Dad'. He's Paul's dad, not yours.

I thought it but didn't say it. I'd learnt long ago to be silent. Otherwise, the repercussions fell on Paul.

'When you've had time to settle down a bit, we'll have to have a talk about where you're going to live. You can't stay in the house, of course.'

Oh, yes I can!

And who, I wondered, was included in the 'we'? Paul had visited his dad in the hospice every day. I suspect he hadn't told his wife or his daughters. Their absence was a blessing to me. Perhaps to him too? He sat in silence beside the bed, holding his father's right hand. I held his left. Day after day, the silence was warm and comforting and said everything that needed to be said.

Two months after the funeral, my first daughter-in-law called me for the last time. 'Hello, Anne. I hope you're well. You've heard the news, of course.'

'What news is that?'

'Paul and I are splitting up.'

Hallelujah!

'Oh?'

'You didn't know? I thought maybe he'd brought the hussy to meet you.'

'I beg your pardon?'

'I thought you knew all about her.'

'I don't know who you're talking about.'

'Don't you? Really? Never mind. You'll meet her soon, I'm sure. Anyway, I'm ringing to say goodbye. The girls and I are moving to Perth.'

As far away as you can get.

Not a word from my granddaughters then or since. I mourn them. I suppose they thought I took their father's part. Well, I did. It was sixteen – no, eighteen – years ago. The silence was hurtful at first. I sent Christmas and birthday cards with cheques in them. No word of thanks. Nothing. Silence can shrivel you into indifference. Not quite. Let's say near-indifference.

Apart from Olivia's daily phone call, the visits from the Inn Home people and the occasional conversation with my stockbroker, I spend much of my time sitting looking out the front window. The house is silent; my mind isn't.

The street is lined with terrace houses. It's one way and so narrow that parking's allowed only on one side. I like watching the comings and goings. The neighbours see me at the window and wave. That's all the company I need. That and the memory of so many people now dead. Silence, I find, makes memories sweeter.

A year ago, a young couple moved into the house opposite. Music blared and a removalist truck blocked the road. Every now and then, a driver would blast his horn and one of the many young helpers would move the truck to let him pass.

Mid-afternoon, a young woman with '*Mais oui*' on her T-shirt and carrying a plate covered in plastic wrap crossed the road and banged on my screen door. Seeing me come slowly down the hall (I don't use my walker in the house), she showed not the least sign of impatience.

'Hi,' she said as I unlocked the door. 'I'm Camille. We're moving in over the road, Harry and me. I s'pose you've noticed.' Her smile was dimpled and cheeky. 'Sorry about the noise and mess.'

'If the noise bothered me, I'd take out my hearing aids and since I don't drive any more, the mess doesn't bother me either. My name is Anne.'

'Well, Anne, I've brought a peace offering. Or let's call it insurance, in case we annoy you in the future. These are my parmesan crisps. Good with a beer.' She looked at me speculatively. 'Or wine. Made 'em for the workers. Gotta get back. See ya.' She twirled around and danced out my front gate and across the road in six leaps.

From then on, I was invited to Saturday night barbecues and my refusals were rewarded with parmesan crisps or ginger bites or chocolate crunchies. My very old teeth have so far survived. I liked it especially when Harry brought the peace offering. Sun-bleached spiky hair, golden skin and blue eyes – he reminded me of Tom when we first met on Manly Beach and I was dazzled by charm and the surfer's body.

The music at the barbecues was always loud. I didn't recognise any of the tunes or singers but that didn't matter. It was happy-sounding and I imagined people dancing in the backyard. At eleven o'clock, the music was cut off and the silence clattered down. The young people, some with babies and toddlers, left in a flurry of kisses and sibilant whispered goodbyes. I'd go to bed, stretch comfortably on my back and sleep peacefully.

Three weeks ago, the barbecues stopped. On the first silent Saturday, I missed the music and commotion and homemade biscuits. Throughout the next day, cars stopped between our houses, deposited middle-aged and white-haired people and came back for them about an hour later. On the Monday, a young man, whom I'd seen before, tightened the straps that held the surfboard on the roof rack of Harry's car. He got into the car and sat for a while with his hands on the steering wheel before driving away. On Tuesday, Wednesday and Thursday, convoys of cars disgorged people who streamed in and out of the house. They brought food containers and flowers.

My hearing aids are sensitive and I stopped putting them in. Even so, the slamming of car doors and hum of voices, pierced now and then by a high-pitched exclamation, made me long for silence.

On the Friday, a shiny black car slid into Harry's parking space. A man dressed in a grey suit and a grey-haired woman in a dark blue dress entered the house. They came out with Camille. I'd never seen her wearing a dress before. I can't remember the colour. I was appalled by her face. She looked as old as the woman in blue. The driver stood by the open back door. The woman eased herself gingerly into the car. Arthritis? Camille slumped forward and crumpled onto the seat beside her. The driver closed the door as the man in the suit got into the front passenger seat.

I moved my computer onto the kitchen table. I didn't want to sit by the window overlooking the street any more. I had fifty-five happy years with a man I loved. I have a loving son and a daughter-in-law of whom I'm very fond. There are two granddaughters who might one day knock on my door. For all I know, there might be great-grandchildren. There's Jason and my stockbroker. My life's reduced from what it used to be, but it's still rich and full. Camille's life isn't at the moment. One day, I hope it will be again.

Now she has the clatter and clamour of the people who step into the silence of the house she and Harry shared. Noise isn't always helpful. You need silence to re-create a face in your mind, to colour the eyes just the right shade of blue, to hear the beloved voice with its teasing tone and the moments when it was tender.

I'm not sleeping well. I keep listening for loud music. I imagine I'm hearing little children protesting about being strapped into car seats. The kitchen is a dreary place to watch stock market shenanigans, so today I'm moving back to the front window.

As soon as I sit down, a car pulls up outside Camille's place. A woman gets out and removes a casserole dish from the passenger seat. She knocks on the front door and waits. She knocks several more times. She puts the casserole in the shade on the veranda and returns to the car, which speeds off as fast as it's possible to speed in our small street.

A little while later, the front door opens. Camille shuffles out – shapeless brown T-shirt, grey trackies, flip flops. She gives a little start when she sees me. She picks up the casserole and clutches it for what seems like a long time. Then she crosses the road.

I make my way slowly down the hall. I unlock the screen door and let her in. It's the first time she's been inside my house. She follows me to the kitchen. I open the fridge door and she makes a place in the well-stocked shelves for the casserole.

As she straightens up, I say, 'I'm about to make a coffee and I have some store-bought biscuits. Would you like to join me?'

I glance at her face and look away. Her eyes are swollen and her skin is pasty. It's been a long time since she washed her hair. Her face is blank.

I take two mugs out of the cupboard, fill the jug with water and put some ground coffee in the plunger. I move slowly around her as she stands still in the middle of the floor. I put milk, sugar and a packet of biscuits on the table. I turn my back on her to pour the boiled water. When I turn round, she's sitting at the table. I put the coffee in front of her. I tear open the packet and shake the biscuits onto a plate. Between sips of coffee, she holds the mug to her chest, as if she's cold. It's summer. Normally, on a day like today, she'd be wearing a pink T-shirt over her swimmers and Harry, in yellow T-shirt and red and orange board shorts, would wave as they jumped into the car to set off for the beach. She takes a biscuit, looks at it and puts it on her plate.

She says nothing. I say nothing. What is there to say?

Goodbye Atlanta, GA

The ceiling of my hotel room is weeping. The bath in the room above me must be overflowing. I call Reception.

Southern diphthongs warmed in molasses flow into my ear. 'We'll send someone right on up, hon. Happy New Year.'

No one comes. My wheelie case traces silver tracks across the sodden carpet. I close the door behind me. The room can do my weeping. Goodbyes have wrung me dry. I'm leaving all I hate and love about Georgia:

fat people feeding out of cardboard buckets;

graciousness and courtesy even from teenagers;

being addressed as 'hon' and 'yew all';

food stiff with batter and saturated with sugar;

people who love me.

In the land that exalts litigation, I can't understand why no one responded to my phone call. I might have slipped, hurt myself, sued and stayed. I fantasise about staying.

The street is howling. I pull my heavy coat more closely around me. An old African-American woman, a ball of rags tottering on unlaced sneakers, head butts the freezing gale and shoves her shopping cart of belongings into it. The wind can do my howling. Goodbyes have clawed me voiceless. I'm leaving all that chills and warms me about Georgia:

young men hunched in hoodies stumbling along the sidewalks;

strangers wishing me Happy New Year in shopping malls;

bare branches scraping the grey belly of the sky;

small, pyjama-clad arms encircling my neck.

'Why can't you stay with us all the time, Gran?'

In the land that celebrates family, I don't have an acceptable answer for a six-year-old. If I let my coat flap, I might catch a cold and have to return to his parents' farm where he can medicate me with Coke and cookies. I fantasise about staying.

The train from downtown Atlanta to the airport is shuddering. A young African-American man slumps in his seat, the crotch of his baggy jeans stretched between his knees. The train can do my shuddering. Goodbye hugs have squeezed me nerveless. I'm leaving all the things that crush and comfort me in Georgia:

rooftops rabid with electric reindeer;

a Charlie Brown DVD, *The Real Meaning of Christmas*, in church on Christmas Eve;

TV presenters urging us to buy safe toys;

TV presenters urging us to donate toys to children who'll otherwise have none on Christmas Day;

fresh-faced kids fighting for democracy in Iraq and Afghanistan saying 'I love you, mom' on TV.

In the land of contradictions, I'm leaving our family for the man I love.

Sydney airport is thumping. The accent of immigration officers bewilders newcomers who have studied English. Unclaimed luggage circles on carrousels. Dogs sniff suitcases. Queues congeal in quarantine. My heart is thumping too. The old American draft dodger is waiting for me beyond the dogs, the queues and the barriers. When he fled Georgia and Vietnam and came to Sydney to marry me, he promised he'd never leave home again. He never has.

Mirrors

Ada did not want to spend the evening looking at herself in a mirror. She was therefore pleased the waiter seated her where a plant blocked her reflection. She'd spent a long time in front of her hotel mirror preparing for this dinner. Her experienced hand ensured powder would not accumulate in the lines under her eyes or lipstick bleed into the fissures surrounding her mouth. The small table lamps, she knew, would be kind to her fine bones and rose complexion. The waiter removed the place setting opposite her and gave her a leather-bound menu.

Ada closed the menu, preferring first to take in her surroundings. A long narrow room, gilt-framed mirrors on wood-panelled walls, crystal-drop chandeliers, two rows of tables covered in stiff floor-length cloths, chairs padded with burgundy velvet – all was as she remembered from long, long ago. The tables were a hand's breadth apart so she could, if she chose, listen to the conversation of the couple next to her. In a mirror, she could see the face of the girl and the back of her companion. The girl had blue eyes. Ada had enjoyed men's admiration of her own blue eyes when she was young.

'What do you want to start with, sweetheart?' The young man's tone was tender, his accent Australian. 'What about oysters?' he continued. 'Mademoiselle Lévèque called them the food of love.'

'Yuck! They look like…'

Ada snapped open her menu to avoid hearing the word.

'I'd like some prawns.' The girl's tone was peevish. 'What's the word for prawns? You'd think they'd have a menu in English.'

'I've forgotten what prawns are. Let's have a look. I might see the word and remember.'

Ada was tempted to say 'crevettes', but that would be an intrusion into an intimate meal in a romantic setting. While the young man studied his menu, Ada observed him over the top of hers. He was in his twenties, open-faced, with bleached hair and squint lines from staring into sun. His clothes earned her approval. Unlike the older men in the restaurant, he wasn't wearing a jacket. Plain links that matched the gold of his wedding band held together the crisp cuffs of his fine white shirt.

Joel was distracted from his menu by a sparkle from the next table. The old lady's ring had a chunk of curiously shaped yellow stone that glinted under the chandeliers. On looking up, he was taken aback to see two huge blue eyes watching him. His Emma's eyes were sky blue. This blue was much deeper. The old lady's splendid eyes seemed to be reading him, recognising depths he had yet to sound. The hand with the curious ring lowered the menu and the old lady smiled. She must have been a looker in her day. She still looked pretty good. Joel grinned.

Ada responded to his raffish charm. 'The word for prawns is crevettes. They're on page three.'

'You're Australian too?'

'Yes.'

'We're from Hobart. We're on our honeymoon.'

'How lovely!' She smiled at both of them.

The girl smiled back and Ada observed the dimples and the pink top with 'Australia' emblazoned across the high young breasts.

Joel glanced at 'Australia' too and shifted on his chair. Later, when Emma looked up at him from the pillow, he would see multiples of his tiny face reflected in her eyes. The old lady's eyes were gleaming with amusement. She knew what he was thinking! Far from being embarrassed, he warmed to her.

I bet she has some stories to tell, he thought. I bet she broke a few hearts in her day. She would have been too much for me. Or would she? She looks as if she likes a joke and a good time. Maybe even a beer on a hot day.

He turned back to the immediate task of ordering dinner and, with Ada's help, chose for Emma the entrée and main course she'd probably like. As he listened to Ada ordering her meal, he decided to try the same entrée.

'I thought you were having prawns like me.' Emma protested. 'What was that you ordered?'

'Foie gras.' His pronunciation was correct. He'd listened carefully.

'What's that?'

'Pâté.'

Ada opened her mouth to explain, but thought better of it and said instead, 'How do you like Paris?'

Joel answered. 'I like all the historical stuff and Emma loves the shops. The crowds take a bit of getting used to. We're hiring a car and driving to the Loire Valley in a couple of days. It'll be real different from driving in Tasmania!'

'Everything's old here, isn't it?' Emma asked. 'Have you been to Paris before?'

Ada noted the link between the girl's two questions. 'Yes, a long time ago.'

'Have you been to this restaurant before?' Joel knew the answer before he asked.

'Yes. Once. It hasn't changed at all.'

'My old French teacher, she came from Paris.' Joel said. 'Mademoiselle Lévèque. She talked about this restaurant. We've come here for a special meal. The food's real different from the steak-*frites* at the restaurant near our hotel.'

He grinned again and Ada felt her heart go light. How lucky I am, she thought: a young man is still happy to talk to me! I won't encourage him. They're here to talk to one another.

Joel saw her smile and then turn her attention to savouring her foie gras. He would not draw her from her pleasure. There was Emma opposite him, getting stuck into those prawns. The waiter brought a finger bowl. Pity! He felt like leaning across the table, taking her hand and licking each buttery finger. It wouldn't be the thing to do here, in this fancy restaurant. He could visualise a young version of the blue-eyed lady, dressed like Catherine Deneuve, extending her fingers across a table towards an elegant man who would slip a diamond bracelet over them.

After Mademoiselle Lévèque's lesson about French movie icons, Joel had borrowed the video of *Belle de Jour* from the Alliance Française. The heroine's tailored clothes with bold geometric motifs would have suited the old lady when she was young. Her dress tonight skimmed over soft curves. Under the glow of the chandeliers, its blue-green material made her eyes look dark opal. Her white hair was styled to emphasise the shapeliness of her head, the back of which he saw in a mirror. Joel wondered about the man with whom she had dined here long ago. A millionaire probably. Someone who appreciated beautiful women. A prince, perhaps. Not a prince of industry – too ordinary. No, a real one. Such people still existed then. A man like that would give a bracelet or chunky ring as easily as a box of chocolates. Emma had pretty hands. Diamonds would look good on them. One day he'd give her some.

After the waiter removed her entrée plate, Ada stood up to go to the ladies' room. She didn't need to go there, but sitting in one spot for an extended period made her stiff. Besides, with her out of the way, perhaps the young man would kiss his wife across the table. He looked as if he wanted to. The girl would taste of garlic and butter.

Emma leaned towards Joel, showing the top of her cleavage. 'That wool crêpe dress must have cost a packet. Why would an old woman get all dressed up and eat alone in a restaurant like this?'

'Nostalgia, I suppose. I bet she always came to restaurants like this when she was young.'

'How boring!'

Whatever the old lady's reminiscences were, Joel didn't think they'd be boring. He hoped Emma wasn't bored. He noticed the back of her head in the mirror. If she got rid of those frizzy curls she spent so much time fussing with, the shapeliness of her head would be obvious.

After Ada's return, the main meals were served and she concentrated on enjoying her *truite meunière*. If she glanced up and Joel happened to be looking in her direction, she gave a small smile, indicating with polite warmth she preferred not to be disturbed. She covertly watched the young wife in the mirror. Emma was eating with relish and picking things from Joel's plate to try. Her eyes sparkled. They were the same shade of blue as the multiple plastic bangles on her arms. Ada ordered a coffee and petits fours to end her meal.

The coffee brought memories of the last time she'd been in this restaurant. Then, as now, she'd been alone. Then, the coffee was the only thing on the menu she could afford. She had come for the atmosphere and the address. One flash of her blue eyes and the waiter had promptly brought her some stiff writing paper and an envelope embossed with the restaurant's name in gold lettering. She had wanted Robert to know exactly where she was when she replied to his proposal.

Tomorrow she would go shopping for something special for Robert. Dear Robert! This trip was his idea. He hadn't come himself. Since his heart attack, he hated flying. But he knew she loved Paris. When she was twenty-three, her father had sent her here in the hope she'd be distracted from two unworthy marriage prospects. Once, when he thought she was out of earshot, he'd called them that bloody barrister and that banal barman.

For her eighty-first birthday, Robert had given her a different sort of present from usual. There'd been no small exciting box, like the one containing the topaz ring she was now wearing. There had been just a plain white envelope and inside, a first-class return ticket to Paris, a reservation for ten nights at the Hôtel George V, a wad of euros and a booking for dinner at this restaurant.

Dear Robert! He'd be camped now near his favourite fishing spot.

Fifteen years ago, she'd been surprised at what he'd chosen for his retirement present. He'd rejected the proposed fancy fishing gear and asked for the money instead. He never told her how much he'd received or what he'd done with it. In the speeches at his retirement party, the most commonly used phrase had been 'a good bloke'. Fifty-eight years of marriage, three children, eight grandchildren, and a great grandchild on the way – yes, she knew he was a good bloke. He was a romantic bloke too. He still wrote on her birthday cards, 'To the Princess who wrote to me from Paris, with love from the Banal Barman'.

Tomorrow she was taking a train to a village on the Marne River. She was seeing a man who had a worldwide reputation for making fishing flies.

Ada signalled for the bill, placed a small wad of euros on the silver tray and asked for a taxi. Responding to a flash from the blue eyes, the waiter offered her his arm. She leant heavily as she turned towards Joel and Emma.

'Enjoy the rest of the evening. I hope for you, as it was for me, Paris is the start of a long and happy marriage.'

Joel watched the waiter escort the old lady towards the door.

'How sad,' Emma said. 'Her husband's dead and she came back to remember a meal they had together here.'

Her light blue eyes glinted like porcelain. Joel shivered. He was sorry he hadn't brought his jacket. The old lady had taken the warmth with her.

'I didn't get the impression he's dead,' he replied. 'He must be some bloke, her husband. A real prince.'

I Do Not Understand

A shadow moves across my newspaper. I look up, thinking perhaps a pelican has flown over. As I lower my gaze, I click onto two big green eyes.

'What's his name?' A chubby finger points to the black moggy stretched along my thigh on the chaise lounge.

'It's a her. Sylvie.'

A chubby hand inches towards the cat that lowers languid lids over golden eyes and allows one gentle finger to touch the white flash between its ears. I'm surprised. I've seen my friends' grandchildren lurch gleefully towards the seemingly sleepy Sylvie and I've leapt to snatch them away from unfurling claws.

'Do you have a cat at home?' I ask.

'Ours died. Mummy runned her over.' Tears glitter in the green eyes. There's a whisper, as if to reassure me. 'She didn't mean to.'

'Of course she didn't. Is your family moving in next door?'

A convoy of utes woke me at six thirty. Unable to linger in bed, I'm having my coffee on the back veranda.

A sudden screech shatters the Sunday suburban calm. The child tenses.

There's a pause and then a series of rapid screeches, powered by formidable lungs, morphs into two repeated syllables, 'Nee Coal!'

The child darts across the grass and disappears behind the hibiscus bush that hides the hole in the fence between the two properties. A few seconds later, more screeching. Prolonged this time. The words are unintelligible. Finally, the same sound having been repeated at least five times, I recognise, '*s'il te plaît*'. Aha! French. I'm taking lessons at the

Alliance Française. It would be nice to have some practice, but my carefully prepared sentences would probably shrivel into heat-blackened gibberish if I tried them out on the owner of the voice.

I decide to go for a long walk and return home mid-afternoon. A bucket brigade is passing cardboard boxes from a ute to the front veranda of the house next door.

A short while later, there's a faint but persistent tapping on my front door. Two green eyes look up at me. 'Mummy says this is for you.' The child is balancing a covered plate on her forearms.

I lift the corner of the tea towel and the smell of baked apples whooshes out. The tart looks professionally made. It's big enough to serve eight. I live alone.

'Tell her thank you. What's your mother's name?'

'Marie-Paule. Daddy Geoff.'

'And you're Nicole?'

A nod.

'Would you like to come onto the back veranda and have a slice of this beautiful tart with me?'

'Will Sylvie be there?'

'Yes, but she won't have any.'

A look of contempt. I've said something silly. Then, for the first time, a smile. I'm forgiven.

'You'd better go and tell Mummy you'll be having afternoon tea with Heather and Sylvie next door. Ask if she'd like to join us.'

'Mummy says she can't come if you arks. She has to feed the helpers.'

Nicole, Sylvie and I sit quietly at the table on the back veranda. Two of us have a slice of tart. We all have cream.

So much has happened since that day. I didn't take a photo and yet I often take out the memory and look at it. It's as fresh and full of colour now as it was then – blue summer sky, vivid green eyes glinting with tears and then smiling at my silliness, sleek black cat sitting tall between us, crisp golden apple slices with toasted edges, intermittent screeches from next door – all elements of what was to come.

The next morning, I'd just stepped onto the footpath when a car came zooming down the neighbouring drive. At the gate, the tyres squealed and the car rocked to a halt. Assuming Nicole's mother to be the driver, I thought of the cat that had been run over. Nicole solemnly waved to me from the child seat in the back. The driver spurted from the car and charged towards me, her hand thrust forward. She grasped my limp right hand and blasted me with rapid vocal fire. At first, her accent was so strong that I wasn't sure whether she was speaking English or French. That problem was resolved when I managed to grab a flying word that turned out to be 'dinner'. I'd been nodding during the barrage and suddenly realised I'd been invited.

'I'm sorry. When?'

'I, me too, I also am sorry. It is very early. *Eh bien*, my 'usband, Geoff. I tell you 'is name is Geoff, isn't it? Yes? *Eh bien*, Geoff, 'e like 'is dinner, as 'e say, on the dot.'

'On the dot of what?'

'I tell you, six zirty.'

'Tonight?'

'But, of course! I make *blanquette de veau* and *un vacherin*.'

'Thank you for the tar—'

'Bof, bof, bof. We are neighbour, no? Nicole tell me you are pleased. Must go. See you tonight. Come early for the apéritif.'

She rocketed into the car and I was left with the impression of a huge zest for every single one of life's joys. I had no idea what she was wearing and couldn't have told you the colour of her hair. (That's irrelevant anyway. It changed often.)

The car engine howled. Nicole, wearing the dark blue sun hat mandatory for local kindergarteners, waved once more. The hat, the wave and her calmness gave her a regal air as she was whisked away by her shouting chauffeur.

Dinner was both interesting and an ordeal. Geoff shook my hand and muttered hello. He was a big man, not fat – well-muscled. He worked in a warehouse. He hardly spoke at all. No need. Marie-Paule didn't stop. By the time we'd finished the exquisite canapés with the pre-dinner drinks, I'd given up making an effort to understand. I ducked beneath the verbal storm and settled for silent observation. I wondered if that was Geoff's strategy too. He concentrated on his food. It was worth concentrating on. Marie-Paule is the best home cook I've ever known. I can't say that *blanquette de veau* is one of my favourite dishes, but what she did to it that night was magic. It didn't take long, however, for a problem to emerge.

''ezer, you will 'ave a bit more, just a teeny bit more, for my pleasure. Geoff, 'e 'as more. I will not give you as much as 'im. You are skinny. You must eat. You eat like a little bird.'

Don't get me wrong. I was never in Marie-Paule's league as a cook, but when Tom was alive, we often gave dinner parties and I did do some dishes well. I appreciate good food; I just can't swallow slabs of it. On the evening of my first dinner with Marie-Paule, Geoff and Nicole, I went home feeling like one of those French geese that's been force-fed. Befuddled and nauseous, I flopped onto my bed without undressing and tried to piece together a tiny incident that had occurred near the end of the main course. Marie-Paule had got up from the table to stir something on the stove. Out of the corner of my eye, I caught a small movement opposite me. I looked across at Nicole and Geoff. There was more food on his plate and less on hers than a few seconds earlier.

Over the next few days, I accumulated leftover veal, the remainder of the *vacherin*, leftover minestrone soup, a chicken casserole, and half a dozen jars of home-made pickles. Nicole brought them so I couldn't protest. I shuffled things from fridge to freezer and felt like a charity case.

When I saw Marie-Paule putting out the rubbish on Wednesday night, I rushed to take mine out too and said, 'Thank you so much for…'

'Yes, yes. Nicole say you say zank you all ze time.'

'It's too much, Marie-Paule.'

She opened her mouth but I held up my hand like a traffic policeman and continued. 'Everything you send is wonderful, but I can't eat
it all. I live by myself and go out three nights a week.'

'I wrap it so you freeze it. The pickles, zey keep. You do not 'ave to
open zem all at once. I do not need ze jars back straight away. I 'ave
plenty more. It is a pleasure. I am not good at many zings, but I make
good food. My Geoff, 'e love what I make. When we meet, all 'e eat is
'amburger, chips, steak, mash potatoes. These are good zings if ze cook
is good, but not for every night. 'e even like Vegemite! I try it once. I
try everyzing. I am not a person who criticise wizout to try. It is like car
grease! It is *une abomination*! 'e 'as a jar in ze back of a cupboard. 'e does
not know I know 'e 'ide it zere. Once 'e give some to Nicole! I say to
'im, Enough! You, yes! 'er no! I do not understand. You Australians,
you 'ave wonderful fresh food 'ere in zis country and you give zis Vegemite to children!'

I backed away. I needed to do some strategic planning to cut off
supply.

On the Saturday night following this conversation, I got home at about
nine thirty, changed into my nightdress and turned on a police drama
on TV. Someone got shot and people screamed. When the scene
changed to the detective's office, the screaming continued. It was coming from next door. I turned off the television. It was a woman's voice.
Marie-Paule's. There were loud thumps and the sound of crockery and
glass being broken. If Tom was still alive, he'd have gone and banged
on their door. My heart raced at the foolish thought that I should do
the same. I wasn't that brave. Geoff was a big man. He'd said so little at
dinner, I'd come away with no idea of what he was like. Marie-Paule
was no bigger than me. As for Nicole...

I reached for the phone near the front window. The screams were
intensifying. Fury or fear? My finger was hovering over the first zero
when I saw a car, lights twirling, pull up outside next door. A police

man and woman got out and crossed the footpath. Heavy banging on the front door added to the crashing and screaming from inside. Suddenly there was silence. Well, not exactly silence. I could hear a murmur of voices and then nothing.

I was trembling. If this was what my neighbours were going to be like, maybe I'd give up dithering and finally sell. How selfish! My first thoughts were for me and not for the safety of Nicole and Marie-Paule. Well, the police were there. They'd call an ambulance and social services if they were needed. No. I wouldn't stay. Friends had been telling me I should downsize. It was getting hard to maintain the big house now that Tom was gone. We'd intended it to be our family home. We'd talked about two, maybe three children. I saw again Nicole's blue hat and my eyes filled with tears. Children hadn't come. Tom and I said we had each other – that was what counted. Indeed it was. But oh, I never told Tom how much I would have liked children. He never said anything either. And then there was cancer.

I was still standing with the phone in my hand when the police car left. Not a sound from next door. I went to bed and tried to read. I fell asleep long after midnight.

The next morning, bringing my coffee onto the back veranda, I found Nicole sitting in her pyjamas on the top of the steps going down to the grass. Sylvie was sitting by her side. I smelt urine.

'Good morning, Nicole. Good morning, Sylvie.'

Nicole acknowledged my greeting by ducking her head and hunching her shoulders, almost as if expecting a blow. I sat down beside her. The smell of urine was stronger. Her pyjama bottoms looked damp. Suddenly, Sylvie licked her forepaw and rubbed it over her face.

'Oh look, Nicole. Sylvie is starting her Sunday bath. She's using her paw as a face washer. She likes to do it here when it's sunny. And do you know what she likes to do next?'

Nicole didn't look at me, but her shoulders relaxed and she shook her head.

'She likes to come to the bathroom door and watch me have my bath. She doesn't come in. She just sits there and stares. I think she's checking to see that I wash my pyjamas properly.'

Nicole snatched a look at me to see whether I was joking.

'Perhaps if you had a bath, she'd come and look at you too.' I added, playing it safe, 'Of course cats don't always do what you expect them to and they can't be made to do anything. Would you like to try and see?'

Nicole looked at me speculatively.

'And then Sylvie can have her breakfast and you and I can have some toast and hot chocolate.'

I wondered why on earth I was creating this confection of partial truths. A responsible adult would have gripped Nicole by the hand and walked her firmly back to her parents. I was not that sort of responsible adult.

I stood up and held out my hand. 'Would you like to try?'

Sylvie had stopped licking herself and seemed, like me, to be waiting for Nicole's answer. Nicole looked from one of us to the other. She stood up and slipped her small cold hand into mine. I hoped against all probability that Sylvie would come to the bathroom door. She occasionally did so when I was taking a shower and her breakfast was late. I never have a bath.

I filled the tub with warm water and opened a packet of bubbles that someone had given me two Christmases ago.

'Can you undo the buttons, or would you like me to?' I asked.

Nicole shook her head and tackled the buttons. She fumbled and took a long time with each one. I had the impression she rarely undid them herself. I sat on the edge of the bath and waited. She pulled off the top and hesitated.

'We'll pop your pyjamas into the bath and give them a bit of a wash and then I'll pop them in the dryer and they'll be all warm and cosy to have breakfast in.'

Nicole turned her back to me and pulled down her pyjama pants.

Naked, she turned towards me and held up her arms to be lifted into the bath. There were no bruises, no marks whatsoever on her body. I was starting to think this was all getting beyond me. I suppose she was the right weight for her age but I found her heavy and was afraid of toppling over. I got her into the bath, tossed her pyjamas in too and sloshed them around. She giggled at the little waves.

I stood up and was about to say I'd better tell her parents where she was when she pointed a foamy finger towards the door. Miracle of miracles! Sylvie was sitting on the threshold.

While her pyjamas were drying, Nicole wore one of my T-shirts that came to her ankles. She showed no impatience for her own breakfast and watched with fascination as I cut up Sylvie's meat and warmed it in the microwave. As I made our toast, she made several trips to put butter, jam, cutlery, plates and mugs on the table on the veranda.

On her last return, she patted my arm. 'Where's the Vegemite?'

'At the back of the cupboard in the corner.'

'That's where Daddy keeps it.'

That afternoon, not long after my return from a walk along Manly Beach, there was a pounding on my front door. I was momentarily alarmed but guessed it was Marie-Paule. Indeed it was. With a big grin and a freshly baked fruit tart. She shifted the tart to her left hand, put her right arm around my neck, crushed me to her chest and kissed me vigorously on both cheeks. This was so intrusive, I wanted to push her away, but was afraid she'd drop the tart. I tried to sound welcoming.

'Hi, Marie-Paule. Come and have a coffee. Or tea if you prefer.'

'Zank you.'

She strode straight down the hall to the kitchen, plucked a knife from the magnet strip on the wall, slashed the tart into quarters, ripped two mugs from their hooks and flung open the fridge door to find the milk. I calmed my irritation at the takeover of my kitchen with the thought, not yet twenty-four hours old, that I was selling up.

She slammed the fridge door and, her face crumpling into quizzical lines, said, 'I zank you for Nicole, but I do not understand. She say you give 'er a bath with ze cat.'

Tears of laughter coursed down her face after I gave an explanation. Although it was getting chilly, I insisted we go onto the back veranda. The volume of her voice, not contained between walls, was less bruising. Too bad if the neighbours heard her side of the conversation.

We discussed how she did the glaze on the fruit tart, much more delicate than anything I've ever achieved, and then got onto the topic of what she was going to prepare for tonight's dinner, homemade pasta and mushroom sauce.

'I make pasta – you know I work in a pasta shop, isn't it? Geoff only eat pasta I make. I do not understand. Last night 'e go to ze pub and he eat 'amburger and 'e come home drunk and 'e not eat ze dinner I make for 'im. I am so angry I shuck 'is dinner at 'im. It take me a long time to clean after ze police leave. Do you see ze police last night? I do not understand. Zey tell me a neighbour ring about ze noise. Zere is not curfew until eleven o'clock. I know ze law. I was angry. I am allowed to shuck zings in my own 'ouse, no? You would be angry, isn't it, if your 'usband come home drunk and not eat your dinner? Oh, I am so sorry, 'ezer. You 'ave no 'usband.'

At the mention of the word 'husband', I stood up and started clearing the plates. That's not the way I like to treat a guest, but I didn't see Marie-Paule leaving without some forceful gesture from me. I was tired from my fears last night, from having to deal with Nicole this morning and from the flood of words this afternoon.

'You 'ave zings to do now? Nicole will bring you pasta so you do not cook dinner.'

'Thank you, Marie-Paule, but I still have some chicken left and, besides, I don't like pasta.'

Tom and I used to love it.

Every Saturday night until my move to Manly, I stayed out until after eleven p.m. and every Sunday morning Nicole 'had a bath with the cat'. After the third time, her pyjamas didn't need to be washed.

When I once suggested to Marie-Paule that Nicole might be upset or frightened by her shouting and throwing things, she laughed. 'No, no, no. She is used to me. She know I bark and I am louder zan ze bite.'

I never mentioned the wet pyjamas. Another responsible adult might have acted differently. I felt I'd be betraying Nicole's confidence. Marie-Paule told me I was her best friend. I didn't feel like a best friend. Although well-intentioned and generous, she intruded into my life. She insisted she'd help me pack and clean the house when I put it on the market. I packed and cleaned while she was at work. Telling lies and modifying my behaviour in order to deal with Marie-Paule made me wonder how Nicole coped. Fanciful as it may seem, I saw her weekly request for Vegemite toast as an act of rebellion against her mother. As for Geoff, he worked, ate beautiful meals, watched sport on TV and got drunk on Saturday nights. It didn't occur to Marie-Paule that I'd leave without giving her my new address. Had it not been for Nicole, I might have done so.

I moved to an apartment in a high-rise in Manly. There was a video intercom at the entrance. Marie-Paule took to dropping in without calling me first. Sometimes, feeling mean and sneaky, I didn't answer the buzzer. As soon as Nicole was old enough to take the ten-minute bus ride on her own, she visited regularly. She always phoned beforehand. She chatted a little about school and then sat quietly on the balcony with Sylvie.

One day when Nicole was in fifth class, Marie-Paule phoned me, so angry and incoherent that I couldn't identify which language she was speaking. Alarmed, I said I'd come over straight away.

Before I'd reached the front door, she wrenched it open, grabbed me in a furious hug, kissed me multiple times on the cheeks and burst into tears. She dragged me into the kitchen, which was in chaos. I stepped gingerly over shards of crockery and glass. It looked as if she'd swept everything off the table – plates, glasses, cutlery, salt, pepper, sugar and jars of sauce.

She shouted, half in English, half in French, sobbing and banging her hand on the wall. I pieced together the essential.

'Ze school, Ze school, zey ring. Zey accuse. Zey say, zey say…I send Nicole to school with no lunch! I do not feed my daughter! My child is 'ungry! Is madness! Is no posseeble! I do not understand. She 'ave beautiful lunch. Every day I make. Every day. I see ze teacher tomorrow. I tell 'er. I do not starve my child!'

The hairs rose on the back of my neck. I brushed some debris off a chair and sat down, wondering. Was Nicole being bullied? One of my friends talked about her granddaughter being made to hand over her lunch to a bigger child. Nicole was small, but I'd always thought she could stick up for herself.

'I tell Geoff tonight. 'e must not go to work, 'e must come wiz me to ze school. 'e will tell ze teacher. My 'usband and my daughter, every day, zey do not leave this 'ouse wizout a beautiful lunch. Fresh, nourishing, delicious. I make it. Wiz my 'ands.'

The following Sunday there was a ring on the intercom. Nicole. She was pale. Two lines dragged down the corners of her mouth, making her look bitter – a horrible look on a child.

'Hi, Heather. Where's Sylvie?'

'Asleep on my bed.'

'Can I…?'

'Of course. Would you like a hot chocolate?'

'Yes please.'

'And Vegemite toast?'

'Yes please.'

I put our drinks and toast on a tray and brought it into the bedroom. Nicole was sitting cross-legged beside Sylvie, gently stroking the white flash between her ears. I looked carefully at Nicole. Her face was plump and her bare arms showed none of the skinniness I've seen in documentaries about anorexia. I'm no expert of course, but she looked healthy to me.

I sat in the armchair with my coffee and asked as casually as I could, 'What do you do with your school lunches?'

She looked at me speculatively and the little girl of our first meeting reappeared. 'I'll tell only if you don't tell Mummy.'

I said nothing. I wasn't going to make promises I shouldn't keep. The suspense was too much. She wanted to tell me.

'I give them away.'

'To whom?'

'Other kids.'

'Why?'

''cos they like them.'

'No. I mean why don't you eat them?'

'I'm not hungry.'

'You must be at lunchtime when everyone else is eating.'

There was a flash of anger. 'No, I'm not! At breakfast I'm stuffed up to here.' She slashed a finger across her throat. 'And I eat till I burst at dinner. You don't know what it's like. She won't listen. I don't want all that food.'

'Did you say that when your parents went to the school the other day?'

A sly look crept over her face. 'I didn't say anything.'

No two things could have infuriated Marie-Paule more – her daughter not eating the lunch she'd prepared and her daughter refusing to explain why. Nicole was waging cold war. Years later, when she was in Year 12, she told me she'd given away her lunches throughout primary and high school. She did it secretly so no teacher ever called Marie-Paule again.

As Sylvie got older and developed cataracts, Nicole visited me more regularly. She read her school texts and let the scrawny little moggy sleep curled on her lap for hours.

One Sunday, she asked, 'You're going to take her to the vet soon, aren't you?'

'I think I'll have to.'

'Will you tell me when and I'll come with you?'

'Yes, I will.'

We cried beside the table where Sylvie lay on her last visit to the vet. That was the only time Nicole and I ever hugged one another.

One Sunday afternoon not long after Nicole finished her Year 12 exams, Marie-Paule leaned on the intercom button and I let her in.

'I 'ave shopped in Manly. I drive Nicole 'ome.'

'She's not here.'

'She 'as left not long ago?'

'She hasn't been here at all.'

'What! She does not visit ze cat?'

'Sylvie died two years ago.'

'Oh! You do not tell me! I do not understand. Why Nicole she not tell me?'

Fury shook me. When had there ever been enough silence for Nicole or me to say the cat had died?

'Now Year 12 is over, she is strange. She come 'ome late last night. She miss dinner. I smell alco'ol. We fight. She say she leave. I say, "If you go, do not come back."'

'Maybe she's taking you at your word.'

'No, no, no. Not posseeble. She know me.'

Marie-Paule didn't stay long. She seemed to blame me for Nicole not being here. Over the next few days I received increasingly frantic phone calls.

''Nicole 'as not come 'ome. She is not wiz you? She 'as not called you? I go to ze police. Zey ask where are 'er cloze. I look in 'er wardrobe. Zey gone. Ze police say she is not a minor. Where is she?'

When I called Nicole's mobile number, a recorded message said it was no longer in use. I waited one afternoon at the entrance to Geoff's work and, when he came out, asked if he knew where she was. He grinned and patted my shoulder. I was relieved. That was the most communicative he's ever been with me.

Over the next few months, despite preparing her usual gargantuan meals, Marie-Paule lost weight. She visited the police regularly.

'Oh, 'ezer. I do not understand. Zey not help. Why she not call? I go to ze school. I ask zem to give me phone number of friends in 'er class. Zey refuse. Why? Can not zey see I lose my mind?'

She expended her increased nervous energy on extra shifts at the pasta shop and more volunteer work at Vinnies (her source of replacement crockery).

It's Sunday morning. The intercom rings. Nicole! When I open the front door, I want to fling my arms around her but restrain myself. She looks well. Her clothes could be described as old or retro depending on your age. She's carefully holding a shoebox.

'Hot chocolate and Vegemite toast?' I ask.

She grins. 'No time. Gotta go. Take off the lid.'

'What is it?'

'Take off the lid.'

Inside, a scruffy black kitten lies limp on a face washer. It has a flash of white between its ears.

'I found her in a dumpster in the street near our squat. I knew you'd take her.'

'Not unless you tell me where you're living.'

'Don't be stupid. Of course you will.'

'Why don't you contact your mother? She's out of her mind.'

'Good! That's where she's always sent me. And Dad.'

'She thinks you might be dead!'

'Typical drama queen. Tell her you saw me on the street. If you say I came here, she'll move in and wait till I come back, which may be never.'

'Will you give me your mobile number?'

'If you give it to Mum, I'll change it and never speak to you again.'

'Now you're sounding like her. She exaggerates but she's not a nasty person, Nicole, and she loves you.'

'How would you like to have her as a mother? The temper, the smashing, the screaming, the force feeding, the not listening. You can tell her I'm not coming home. Ever.'

'And your father? Are you in contact with him?'

'She hasn't bothered, not once, to ask him if he knows where I am. It's all about her.'

'Where's this squat?'

'Too many questions, Heather. Bye.'

She spins around and strides towards the lift. She's wearing what I'd describe as combat boots! I'm so relieved, my knees feel weak. Clutching the shoebox, I stumble into the living room and plonk down on the couch. The phone number! I didn't get the phone number! I snatch up my mobile. Thank God! She's just sent it. Tears wet my cheeks as I stroke the kitten with one finger. It opens its eyes and yawns, exposing tiny ferocious fangs.

I make up my mind. For once, Marie-Paule will come to my home, sit where I instruct her to, eat my chocolate cake and listen to my understanding of what it would feel like to be her daughter. And I'll insist she pronounce my name properly. Before making the phone call, I feed the kitten and watch her fall asleep on Sylvie's old blanket.

Last Day of Term

'Bye, Miss Braithwaite. Have a nice holiday!'

'Bye, Miss Braithwaite. See ya next term.'

'Goodbye, Geraldine. Goodbye, Tim.'

'Bye, Miss Braithwaite. Be good!' Joe Mann winks as he darts out the classroom door.

'Here, miss.' Con Demetrious shoves a creased piece of paper into her hand. He hurries past her but stops just inside the door waiting for her reaction.

The last few pupils scramble out and Gail looks at the paper through the reading section of her bifocals. It's a caricature of her. That's what he must have slid into his folder when she strolled menacingly towards his desk this morning.

In the sketch, she's wearing a black top with 'Teecha' emblazoned in lightning strikes across her chest. Con knows how to spell. He's winding her up. Wiry grey hair corkscrews out from her head. Goggle glasses skid down her Pinocchio nose and a huge grin exposes a regiment of teeth. Her cat, Percy, also grins. Sometimes, she tells stories about Percy to the class. Friday afternoon is a good time to invent his adventures. In Con's drawing, Percy's front paw pinions a snarling rat.

The combination of the last day of term, the waiting boy and the rat reminds her of another last day of term, another boy, another rat, a real one, and a teacher who influenced her life. She looks up from the drawing and, instead of walls covered with children's paintings, sees the institutional green walls of a classroom from long ago.

Nothing brightened that classroom. The dark wooden sills of the paned windows were well above the children's heads. Through the window above Miss Thomas's desk, the skeletal branches of a dying tree groped at the sky that in Gail's memory was always grey. The double desks, their wooden lids deeply scored with names, were heavy to move, so dirt accumulated around the bottom of their metal legs. Lolly papers and brown apple cores were jammed into the inkwell holes. Over the cracked blackboard at the front of the room, dust blurred a framed photo of Queen Elizabeth wearing a diamond tiara and a yellow evening dress with a sash across it. On top of the bookcase, a world globe featured all the countries of the British Empire in red. The noticeboard was the colour of peanut butter, which Gail hated. Curling around its pin, a list of monitors' duties mentioned her name for the teachers' tea.

Miss Thomas's voice droned on about bushrangers. How boring she made them sound! Gail knew better from the book she had on her lap. When the pupils in Grade 5 finished their work, they were supposed to read a book from the bookcase to stop them disturbing others. If they brought a book from home, they had to show it to Miss Thomas for approval.

When Gail had shown her birthday present, *Robbery under Arms*, Miss Thomas raised her bushy grey eyebrows and said, 'That's a classic, but I think it's too old for you. If you find it too hard, you can borrow a book from the bookcase.'

'Why does she think I'll find it too hard?' Gail whispered indignantly to Renate, who sat next to her. 'I've read every book there, twice!'

Robbery under Arms was the first novel Gail had read about adults. It was a relief not to read about cute children or talking animals.

'Gail Braithwaite! You're not listening! What did I just say?'

Renate nudged her. Gail was aware the droning tone had changed but hadn't been listening to the words.

Sitting up straight, her hands clasped on the desk lid, she recited, 'Grade 5, open your exercise books, rule a one-inch-wide margin with your pencils, write the date – it's Friday, 27 August 19 hundred and 54 – copy the heading and questions from the board leaving three lines for each answer, write your answers in complete sentences and do not talk to one another.'

The recitation was not an exceptional feat of memory. Miss Thomas said exactly the same thing each time the class became restless.

A ball of paper suddenly landed on Gail and Renate's desk, probably catapulted from Graham Johnston's rubber band. A murmur was rising from the boys' side of the classroom. Gail smoothed the paper and read the note: 'She looks like she smells something bad – herself.' Gail sucked in her cheeks to stop a giggle. Miss Thomas did have a bad smell. Gail and Renate talked about it. Miss Thomas didn't smell like Mr Edwards, who taught the dumb Grade 5 class. He smelt of sweat and cigarettes. That was all right. At least the two girls knew what he smelt of. Years later, when Gail was teaching in an economically deprived area of Melbourne, she recognised Miss Thomas's smell on some of her pupils, the ones whose bodies and clothes were never washed.

Miss Thomas snapped, 'Get on with it then!' and was about to resume writing on the board when she noticed the crumpled paper. 'What's that on your desk?'

Gail was tempted to say, 'My exercise book,' but knew she'd be pushing too far. She never misbehaved and, because she always answered the questions on the board correctly, Miss Thomas had told her mother she was 'an exemplary pupil'. Exemplary status entailed the privilege of being tea monitor. This meant that she left the classroom five minutes before the beginning of recess and lunchtime to make the teachers' tea. She looked forward to the twice daily escape from boredom.

'Rubbish, Miss Thomas. I'm just going to put it in the bin.' As a diversionary tactic, her trip to the bin failed.

'Graham Johnston, bring your rubber bands, all of them, and put them on my desk!'

Graham winked at Gail as he brushed past her desk. She tossed her head, making her plaits swing, and pretended not to watch him. She wondered how long he would have to stand facing the wall this time.

Silly Graham! He made himself a perfect target for Miss Thomas.

He never listened and, although Gail suspected he always knew the correct answer, he couldn't be bothered to spout it when picked on. He wasn't the only boy who did things Miss Thomas said were bad.

When she couldn't identify a culprit, she picked on Graham because he'd usually confess. He always confessed when the bad thing was going to be punished by the strap. Miss Thomas would send him with a note to Mr Edwards and a few minutes later he would stroll back with his hands in his pockets. The other boys were always eager to see his cuts.

Each boy reacted differently when he was sent to Mr Edwards. Ian Peters went red in the face but he didn't cry. Andy Scarborough cried. He'd start to blubber before he left the room. Snot ran from his nose and he wouldn't wipe it away. Once, he wet his pants. Gail saw the urine running down his leg. Miss Thomas hissed, 'Go to the lavatory at once!' As Andy headed for the classroom door, he thrust his forearm across his eyes and howled.

Graham's current punishment, Gail thought, was probably worse for him than the strap. Having confessed to catapulting the paper ball, he had to spend lunchtime in the boys' shelter shed and was not allowed to play football.

Gail tossed her plaits again. She had no time to feel sorry for Graham Johnston. If she answered the questions quickly, she could get back to *Robbery under Arms*. By the time she finished them, however, there was only a minute left before she had to prepare the teachers' tea. She spent it gazing at the dead tree through the window.

After three terms in her class, Gail avoided looking at Miss Thomas. Graham Johnston liked to draw funny pictures of her. Gail was good at drawing too, but she wasn't going to waste her few precious Derwent pencils drawing Miss Thomas. No pencil could reproduce the creepy contrast between the white scalp and the shoe-polish brown of the dyed hair. Graham always hatched heavy creases around Miss Thomas's mouth. Her dentures fitted so badly that she had to purse her lips to hold them in. Gail could have drawn every item of Miss Thomas's wardrobe from memory. Today, she was wearing her grey pleated skirt. After lunch, when she sat on the lid of her desk, the girls would be embarrassed and the boys would snigger at the wrinkles and darns in her thick brown stockings. Today's flat brown lace-ups were more deformed by her bunions than the newer black lace-ups. She'd taken off her cardigan and had draped it over the back of her chair. Hand-knitted in camel-coloured wool, it had sagging pockets where Miss Thomas kept her handkerchiefs, fresh ones in the right pocket, used ones in the left.

'Gail Braithwaite! You're daydreaming again. Have you finished answering the questions on the board?'

'Yes, Miss Thomas.'

'Well, it's time to get the tea. And this will be the last time. Next term, there'll be a new tea monitor. You need to stop daydreaming and make good use of every minute you're in this room.'

Gail felt her freckles burn. She put her exercise book, pencil case and ruler neatly in her desk and, after wrinkling her nose at the sympathetic Renate, left the room. No more twice-daily escape from boredom! For the rest of the year, she was going to have to stay with the others until the bell. She didn't hate Miss Thomas, not really. She felt sorry for her. She was old and had dentures and her feet hurt. Gail just hated being in her class.

While she set out the cups and saucers for the teachers, she thought of the only other relief from boredom, too rare even to look forward to. Miss Thomas occasionally put her class in with Mr Brown's to be minded. For a few exciting minutes, the pupils squashed into his classroom four to a desk. Miss Thomas had the top Year 5 class, Mr Brown had the middle class and Mr Edwards had the dumb class. Gail's friend, Helen, had been put down into Mr Brown's class because she answered back to Miss Thomas 'once too often'.

Mr Brown had lots of smile lines. He had frown lines too. He frowned when pupils were bad, but he didn't hit anyone. He listened to pupils and didn't mind if they took a long time getting to the point.

He spoke to them as if he were having a grown-up conversation and sometimes used big words. He wrote the big words on the board, 'in case,' he said, 'anyone wants to look them up in the dictionary'. Gail always did. She'd often been tempted to answer back to Miss Thomas, but wasn't sure she'd have the same luck as Helen and be put down into Mr Brown's class.

The lunch bell rang just as she was pouring boiling water into the big metal tea pot.

By the time Gail collected her lunch and found Renate, a seething mass of boys was jostling around Graham Johnston at the entrance to the boys' shelter shed.

'What's he got?'

'Let me see! Move your head!'

'What is it?'

'It's a mouse.'

'No it's not. It's a rat.'

'Where'd he get it?'

'Under the seat in the shelter shed.'

'Is it dead?'

'No, it's moving.'

'That's maggots, idiot!'

'Let me see. I want to see the maggots.'

Gail and Renate screwed up their faces. 'Ew!' It was good they had to stay on the girls' side of the yard. They couldn't have resisted looking.

'Watcha gonna do with it?'

'Put it in her desk.'

'She'll scream. They all do.'

'Maybe she'll faint. My mum fainted when she saw one.'

Stupid Graham! Gail thought. Whatever Miss Thomas did to begin with, he'd be in really big trouble. She shoved her clenched hands into the pockets of her pinafore. She could feel the slice of the strap, even though girls never got the strap.

After the bell at the end of lunchtime, an alert quietness electrified the class. Gail found the tension almost unbearable. It could last all afternoon. Miss Thomas might not open her desk until she took out the roll at three twenty-five. She kept pacing up and down the rows. She suspected something. The unpleasant smell of her passing heightened Gail's sense of foreboding. Stupid, stupid boy! So what if Miss Thomas had hysterics! The consequences wouldn't be worth it. By three fifteen, Gail was so wound up that she couldn't finish the questions on the board and had no interest in *Robbery under Arms*.

Three twenty-five. All eyes followed Miss Thomas to her desk. She raised the lid, tilted it back and then snatched her hand away so violently that she hit herself on the chest.

Slowly she looked around the class, her slitted eyes finally fixing on Graham Johnston. 'Whoever put that thing in there come and remove it!'

The silence stretched like a rubber band and snapped with the sound of pencils falling and rolling on the floor. All eyes swivelled towards the owner. With open-mouthed fascination, the class watched Gail walk towards the teacher's desk, scoop out the rat with the bottom of her pinafore, fling it into her wooden pencil case and slide the lid shut.

'You! You?'

The voice was a squeak. The class was exultant. This was even better than hysterics!

Throughout her career, whenever a pupil disappoints her, Gail remembers the eyes filling with tears, the wobbling chin and the hideous fear that the trembling mouth might not be able to hold in the dentures.

She hadn't thought of confessing until she found herself doing it. She got what she wanted. Almost. Mr Brown's class had been too much to hope for. Mr Edwards was all right. When he wasn't strapping the boys for other teachers, he sometimes made jokes and he let her read whatever and whenever she wanted.

Con shuffles his feet. He's poised to flee. He'd expected a quicker reaction to his drawing. Coming back from far away, Gail turns to him, eyes slitted with memories. He edges into the corridor.

She smiles. 'What a fantastic drawing! I'm going to find a frame for it and put it on my mantelpiece.'

He bursts into a grin. 'See ya, Miss Braithwaite!'

Lemon Meringue Pie

June 1964

'Ya stinky old witch.' The child stands in front of my gate, barring my way in from the street. His grey shorts are too small for him and his thighs are mottled with cold. He has picked at the scab on his knee and blood oozes towards his crumpled grey sock.

I step forward. He sticks out his tongue and darts away. One of the Ferrises from down the street. Mr Ferris is a wharfie. He's often at home, either out of work or on strike. Mrs Ferris is always pregnant. She has no money and no time to get dentures.

'Old' I accept. I'm old enough to be the boy's grandmother. 'Witch' I accept. Any grey-haired woman would be a witch to the Ferris children. One or two grey-haired women come to their house almost every Friday. 'Stinky' I don't accept. It's a struggle on the pension, but I always pay my gas bill so I can heat the boiler and have a bath every day.

I push the gate open, plop my shopping bag on the brick path and pick up the lolly papers and cigarette butts that have been tossed over the fence onto the rectangle of dirt. Not enough sun gets to it for flowers but I try. Geraniums sometimes last through spring into summer.

Inside, I put the rubbish in the bin under the kitchen sink and the groceries on the table. I light the oven so it will heat up for the lemon meringue pie. I always make one on Fridays. It's my daughters' favourite, the only thing they ever agreed on, apart from wanting to get away from St Kilda. As soon they got married, they moved to a nicer suburb. If one of them comes to see me, it's always on a Friday. If neither comes, the pie lasts me until Tuesday.

I love the smell of grated lemon skin and freshly squeezed juice. I wonder if the little Ferrises and the other children who yell at me in the street ever get lemon meringue pie. I don't think so. Their mothers are too busy to bake.

I put the egg whites in the Mixmaster and beat in the castor sugar. When my daughters were children, part of the fun of lemon meringue pie was seeing how high I could make the peaks. The more peaks the better, and they had to be browned just right.

I've done well today. The peaks are about seven inches tall. I hope one of my daughters pops in. Perhaps if I'm lucky, both will come. It has happened once or twice before. The oven sends a warm blast onto my face. I slide the pie in and close the door gently to avoid blowing out the jets.

While the pie is baking, I'm warm enough from the heat in the kitchen to go into the icy front room and make my bed. As I tuck in the blankets, I look through the window at the Friday sharks gliding along outside: truant officers, rent collectors, the minister and the priest. No police or debt collectors yet. They'll come trawling tonight.

The Ferris boy should be in school. I'm never sure how many children live in each house because they're constantly being taken away and brought back. The women don't speak to me. They're too busy. I shop, cook and clean just for myself. That's something else that makes me peculiar, the 'witch' of Dudley Street.

A car stops outside the Ferris house and a grey-haired woman gets out. The pie should be done. I don't want to watch Mrs Ferris being harassed again. The smell in the kitchen is delicious: warm pastry, sharp lemon and sugary meringue. Using a folded tea towel, I take the pie out of the oven and put it on the sink under the window. There's a small shadow beside the toilet in the backyard, a child, the Ferris boy. He's crouching to make himself smaller than he already is. He has climbed the fence and is hiding from the truant officer. I leave the oven on, open the back door and sit at the kitchen table.

I hear a small noise in the yard.

'Come in, if you want,' I call out.

Silence. I sit still and wait.

'You can have a piece of pie, if you like.'

Silence. I don't move.

'I'm going to shut the back door soon. The pie is getting cold.'

A rustling sound.

'I'm making myself a cup of tea and cutting a slice of pie.'

I fill the kettle and light a jet on the stove. I put two cups, saucers, plates and spoons on the table with more noise than necessary. I'm not looking at the doorway, but I feel a presence there. I take out the sugar and a bottle of milk.

'If you want a piece of pie, come and sit at the table. Close the door behind you to keep the warmth in.'

The kettle whistles. I swish boiling water in the pot, spoon in the leaves, pour the water, put on the lid and cover the pot with the knitted tea cosy. When I turn towards the table, I see him hunched on a chair.

'What's your name?'

'Jimmy.'

'Mine's…' I hesitate. Normally I'd say 'Mrs Scrafton' to a child. 'My name's Iris. Would you like milk or tea?'

He nods and wipes his nose on his unravelling sleave. His nails are black-rimmed and his fingers red. He probably has chilblains.

I pour milk into a glass and put it in front of him. He grabs the glass and the milk disappears as if poured down a gully trap.

'Put your glass down and I'll cut us both a piece of pie. In my kitchen, if people eat pie with a spoon, they can have a second slice.'

He snatches up his spoon and holds it upright in his fist. Each of his knuckles has raw-looking cuts.

I serve tea and pie until pot and plates are empty. Too bad if one of my daughters visits today. She'll have to make do with yesterday's Anzac biscuits.

'If you come after school on Monday, there's apple pie and ice cream. No point coming during school time. I only make apple pie in the afternoon.'

The chair is scraped back over the linoleum and the back door bangs. If he doesn't come on Monday, the apple pie will last me to the end of the week. I start a new shopping list with 'Carnation milk'. It's cheaper to make ice cream with that than to buy a block.

June 1974

I jerk awake. Someone's banging on the front door. It's been a long time since any of the teenagers have done that, and they never did it after midnight. I lie under the blankets trembling. The teenagers used to bang on the door and run away. This noise doesn't stop. I sit up and reach for the dressing gown that's on top of the blankets. I slide out of bed. Even with my bed socks on, I feel how cold my slippers are. My bad knee begins to ache as I shuffle into the hall. The banging stops. I turn to go back to bed and hesitate. There's scuffling outside.

A croak: 'Iris. Iris.'

'Who is it?'

'Jimmy.'

I open the door. He sways and almost falls on top of me. With the streetlight behind him, his face looks black. I stand to one side and he staggers along the hall and slides down, making a black smear on the wall. He lands on his bottom with a thump and topples onto his side. I switch on the light and bend over him. His face is covered in blood and his clothes are soaked. He opens his eyes but doesn't seem to see me.

I pull the top blanket off my bed, tuck it around him and say, 'Hold on, Jimmy. I'll get help. Back in a tick.'

I take a jug out of the kitchen cupboard and empty a tray of ice cubes into it. At the front door, I hook my walking stick over my arm. I may not need it, but it will make more noise than my fist. I pull my dressing gown sash tight and hobble across the road to the house opposite. I knock on the door. No answer. I try the knob. It turns and I open the door. The stench hits me in the face and I grope for the light switch. Nothing happens. They must have cut off the power. I head towards the smell and enter the bedroom. The gaping curtains let in enough streetlight for me to see Mick sprawled on top of his bed. Dark liquid from an overturned bottle stains the carpet that squelches under my slippers.

'Mick. Mick. Wake up. I need your help. Do you hear me? Wake up, Mick.'

I tap his cheek and he turns his head away, making a slopping noise with his tongue.

'Mick, I've brought some ice and you know I'll use it. Get up! Now! Jimmy Ferris is injured. Looks bad.'

Mick grunts and smacks his lips together.

'Mick, the ice.'

'No, no. I'm coming. Old witch.' He heaves himself into a sitting position and almost slides off the bed.

I back away, afraid he'll knock me over. Mick O'Toole was struck off years ago but keeps himself in plonk by patching up the neighbourhood kids. He totters with me towards the front door that I left ajar. He's groping for his bag under the hall table when I hear a car approaching. It's the night sharks, the police, possibly looking for Jimmy. I touch Mick on the shoulder and he drops his bag and slumps against the wall. Headlights slide by. When the street is empty again, I pick up his bag and we shamble across the road and into my place. Mick helps himself to my walking stick and lowers himself onto his knees beside Jimmy.

I always marvel at how steady Mick's hands become when he touches an injured boy. His fingers float over Jimmy's face and torso and then probe harder. Finally, he sits back on his heels and growls, 'Nothing broken. Lots of blood. Cut with a bottle. Stitches.'

I know the drill. Mrs Ferris said years ago she'd have no more of Jimmy bleeding in front of the little ones. I boil the kettle and several saucepans and while Mick washes his hands and the needle, I cut away Jimmy's shirt and sponge the blood off his chest. I sit on the floor and hold his head steady. Pain gouges my bad knee. Jimmy doesn't murmur during the sewing. Over the next five days, he sleeps on my couch and whinges like the big kid he still is.

Fortunately, my daughters visit even less than they used to. My grandchildren are too small to leave at home by themselves and my daughters don't like them seeing the derelicts hanging around the Salvation Army hostel down the street. During the week, I make Jimmy's favourites: minestrone soup, sausages and mashed potatoes and baked beans on toast. I know he's getting better when he asks on Friday morning if I'm going to make a lemon meringue pie. He likes high peaks too.

June 1986

My daughters are going to visit me today. They did last Friday too. They said they're going to bring someone. They smiled as if it would be a nice surprise. It would be a lovely surprise if one of the grandchildren came, but that's unlikely. It'll probably be that shark developer that's been cruising around and buying up everyone in the street.

I've made a lemon meringue pie. If Jimmy comes when my daughters are here, he won't stay long. He might not even have a piece of pie. He didn't last Friday. I have the impression he doesn't like former residents of Dudley Street who have children in private schools. He can stand only so much respectability. I like to think I'm respectable but I'm old and he's used to me. His fingernails are clean now and he tells me his shoes are made in Italy. Very smart they are too. I like nice shoes. Not that I can wear any kind of shoes any more. It takes me all my time to get my feet into slippers, what with the bunions, the swelling and the arthritis. Jimmy's certainly not going to stick around if that shark developer comes.

I've put the electric heater on. My daughters gave it to me. It's not as cosy as the oven, but they tell me it's dangerous as well as wasteful to use the oven for heating. My pension still pays for the gas. I use the heater during their visits.

I might be shaky on my legs but there's nothing wrong with my ears. I hear the swish of Jimmy's little red sports car stopping outside. Although Dudley Street is short and narrow, there's always a parking spot in front of my place on Fridays. I've left the front door unlocked and he comes in.

'Hello, Iris. What's the gossip? Who's sold up this week? Is there a cup of tea going?'

'Only your mother, but you know that already. The tea's where it always is.'

'Yeah. I made sure she got a good price. She wants to go into that fancy retirement village near St Kilda Junction. I'm teeing that up too.'

'My daughters say if I move into the council retirement home, I won't need an oven. What would I do without an oven? Did you put that notice in the paper about Mick?'

'Yeah.'

'Were there many at the funeral?'

'All the mates.'

Jimmy is taking the tea canister out of the cupboard when we hear footsteps coming up the path. He closes the cupboard door and lounges against the sink next to the cooling pie.

A voice calls, 'It's us, Mum,' and then lowers for, 'Come in. She'll be in the kitchen.'

A smart-looking young man halts at the entrance from the hallway and, in an oddly proprietorial way, stands back to allow my daughters to enter the kitchen. Margaret, dark and olive-skinned like her father, flicks a look at Jimmy. Her smile shifts and then fixes. Kathleen, a wispy blonde who faded quickly like me and now uses tanning cream, nods at him.

Margaret takes charge. 'Ray, this is my mother, Mrs Scrafton.'

'Pleased to meet you, Mrs Scrafton,' he booms as if I'm deaf. He has unnaturally white teeth, like the people who advertise toothpaste on TV.

He holds out his hand and before I can respond, Jimmy steps forward and grasps it.

'Jimmy Ferris, and you are Ray...?'

I've never seen a shark turn into a guppy before. Jimmy's name and photo are often in the papers. I don't read the articles any more. They're about gangs and fights. The guppy must have read them too.

'Ray Cavendish of Morton...'

He gabbles a list of names. Jimmy keeps hold of his hand.

'Ah yes, Ray. We were expecting to see you today.'

It's interesting to see a guppy turn pale. I don't put the kettle on. I don't want to miss a moment. Who does Jimmy mean by 'we'?

'I won't beat around the bush, Ray.'

Margaret opens her mouth as if to protest or take command again. Jimmy ignores her.

'Mrs Scrafton promised if ever she puts this house up for sale, she'll give me first dibs and I'm holding her to it.'

I've never said any such thing! It's peculiar to hear Jimmy call me Mrs Scrafton. Telling lies is wrong, but lying to a fish doesn't count. Jimmy suddenly opens his fist and Ray's hand falls and dangles by his side.

The guppy turns to Margaret and says, 'You have my number. The offer...'

Jimmy moves closer to me and puts his hand very lightly on my shoulder.

The guppy veers towards me. 'Goodbye, Mrs Scrafton. Nice to meet you. I can see myself out,' and he swims into the hall.

Margaret's about to let fly and I decide to play the helpless old lady.

'Why are we all standing? I need to sit down. Can someone else get the tea?' I shuffle to the table, put my two hands on it and lower myself more slowly than necessary onto my chair.

Self-restraint turns Margaret purple and Kathleen's tanned face is darkening too.

'I'm a little tired with so many visitors all at once and I haven't had my tea. I'll feel better after that.'

Margaret's stare blazes across the table at Jimmy, willing him to leave.

He says, 'Coming up, Iris. Are you ladies having a slice of pie too?'

'I think it would be better if we came back tomorrow, Mum.'

'I'll be here, dear.'

A visit on Saturday! Unheard of!

Kathleen has to squeeze past Jimmy to get to the hall. His hand hovers near her bottom. I make a 'tsk' noise with my tongue. He drops his hand and gives me a grin that cracks the scars on his face.

'See you tomorrow, Mum.'

'Yes, bye, Mum. And have a snooze after your tea.'

They both glance at Jimmy, the only goodbye he's going to get. Their clatter down the hall doesn't cover one of them hissing, 'Silly old witch.'

Jimmy puts the kettle on and sets the table for tea. The kettle whistles. He swishes boiling water in the pot, spoons in the leaves, pours the water, puts on the lid and covers the pot with the knitted tea cosy. He sits down, picks up a spoon and holds it upright in his fist. He intends having a second slice of lemon meringue pie.

Joy

I wake up gasping for air. Edward's lying on top of me, his hand on my throat. Thoughts flash. He's going to kill me. Try to knee him? If I move, that'll alert him. He'll react. Violently? He's a big man. The pressure's firm. He isn't squeezing. Stay calm. Stay rational.

I take shallow breaths. Not enough to scream. Useless. Who'd hear?

With stocked-up breath, I whisper, 'Edward, darling, get off me.'

No reaction. I stock up more air.

'Edward, your side of bed. Roll over.'

He does. I lie still. I gulp air as quietly as I can. When I hear a snore, I ease myself out of bed. Not bothering to pick up my dressing gown, I flee to the kitchen. I unlock and prop open the door into the backyard just in case. Trembling with cold, I creep into the hall. It stinks. I put on my coat and boots and take my handbag back to the kitchen. Closing the door between the hall and the kitchen only partly cuts off the smell of urine. I don't dare turn on the coffee maker. It'd make too much noise. I boil water in a saucepan. My hand shakes as I spoon instant coffee into a mug. I pour the water and sit at the end of the table nearest the back door.

Thoughts dart. This is it. No more shilly-shallying. I'm making the decision this very minute. I'll phone at nine. The director will be there then. Edward has to go today.

I've been dreading having to make the decision, but oh, the relief! My next thought – I'll rip up the carpets. It's funny what irrelevant things jump into your mind. No, not really irrelevant. Edward uses the plant pots, the sinks, any bowl-like object to urinate in. He often misses and hits the carpet. I can't keep up with the cleaning. I can't remember the last time I invited someone to the house. It smells of urine and dis-infectant. The doctor warned me Edward might become violent. I only half believed him. Sitting with an instant coffee in our cold kitchen at three thirty a.m., I believe, I believe. Five and a half hours to wait before I can phone. A dementia ward – what horror! How much will Edward be aware of it?

That was three years ago. Several friends who are looking after their ailing husbands at home criticised me for giving up. I haven't told anyone what precipitated my decision. I want people to remember the true Edward, the gentle man who ran a highly respected legal practice and retired with the intention of conducting daily phantom Wagnerian concerts in the sound room he'd built behind the house. The same friends argued that he'd have given me anything. That's true.

But, oh, those judgemental friends, they know nothing of the decision I made decades before Edward started to frighten me. They'd have applauded. That decision was also about my life. At the moment of highest need, obsession even, why is it that someone appears on your path and a new beginning becomes possible?

Edward and I had a good marriage. We didn't fight. We didn't disagree on most things. We even gently ignored each other's football preferences. As a lifetime resident of Sydney's northern beaches, I supported the Sea Eagles. As a former Melbournian, Edward went on an annual pilgrimage to the AFL grand final no matter which teams were playing. And we didn't have children. Sometimes my body ached for a baby and I told myself it was my imagination. I didn't convince myself.

Edward said, 'It'll happen.'

Three years, five years, ten years of marriage and it didn't happen. We went to doctors. They said there was nothing wrong with either of us. I said I wanted IVF.

Edward said, 'It's not natural. Let's give it a little more time.'

I said, 'How much is a little? I'm thirty-seven. The IVF program has an age limit.'

Edward conceded graciously. I was exhausted from arguing and delirious with anticipation. I intended giving up work the moment conception was confirmed. No need. The attempt failed.

And then there was Paddy. What a clichéd story! The sad wife approaching forty and the handsome freelance pilot who could charm the eyes off butterfly wings. We met in the bar of a city hotel. I was waiting to have a drink with friends after work. He was approaching his second divorce. I became giddy. I took risks. All kinds. I answered the phone when I knew it was Paddy and Edward was home. I said 'Yes' and 'No' as if a girlfriend was asking my advice on a recipe, instead of being asked if I'd rather he kiss my left or right breast first. I lied to Paddy and said I was taking the Pill and hoped I'd fall pregnant. I thought no further than our next meeting in the next hotel room.

And suddenly a decision had to be made. The IVF clinic phoned and asked if we wanted to try again.

Edward said, 'Let's do it!'

That very afternoon, Paddy said, 'I've got a job in Sri Lanka. Come with me, Joy. I don't have a home, but I earn good money and you can spend it any way you like. We'll have fun.'

It felt like my last chance. At everything. At a baby or at life with a man I loved with total irrationality. Oh, I agonised. I put off deciding for ten days. I cried and became hysterical and acted like a hormonal teenager.

And in the end – I blame it on exhaustion – I made a rational decision. I stayed with Edward. We had another go at IVF. By the time that one failed, Paddy was in Sri Lanka. Address unknown. Again my body ached. This time I knew it was for him. Wine brought numbness, as did a busy career, ironically in family law.

The numbness lasted almost until now. Except, except… There were postcards. Every Christmas, from Colombo, Nairobi, Guangzhou, Vientiane, Buenos Aires, Karachi, Churchill on Hudson Bay. Always addressed only to my first name. No surname, no message, no signature. But I knew they were from him. It's not much to fill a life, is it? Blank postcards. Thirty-one of them. But he hadn't forgotten me. Not until three years ago.

In all the complications and adjustments following the diagnosis of Alzheimer's, I almost forgot about the postcard that year. On Christmas Day, while I watched wine dribble from the corner of Edward's mouth, I suddenly realised – there'd been no card. I was bereft. Had Paddy forgotten me? Had he died? Selfish of me, but there you are. Edward was sinking into emptiness and all I could think of was a blank postcard.

It's funny how some things coincide, just by chance. That seems to have been my story. After no postcard for three years, Edward goes into the nursing home. A month later, I receive a phone call. It's from someone called Justine. She says she's Paddy's wife, his fourth. They're in Bangkok. He's asking for me. He's in a hospice. He doesn't have much time. Would I come? Would I be as brave as Justine and make such a request? I suppose a person doesn't know until she's tested.

Edward has no concept of time. I'm not sure he recognises me when I visit. I say I'll see him soon. I take a taxi from the nursing home to the airport. In Bangkok, I take a taxi from the airport to the hospice. A receptionist shows me to Paddy's room.

A woman stands up from the chair by his bedside. She's at least ten years younger than me. That doesn't make her young. 'Thank you for coming,' she says. 'I'll go and have some tea.'

I sit on the chair she's just left. I take his hand.

'Hello, Joy,' he whispers. The lovely Irish accent.

No tears. Not yet. I open my handbag and take out the last postcard. I ask, 'Can you sign it?'

He raises his hand. I put a pen in it. I put the card on the novel I brought but didn't read on the plane and hold it steady while he writes. It takes a long time. His hand shakes.

He's written, 'Joy. All my love, always, Paddy'.

Maybe he'd have left me for his fourth wife. What does that matter now? Regrets? At seventy-two? What a waste of time! We hold hands and wait for Justine to come back from her tea.

Small Man, Big Man

Melbourne 1958

Tony Johnson trembles and his chest feels so tight he can hardly breathe. Every nerve strains to listen. The four gang members aren't thinking about him yet. If he's lucky, their game will continue until the bell rings. Then he'll dart into the red-brick building and be first in line to file into the classroom. They'll pinch and jostle him for sucking up to the fat cow, but they won't do anything obvious. Nothing she'd notice.

'The fat cow' is the gang's name for the teacher. Tony doesn't call her that. His father uses the word 'cow' whenever the latest house keeper/child minder moves out of the spare room, high dudgeon heightened by the indignity of having to bump her bulging suitcases down the stairs. Tony calls the teacher Mrs Curtis. He's been called names too often to do it to someone else, even if that person's been horrible to him.

He listens to the shouts and the thwack of ball on bat until a triumphant 'Out!' signals it's his turn. They'll come looking for him. He's part of their lunchtime fun. Already their voices jangle in his head. Whether in his imagination or in reality, it makes no difference.

'Titchy Johnson farts and stinks. Teacher's piss he sucks and drinks.'

That's an O'Donnell chant and they love it. O'Donnell doesn't join in the punching and kicking. He sniggers and uses words instead. Tony fights the other three. He bites, scratches and jabs with elbows, feet and knees. In the part of his mind that remains rational, he wonders how he'll be able to keep fighting if the bell for the end of lunchtime is late or doesn't ring at all. When it does ring, he curls up on his side to make as small a target as possible for the parting kicks. Hearing the three run towards the school and aware of O'Donnell watching him, he straightens his body and heaves himself onto one knee, then the other, one foot, then the other. He ignores the bruises. He won't cry in front of O'Donnell.

'Bell's gone,' O'Donnell always flings over his shoulder before tearing across the grey asphalt.

Tony, a small grey shadow, stumbles across the asphalt in time to bray with the rest of the class, 'Good afternoon, Mrs Curtis.' He enjoys the small victory of depriving the others of the pleasure of seeing him get into trouble for being late.

Today, hiding under a bush between the garbage bins behind the canteen, Tony feels the familiar rage and fear coiling together in his stomach. He gulps great breaths. O'Donnell will find him. He always does. The other three just follow.

The chanting is not in his imagination; it's real. He hears the slap of shoes on asphalt at the side of the canteen. O'Donnell has guessed where he is. It's not hard. There aren't many hiding places. He crouches lower. Maybe they won't see him. The bush is thick. He thinks of climbing inside one of the metal garbage bins but they'd jam the lid on and roll it around the playground. He prefers to see and feel them. Several times, he succeeded in hiding until the bell by lying along a branch of a tree. Being the smallest boy in the class has occasional advantages. It didn't occur to O'Donnell to look up. At the end of several frustrating lunchtimes, O'Donnell lingered in the shelter shed at the risk of getting into trouble for being late and saw Tony drop out of the tree. That was the end of that hiding place.

The shoes and voices are close. 'Titchy Johnson lick my shoe. Kiss my bum and eat my poo.'

They aren't hunting. They know where he is. They're tracking.

Tony's not sure how much time there is before the bell. He guesses a few minutes. He doesn't wear the watch his father gave him for his birthday. They'd rip it off him and stamp on it. The teachers are coming out of the building and making the boys pick up rubbish. O'Donnell and the others are far enough behind the canteen not to be seen. They come straight to his bush. Lang bends over, grabs his arm in both fists and drags him onto the dust and food scraps between the bins. With more effort than necessary, given the difference in their height and weight, he wrestles him flat onto the ground. Tony manages one kick to the shin.

'Hold him. Kick him. Get him where it hurts.' O'Donnell.

The three fall into a frenzy of kicks and punches. Lang suddenly stands up straight and Tony sees him remove his belt. It's new. He's been showing it off all morning. It has an eagle on the buckle. The boys aren't allowed to wear fancy belts to school but Mrs Curtis hasn't noticed this one. The belt swishes. Tony rolls to the left. The buckle hits him on his bruised arm. He shrieks. The belt swishes again. He jerks himself into a tight ball and flings both arms over his head. The prongs of the buckle open the cuts Ward made yesterday with the point of a compass.

'Stop that now! Now! Do you hear me? Lang, Ward, Flego – go and stand outside the headmaster's office and wait for me there. Move! O'Donnell, what's going on?'

'They're ganging up on him, Mrs Curtis.'

'Yes, O'Donnell, I see that. You can go to the headmaster's office too. You can explain to him what the four of you were doing. Let's have a look at you, Johnson. Dear, oh dear. Your arms are covered in blood. What a mess! Come with me. We'll get you cleaned up. They're big boys. You shouldn't provoke them. Do you know what "provoke' means?'

'Yes, Mrs Curtis.'

'Of course you do. You're an intelligent boy. That's why I don't understand why you always get into fights. Your mother is going to have to buy another shirt. This one is ruined.'

Bitterness at the mention of his non-existent mother overrides relief at being rescued. The relief is only temporary. Already he's thinking about tomorrow. If he does something bad, maybe Mrs Curtis will keep him in at lunchtime. Once, when he brought a comic to school, Flego grabbed it at recess and stuffed it down the toilet. Just before lunchtime, Mrs Curtis and the headmaster had a whispered conversation outside the open classroom door. When Mrs Curtis came back, she stood on the platform in front of the blackboard and asked who had blocked one of the toilets at recess. Since no one else put up his hand, Tony knew he was expected to. He had to stay in at lunchtime and write a hundred times, 'I must not vandalise the toilets.' Although he wrote as slowly as possible in the hope of staying in the classroom until the bell, ten minutes before it was due Mrs Curtis said, 'You can finish the rest for homework. You need to go outside and get some fresh air and go to the toilet.'

The gang was waiting for him.

The day after Mrs Curtis rescued him, Tony spends the morning trying to think of a new place to hide. There are the toilets, but the doors don't shut properly and he doesn't want to be trapped.

He once entered the toilet block when the gang was taking revenge on Robin Cartwright. Tormented because of his sissy name, Cartwright had dobbed to his mother, who had complained to the headmaster, who had used the strap and made the four of them cry. Lang and Ward were holding Cartwright's head in the toilet bowl while Flego urinated on him, splashing their hands. O'Donnell leant against the door frame and sniggered. Happy not to have been noticed, Tony crept away.

No, the toilet block is not a place to hide. He prefers being punched to peed on. In the end, partly out of desperation and partly out of defiance, he stands conspicuously on the sidelines of the lunchtime game. They won't have to seek him out. Maybe the noise will attract the teacher on duty. Small chance of that! It's Mr Logan's day. He spends most of his duty time smoking behind the tree near the back gate. Tony trembles as he always does during a game, but now curiosity spices his dread.

A series of lucky catches and an LBW end the game early. Lang, Ward and Flego converge on Tony. O'Donnell lounges beside the dustbin stumps. The other players, aware that something's going to happen, form a loose circle.

Lang puts up his fists. What an idiot, Tony thinks. His reach is far longer than mine. He doesn't have to pretend he knows how to box. A stinging blow to the head sends him into a stumbling spin, then Flego puts out his foot and trips him and he's down. Three bodies fall on top of him. He can't scream because the weight presses the air out of him and there's a forearm across his throat. He sees black with darting pinpricks of white. Through the surf surging in his ears, he hears a deep voice. He can't make out the words.

Then the weight on top of him shifts and the voice speaks again. 'Get off him. Pick on someone your own size.'

He feels a few half-strength kicks and he's lying on his back, alone. A dot of light expands like the opening of a television picture. He squints up at a dark head surrounded by sunlight. A hard hand grasps his and pulls him to his feet. Frank Enderby.

The circle of boys breaks up. Some drift away; others mill around out of respect for the biggest boy in the class. Enderby is repeating Grade 6.

O'Donnell moves away from the dustbin. 'Show us ya muscle, Enderby,' he commands.

The big boy obligingly rolls up his sleeve and flexes his muscle. Even O'Donnell is silenced by the impressive bulge. Tony hovers close enough for protection but not so close as to be a nuisance. Enderby is reputed to have four hairs on his chest, but Tony has never seen them. He's always excluded from the good things.

Enderby cuffs Lang, Ward and Flego with familiar playfulness. Unhurt, they duck and cry 'Ow' in deference to his manly superiority. He also cuffs Tony to be fair. His hand does not connect with any bruises and Tony does not cry 'Ow.'

The bell rings. Mr Logan comes flapping into the centre of the playground, shouting at the scattering boys to pick up rubbish. Enderby droops. Tony follows his dragging steps towards the school building. Enderby has saved him. What can he do in return?

Every day after lunch, there's spelling. Each pupil has to stand up and spell aloud a word that Mrs Curtis chooses from the reading book. She usually gives Tony a big word. He gets today's word right and hopes she won't praise him. Tomorrow he'll get it wrong so the gang will have one less thing to pick on. Now it's Enderby's turn. He scrapes his chair back from the desk that's too small for him and lurches to his full height.

Mrs Curtis seems to sigh. 'Your word is "cricket".'

Enderby shuffles. The boys around him put their elbows on their desks and support their chins in their hands to hide their smirks.

'Come on, Enderby, we had the word this morning.'

Enderby hunches his shoulders.

'It starts with a k sound. What letters make a k sound?'

There's a snort from the back of the room.

'Come on, Enderby, there are fifty-five pupils here, all waiting their turn.'

Tony stares at his maths textbook in an effort to block out what's going on. He can't whisper the letters to Enderby. The others would tell and Enderby would be given another word.

'Sit down, Enderby. We can't wait all day. O'Donnell, your turn. Spell "cricket".'

Tony's relieved. Mrs Curtis hasn't made Enderby go to the blackboard and write the word while she spells it. In fact, she stopped doing that some time ago. Maybe she's realised he can't write.

The next day at recess and lunchtime, Tony hovers close to the big boy for safety but far enough away so no one will call him a suck. He doesn't want Enderby to be annoyed and tell him to get lost. That would be the end of hope.

At lunchtime, Enderby starts the batting. He hits the ball hard, usually in the same direction. The fielders clump where the ball is likely to land and get in each other's way.

After thirty-two runs, Enderby is caught out. He reverses the bat and thrusts the handle at Tony. 'Here, Titch,' he says. 'Have a go.'

Tony's heart thumps. He must get some runs. He mustn't disgrace Enderby. He takes the bat in both hands. Walking towards the dustbin stumps, he tries not to show how heavy it is. Once in position, he taps it several times on the asphalt, the way he's seen cricketers do on the newsreels. Its good balance surprises him. He hears some jeering voices but pays no attention. The fielders are clumped to his left, jostling one another and giggling. He taps the asphalt several more times and looks at the bowler. Lang rubs the ball against his groin. Tony noticed his bowling to Enderby was inconsistent. Now Lang walks backwards to where he'll start his run, tossing the ball from one hand to the other. He stops, bends forward and breaks into a jog, then a trot, then a run. Having watched English and Australian bowlers on newsreels, Tony is wary but not intimidated. The ball goes wide. And the next. The third ball is slow and straight. Tony angles the bat and – whack – the ball sails straight past Donnelly, who's sticking his chewing gum wad on a tree.

Tony hears, 'Run, Titch,' and, hefting the bat, he scrambles towards the dustbin in the distance. When he reaches it, he hears, 'Good on ya, Titch.' Enderby.

Eighteen balls. Eleven runs. Tony's wrists hurt. He gasps for air through his burning throat and rubs the sweat off his face with his shirtsleeve. He purses his mouth and looks around at the fielders. They've spread out. Lang is showing off less and concentrating more. This time, his run is shorter, tighter. The ball spins. Tony hefts the bat, hears the whack and sees Flego reach up.

'Got him! Out!' Donnelly.

'Good innings, Titch.' Enderby.

Tony's arms tremble from the weight of the bat. He's frightened he'll drop it when handing it to the next batsman. He doesn't. He hasn't disgraced Enderby, but it's not enough.

It's not until Melbourne Cup day that Tony finds something he can do for Enderby. Until then, whenever the big boy notices him on the fringe of his entourage, he calls out, ''ow ya goin', Titch?'

Tony loves hearing him use the nickname that he hates from everyone else.

Arriving at school just before the morning bell, Tony sees Enderby in the middle of a crowd of boys who are pushing money at him. He's running a sweep.

Donnelly flicks a ten-shilling note. 'Why don't cha run a proper sweep – like ten bob? You think you c'n work out the winnings?'

'You betcha,' Enderby says.

Tony believes him. He wriggles through the crowd until he stands by Enderby's elbow. 'I'll write the names if you like.'

'Orright, Titch, you're the bagman. C'mon, yous. Get into line. A shilling here, five bob here and ten over there.'

His ears ringing with the word 'bagman', Tony draws columns in his maths exercise book.

So begins a partnership: bookie and bagman. Enderby, having learnt from his uncle, teaches Tony how to run a book. Until the end of the school year, Tony slips the form guides out of his father's newspapers. Every Friday he records the class's bets and every Monday he stands beside Enderby, ticking off names and amounts as the big boy pays the winnings. One time, Tony makes up the short fall from his pocket money. Several times, they break even. Usually, they win. Tony would have been happy for Enderby to keep all the winnings. Enderby says, 'Fair's fair, Titch. You've earned your share.'

The gang no longer waits for Tony at lunchtime. Occasionally they hum one of the old chants if they're out of Enderby's earshot, but they never sing the words. Tony bides his time. Being partners with Enderby is good, but it isn't enough. His debt is huge. One day, he'll pay it in full.

Melbourne 1992

The voice of Tony's PA comes through the intercom. 'The next applicant is here, Mr Johnson. Shall I send him in?'

'Two minutes please, Mrs Black.' Tony checks his list, knowing full well the name of the next interviewee. The hide of the man! He must know I'm the owner. Perhaps he thinks I'll still be a pushover.

A wave of nausea surges up from his stomach and sluices his mouth with bile. 'Titchy Johnson farts and stinks.' No one calls him Titchy Johnson now. Nowadays, they show respect. That's how it should be. He pays the wages. And damn good wages too. Above the awards. No one can say he doesn't pay well for work well done. 'Fair's fair,' as Enderby always says.

And now, O'Donnell, O'Donnell of all people, has applied for a job. Well, Tony will interview him. He'll see what O'Donnell has to say for himself. He doesn't have to employ him. There are plenty of other applicants. O'Donnell looks good on paper. He's up there with the best applicants – on paper. It won't do any harm to see him. Will O'Donnell bring up their schooldays? If so, what will he talk about – Mrs Curtis, cricket, the betting with Enderby? Tony isn't going to be drawn into any discussion about Enderby. He's calling the shots now. He has something O'Donnell wants. Primary school was a long time ago.

Tony looks around his plush office with its Turkish carpet covering the whole floor. He'll say this much for Anne. When she decorated it, she'd given it class. She certainly had that. It's one of the things he'd liked about her. She knew about art and what to order in restaurants. Before their marriage, she'd mentioned love, but what she'd really been after was his money. Three years later, she'd left both him and the baby she said was his and went off with one of the salesmen. And got a sizeable settlement into the bargain! Tony wasn't going to add to his humiliation by squabbling over money. He had a baby and a business to look after. His daughter, now twenty-two years old and flatting with uni friends, is the subject of the portrait in a gold-leaf frame that hangs behind his antique oak desk. He'd commissioned that fellow who always enters the Archibald and it had cost a bomb. That was him all over – never spared money when it came to buying quality.

There's a small tap on the door. Mrs Black ushers in Jerry O'Donnell.

In a moment of panic, Tony wonders whether to stand up and shake the man's hand or remain seated behind his desk. He can tell a lot about applicants by the way they react to his shortness. Some bend their knees and go into a sort of squat. Some lean over him. Some manage to give the impression they're on the same eye level. He likes that. No, he'll treat this interview like any other. It is, after all, a matter of a job. He's running a business. Always prides himself on giving a job to the best applicant. Curiosity's overcoming nausea. Will O'Donnell be the best? If he interviews well, there'll still be the referees to check. Nausea rises again.

He extends his hand. The dampness of his palm makes him cringe. O'Donnell's handshake is firm and hearty, well calibrated as a good salesman's should be. Tony wonders if O'Donnell gives no flicker of recognition in order to put him off balance. He returns to the executive chair on a small platform behind his desk and motions O'Donnell to the chair in front of it. He's glad to have the routine of the normal interview questions to fall back on. O'Donnell follows his lead, answering with the confidence and frankness of an experienced salesman.

Tony notes with satisfaction that O'Donnell is carrying a lot of weight. He looks as if he lives well: high colour, the start of jowls, good suit, probably tailored in Thailand. Exactly what you'd expect in a high-flying salesman. Oh yes, he's certainly that. Gift of the gab. Could sell fridges to Eskimos. Why is he changing jobs?

'I like to go where there's a challenge and the money's good.' O'Donnell says. 'To be perfectly frank, I'm being laid off by Lindsay's. They're having a hard time and need to downsize to keep afloat. My kind of selling is too rich for them. Don't want to pay my expenses. You have to spend money to make money. If I stay at the Windsor in Melbourne, it's because my clients expect me to. If you ring old John Lindsay, he'll give you the low-down on my sales record. I've told him I'm applying here. Said he'd be glad to speak to you.'

Yes, Tony thinks. I'll phone John Lindsay. I'm nothing if not thorough. And fair. O'Donnell warrants a follow-up. He's the best so far.

The half hour is almost over. Tony wonders if they'll finish without any reference to school. He doesn't know whether he'd be pleased or disappointed. He stands and extends a damp hand.

'Thanks for coming in. I want to fill the position as soon as possible. I'll let you know by Friday. Don't like to keep people dangling.'

O'Donnell springs up, taken slightly off guard by the suddenness of the end of the interview.

Tony opens the office door and nods pleasantly.

'Great to see you again, Johnson.' O'Donnell contrives to look him in the eye as if they're the same height. 'Great to see how you've put that mathematical brain of yours to good use.'

O'Donnell grins and beyond the incipient jowls and expensively styled hair, Tony sees the sly smile of the eleven-year-old. He clutches the door handle.

O'Donnell nods at the painting. 'Your daughter?'

'Yes.'

'Good for you. I've got two of them.'

Maybe it's an attempt to find common ground, but to Tony it sounds like one-upmanship.

The ever-attentive Mrs Black ushers O'Donnell out. Tony shuts the door, stumbles back to his desk and collapses into his executive chair. The buzz of the intercom makes him jump. The red light shows it's the stock room. His hand shakes as he presses the button.

'Yes, Neville.'

'Hello, Mr Johnson. Just thought I'd let you know. Frank Enderby hasn't come into work again today.'

'Have you phoned him?'

'Yes. There's no answer.'

'Thanks, Neville. I'll deal with it.'

Tony walks up four flights of concrete stairs. He doesn't like using the lift. Pine disinfectant loses the battle with the smell of urine. The grimy walls of the stairwell, spattered with half-finished graffiti, ooze hopelessness. He walks along the concrete balcony to Unit 48, shifts his plastic bags into his left hand and knocks on the door. There's no answer. He knocks again. Silence. The whole building is silent. It's as if not one person breathes inside any of the dozens of small flats. He pushes the door and it swings open.

'Frank? Hello? Frank, it's me, Tony. I'm coming in.'

Across the dark space in front of him, a slit of light shines beneath a lowered blind.

'Frank, are you there? I'll put the blind up a bit. All right? Get some more light. I won't put it up all the way. You all right, mate?'

Tony edges towards the window, brushing his hand along the wall, reluctant to lift his feet in case he trips on something.

'Here goes. A little more light. I'll open the window too. All right, mate? Don't worry. Not too wide. Get rid of some of the stuffiness.'

An indistinct noise comes from a mound of shadow looming in the dimness. Tony grunts with relief.

'I've got some ice cream here. That chocolate cherry one you like. There's bread, marg and Vegemite too. I'll put them in the fridge and then we'll see about a shower.'

This time, the noise, although slurred, is recognisable. 'Ta, boss.'

Tony takes off his suit coat and hangs it on the back of the single kitchen chair. He empties the contents of one plastic bag onto the Formica table and puts the ice cream and margarine in the empty fridge. He takes a tracksuit and towel out of the other bag and balances them on top of his coat.

He turns towards the shape on the couch. 'All right, mate, let's get these clothes off. Come on, Frank, stand up, mate. You know I can't pull you up. Put your hands on the seat and push. That's it. Whoa. Steady. Put your hand here on the wall. There you go. Let's get this shirt off. I've brought some trackies for you to put on after your shower.'

Frank towers waveringly over Tony, who reaches up and pops the buttons on his sodden shirt.

'Okay, mate. You have to help me here. Push it off your shoulder. There you go. Now the other one. That's it. No, leave it on the floor. Pants next. Can you manage? Good man. One leg. Steady. Whoa. Hang onto the wall. That's it. Push them down. Okay, mate. Hand on my shoulder and let's get to the shower. Not too heavy, mate, or I'll end up on the floor. Here we go. Hang onto the rail. Got it? I'll get the water going. Don't want it too hot, do you?'

'Na, boss.'

Tony fiddles with the taps to get the right temperature, at the same time rinsing the vomit off his hands.

'Keep hanging onto the rail, mate, and step in. That's it. Here's the soap. Got it? You right now?'

Tony's wet shirt clings to him and he slips a little as he steps back from the shower recess. Water cascades down the hulk of the ruined body.

Leaving the bathroom door open, Tony returns to the living room. He stuffs the discarded clothes into a plastic bag, picks up bottles from the floor and stacks them under the sink. He takes the new tracksuit and towel to the bathroom.

'You right there, mate? Don't go to sleep. You haven't gone to sleep, have you, Frank? Frank!'

'Na, boss.'

'You ready for the towel?'

'Yeah, boss.'

'Here you go, mate. Missed your AA meeting, did you?'

'Yeah, boss. Had a win. Had to shout me mates. Stayed too long at the pub.'

'Yes, well. Neville's your mate too, isn't he? He'll be going to the meeting tomorrow. What if I call him up and see if he can stop in here on his way? Make sure you get there. That okay with you?'

'Yeah, boss.'

'Good. I need you back in the storeroom. No one knows where everything is like you, do they?'

'Na, boss.'

'Right, well, you get into your new trackies while I call Neville and then we'll see about some toast.'

By the time Tony drives into his garage, he's shivering convulsively although he's had the heater blasting. He turns off the ignition and sits still.

No one to hurry inside to. The housekeeper will have left his dinner in the oven. Mrs Curtis's youngest, she is. Frank had said she needed a job. A disgrace to the family apparently. Something about a baby having to be given up. He doesn't know the whole story and won't ask. What matters is that his house is spotless, his shirts impeccable and his meals prepared the way he likes them. Frank had said she could cook.

Frank. The episodes are happening more frequently and lasting longer. So much for all his money and the successful company and the big respectful staff! He can't even look after his mate.

And what's he going to do about O'Donnell? Great salesman. Ringing his referees will only confirm that. Fair's fair. That's what Frank always says. Would it be fair to give the job to an inferior applicant? Tony prides himself on always choosing the best person for the job. It doesn't matter if he dislikes the person. He's hired people he dislikes. He's never hired anyone he's afraid of. Afraid? He wonders if he really did see flashes of the eleven-year-old manipulator during the interview. The basic question is, would O'Donnell be good for the company? Tony suspects he'd either spur on the other salesmen to compete with him or sit back and watch whatever trouble he's stirred up. Tony's dealt with trouble all his working life – unions, the rise of the dollar, his wife leaving. He's always tried to put on a brave front. And now? O'Donnell and Frank will inevitably cross paths. And Frank will be delighted to see his old mate. He won't notice the sniggering. Tony wonders if protecting Frank is merely an excuse, an unbusinesslike reason, for not hiring O'Donnell. Will he be a coward if he doesn't hire him?

Wearily, he heaves himself out of the car and enters his empty home. He puts on his pyjamas and dressing gown and dutifully eats the dinner that's been left in the oven. He has to keep his strength up. People depend on him. Not O'Donnell. Tomorrow, he'll look more carefully at the other applications.

Mother Behaving Badly

'No!'

'Oh, Mum, be reasonable!'

My daughter thinks it reasonable that I'd share a room with her father!

'Mum, his wife's just died. He's grieving.'

Silently, I correct her: his *second* wife. It's been a long time since I've corrected her aloud. I stopped so that Michelle would stop saying, 'Get a life, Mum. You should be over it by now.'

Sitting at my daughter's dining table, I don't like hearing the implication that I'm mean and uncaring. I am, but I don't want to argue about it.

'Michelle, the answer is no. He can stay with one of their children.'

'But Mum, they've all got little kids. You can't inflict a grieving man on his grandchildren.'

I snap. 'But you can inflict him on me? No. The subject's closed. I'll help you go through the catering arrangements if you like. Otherwise, I'm leaving.'

'You're taking your bat and ball and going home!'

'Yup.'

I don't like the derisive tone either. And I'm fed up already with this wedding. I'm turning into a grumpy old woman. It feels good. All this fuss: the dress, the flowers – natives or her favourite camellias? Three, four or five bridesmaids? Should the flower girls and pageboys be just the grandchildren? What about their friends' children? There's the photographer, the video, the chapel, the reception place, the caterers, the minister. Oh yes, the minister, an afterthought. There are compulsory meetings or lessons or indoctrination sessions because the bride and groom aren't members of the parish. I don't think they're even Christian! There's also the cost of staying overnight. Why does the wedding have to be in the Blue Mountains? The bride and groom and all the guests live in Sydney. Maybe it's a conspiracy: Michelle and Pete needn't invite the people who can't or won't pay for the guest house they've booked. Mean, and cynical too – that's me.

I'm not talking about the first flush of young love. Michelle's forty-two, Pete's forty-five. Nothing romantic about this wedding. It's a business plan. Baby number 1 is scheduled for March. I'm delighted. My first grandchild. I'm reminded of Michelle's father.

'Isn't it time we settled down?' he said. 'We need to think about kids. We're getting on.'

We were twenty-five! We'd been lucky. After graduating from teachers' college, we landed jobs in the same high school. We spent our summer holidays travelling. One glorious summer, '69, we spent the whole holiday pretending to be flower people in wintry San Francisco. No wedding fuss for us. Just a registry office. We were happy, in love and 'working on having a bub'–– Jim's words, not mine, but they made me laugh. I laughed a lot in those days.

Michelle was a perfect baby. She rarely cried. Daisy fingers played with invisible butterflies. She fed when it was feeding time. She burped on cue. I whispered, 'Go to sleep, baby,' and she did.

I was not a perfect mother. Looking at Michelle's dimpled cheeks as I held her in my arms, I felt stomach-turning revulsion. I had to be abnormal. I cried constantly. My breasts hurt. The smell of my body revolted me. I had no energy. Between feeds I slumped on the couch. I dragged myself up when the alarm signalled the next feed. I forced myself to eat. The sight, smell and taste of food nauseated me. When Jim came home from school, I handed the baby to him like a parcel. I lied and said I'd changed her nappy half an hour ago. I couldn't remember how long ago it had been.

When Jim made moves in bed and said, 'Isn't it time we got back

to normal?' I turned my back on him and sobbed. After weeks, months
– I can't remember – he became insistent. 'I'm the one working all day.
All you're doing is staying home with the baby.' I couldn't be bothered
resisting and let him paw me. He entered me and climaxed immediately.
After a few such episodes, he gave up. I assumed it was horrible for him
too.

In those days, postnatal depression was a barely acknowledged medical concept. Jim's mother, who'd had five kids, told him, as he reported
to me, that I 'should snap out of it and stop being a prima donna'. My
own mother was sympathetic but distracted by my father who was sinking into early onset Alzheimer's. That too was a little understood medical condition.

Jim and I staggered on until just before Michelle's first birthday.

One evening, after I'd listlessly mentioned a party, Jim said, 'Listen,
Soph. You and I've always been honest with one another.'

Had we? I suppose so. His tone was strange.

'We haven't been getting on.'

We certainly hadn't. I felt rotten all the time. I couldn't blame him
for losing patience with me.

'I've met someone else.'

At first, the words made no impact. I repeated them in my mind
and became alert.

'We're in love.'

Love? I'd stopped thinking about love. My focus was to stay alive
to keep Michelle alive.

'You and I can get a separation. We'll have to give up the house.
You can keep the rental deposit. That'll keep you going for a while. Your
parents have plenty of room.'

My parents! This had been carefully planned. I couldn't think
straight.

'We want to get married. You and I can get a divorce on the grounds
of separation. Gloria and I can wait.'

'Gloria? You mean Gloria from school?'

The receptionist had always beamed at Jim when we arrived in the morning and barely acknowledged my existence. I'd had an existence then.

'Yes. And she's happy to take Michelle, since you're not coping.'

'What!'

'You can hardly say you're a fit mother!'

I reared up from my chair. Jim was so startled he leapt up too. I was shivering and ablaze.

'That'll sound good in the divorce court: a man takes his child from his wife and gives her to the whore he's screwing! How long's that been going on! Were you fucking her before I got pregnant?'

I didn't deliberately spit but my accumulated saliva sprayed his face. I looked up at him with – I don't know – disbelief, fury, loathing. I felt like shit, but I'd walk over upright razor blades before I'd let him steal my baby.

He clenched his fists.

'Go ahead,' I snarled. 'Hit me. Bruises, black eyes, broken nose, smashed jaw – I'll show the police, the headmaster, the staff, your parents, your friends. They'll see you for what you are – a disgusting, cowardly brute, a slimeball not fit to be near a child.'

He raised his right fist. I raised my chin and looked him in the eyes. The venom I saw matched my own. If a kitchen knife had been within reach, I'd have used it. Even now, I marvel to think how daring or foolish I was. He lowered his arm. He was too calculating to be physically violent. He bent over me. I leant backwards but didn't move my feet. He opened his mouth. Words didn't come. I think he was so shocked at my reaction he didn't know what to say. He straightened up. So did I. We were inches apart. He threw up his hands. I flinched. Fear coursed through me.

'I knew you wouldn't be reasonable!' he flung at me.

Reasonable! I almost laughed. He slammed out. The car roared down the driveway. I packed Michelle's things and took the bus to my parents' place.

This was pre-1975. Divorce was still based on one party being at fault. Jim's parents paid for an expensive lawyer and divorce was granted on the grounds of my desertion. I didn't care about the grounds as long as I kept my baby.

Reasonable! Michelle uses that word a lot. She got it from her father. She stayed with him and Gloria and their three children on weekends and school holidays. It was part of the deal worked out by my legal aid lawyer. In return, Jim was supposed to pay a 'reasonable' amount for her upkeep. The amount never increased from the time he started paying it. I deposited every cent in an account and gave the total to Michelle when the payments stopped on her eighteenth birthday. She thought it a lot of money until she learnt it was enough to buy an old small car, not a new one.

After the divorce, I went back to teaching. During the day, my mother looked after a toddler and a sick man. When I came home from school, I took over from her. I cooked and cleaned, marked my students' work and prepared my lessons. After Dad died and Michelle became an unusually non-aggressive and happy adolescent, we both looked after my increasingly frail mother. Several affairs fizzled out. I didn't have the time or energy to sustain them.

After Michelle moved in with Pete, I applied to be head of English in a senior high school. That kept me fully occupied until retirement a year ago. Whenever I mentioned children, Michelle would lecture me about the importance of a career to a woman's identity and Pete would suddenly decide the dogs needed to be taken for a walk. A series of rescue dogs; no children.

And suddenly, whammo! A huge wedding, a baby on the way and the expectation that I'll share a room with a once loathed man. Age has brought indifference. Today, I'm even edging towards pity. Seeing Jim at the wedding rehearsal was a shock. His face is scribbled with purple veins. When he tried to kiss my cheek, I reeled back from the alcohol on his breath. I'm not sure he knew who I was! He looks old. We're the same age. Do people think I look old? I suppose so.

Did Jim ask Michelle to ask me about sharing a room? I doubt it. It's her bizarre idea.

In a futile effort to persuade me, she said, 'I'll book the room, Mum. You don't have to bother. I'll make sure it's big and has single beds, of course. You'll both save money and it'll free up a room. We're having trouble fitting everyone into the guest house.'

She was crestfallen at my emphatic 'No!'

Save money! Two sex-dead oldies, one half-sozzled, simultaneously needing the shared bathroom! She'd conjured some sentimental dream about her parents getting together. Gloria died a year ago. How did Michelle imagine Gloria's children would react? My daughter has many wonderful qualities. Emotional understanding isn't one of them. She expects people to be kind. I'm not kind.

Wedding day. I've been dreading it, but now it's here, I'm quite looking forward to the whole shebang. I'll be polite to Gloria's children, as always, and say pretty things to her grandchildren. But I won't be a twittery mother of the bride. I'm wearing a red cheongsam and glittery high-heeled red shoes.

Michelle wails, 'Oh, Mum, you can't. It's too daring!'

'What do you mean "daring"? It's got a high neck and comes below my knees.'

'The splits go up your thighs!'

'I've got the legs for it!' (With support hose!)

Pete says, 'Right on!'

Michelle throws him a reproachful look.

In the church, Jim's tribe occupies the front row on the right side of the aisle. I sit with Pete's family on the left. Just before the organist crashes into the bridal march, a fit-looking grey-haired man slips onto the end of the pew. Pete's family greets him warmly. Jim shuffles down the aisle beside my daughter.

The minister keeps the ceremony mercifully short. Michelle and Pete look touchingly delighted. When the minister says, 'You may kiss the bride,' one of the pageboys, a grandchild of four, inspired by Pete's enthusiastic embrace of Michelle, kisses the flower girl next to him. Following Michelle's example, she puts her arms around his neck and kisses him back. Love all around. I'm eager to get stuck into the champagne.

I discipline myself to wait. I have a speech to make. The bride's father might shuffle, but her mother mustn't slur. I drink water during the ordeal of delicious hors d'oeuvres and beautifully cooked chook without wine.

Jim stands and holds up his glass. He manages to say, 'To the bride and groom,' and slumps onto his chair while the guests are still getting to their feet.

When it's my turn to speak, I let rip. I haven't spent four decades in classrooms full of Shakespeare-hating, mutinous, angst-ridden teenagers without learning how to grab an audience. The kisses of the pageboy and flower girl inspire me to start with Michelle aged four. Blue eyes, blonde curls, she holds my hand and stares at an elderly woman at a bus stop.

The woman coos, 'Hello, sweetie. What's your name?'

'You're mad. You're mad. Your feet stink.'

Michelle had been put up to it by Mario, her paramour at kindergarten. Money was involved. Ten cents.

By the end of my speech, the guests are roaring, Pete is kissing Michelle's hand and she's scarlet with embarrassment. I head towards my reward – champagne at the outdoor bar.

The man ahead of me is the one from the end of the pew. He turns and grins. 'Great speech. I'm Seamus, Pete's boss.'

So he's a vet.

A small commotion makes us look through the terrace doors into the reception area.

'Your husband's looking a bit unsteady.'

'Ex-husband.'

Jim's foot is tangled in a flower girl's fallen flowers and he's swaying. Gloria's daughters surge to his side and sit him on the nearest chair.

Seamus says, 'All sorted. Why don't we take the bottle and sit over there?' He points to a small iron lace garden table and two chairs.

'Good idea.'

The table top is uneven and my champagne glass almost topples. Our hands touch as we steady it. Am I imagining it, or does his hand cover mine slightly longer than necessary? I wouldn't mind. He's a nice-looking man.

'Like you said in your speech, Pete's a great guy. My wife didn't know him. He joined the practice after we split. She's allergic to cats, would you believe? We're still good friends. Enough about exes. What'll we talk about?'

'Birds versus fish? Dogs versus cats? Horses versus ponies?'

'Okay – a very important question.' He pauses and elaborately crosses his fingers on both hands. 'You prefer dogs or cats?'

'I'm a cat person.'

He breathes an exaggerated sigh of relief, tops up my champagne and regales me with stories about the sophistication of cats and the stupidity of their owners. I laugh until I gasp for breath. The light fades, our second bottle is empty and the waiters are hovering to collect our glasses.

Seamus asks, 'You staying at the guest house too?'

'Yes.'

'Like to share an Uber?'

At the guest house, we tumble out of the car. I feel light-headed and not totally in control of my high heels.

He asks, 'Your room or mine?'

'The nearest.'

'Mine's upstairs.'

'Mine's first door on the left.'

I fumble with the key. People clatter in the hallway behind us. The place is full of wedding guests. They probably recognise us. I don't care.

No sooner have we pushed the door shut than he's leaning me against it and we're kissing, alternately hard then gently.

He says, 'Turn around.'

I face the door and the zip of my dress slithers down my back. Goose bumps pop all over me. I'm glad I'm not wearing my usual serviceable underwear. I bought red lacy panties and matching bra to go with the dress. They looked glamorous in the shop; I hadn't expected anyone else would be seeing them. Even the support hose feel sexy as he slides them down. He puts one arm around my shoulders and one at the back of my knees and swings me up.

'You're showing off,' I say.

'You're impressed?'

'Yes.'

'Goal achieved.'

He staggers six steps, drops me on the bed and lands on top of me.

'Sorry!' he says. 'I intended to lay you down like a princess. Champagne's knocked the muscle out of me.' He grins. 'Don't worry, I'm up for the rest.'

I chuckle. Did he intend the play on words? He kisses my ear, rolls off the bed and stands beside it. He undoes his belt and shirt buttons in a slow striptease. I touch the bulge in his pants.

He brushes my hand away and says, 'No need to hurry. We've got territory to cover before getting to the basics.'

I laugh. Territory? There's a lot of it and neither of us is overweight! He knows what he's doing and I know what I want and never had. I make discoveries: like laughter is so erotic, like being on top is fun, like licking everywhere requires a lot of saliva! I tingle and tremble and give instructions. He's an obliging man.

Finally, we roll apart, panting. I fight sleep and lose. I wake up with a dry mouth and a headache. The bed looks like it's been under a rugby scrum. I go to the bathroom, swallow two glasses of water and two painkillers and only then do I remember. I rush back into the bedroom to check that he really isn't there.

My next decade will be my eighth and for the first time in my life I've had a one-night stand! I plonk down on the bed. What we did last night – that was fun: no promises, complications, baggage, guilt, responsibilities, excuses – none of the paraphernalia of marriage. For one pulse of eternity, I was happy. It no longer bothers me that happiness is ephemeral. I straighten the bedclothes and hum while I shower, dress and prepare to face the other guests at breakfast. I pick up my handbag. A piece of paper's sticking out of the side pocket. There's a mobile number and a message: 'Call me.'

Flames

The battered four-wheel drive judders to a halt in front of the apartment building. A young man, the top half of his wetsuit flopping around his waist, hops out, removes his surfboard from the roof rack and gives the driver the thumbs up.

'Dunno why you don't leave your board here. Your gran's right at the beach.' The driver's tone is envious.

'Too many strings,' the young man answers. 'Dunno how long I'll be. See you out there.'

His flip-flops slap up the sandstone steps and he presses the security buzzer.

'Is that you, Andrew?' The voice trills through the intercom.

'Yes, Marianne, it is I.' Andrew makes a mock bow to the intercom.

'Have you brushed the sand off your feet?'

'Yes, Marianne.'

Useless to explain he's going to the beach, not coming from it. It's a matter of indifference to his grandmother. He lays his board behind the potted palms in the vestibule and, ignoring the art deco lift, trudges up the stairs.

The air conditioning in the apartment gives him goose bumps. Apart from the freezing cold in summer and fierce heat in winter, he's never been able to identify why the place makes him uneasy. He hasn't the energy to think about it now. The apartment has a splendid view over the Norfolk pines along Manly Beach, minimalist Swedish furniture and violent contemporary art. Today, amidst the crisp white walls and pale wood, the slash of red in the photo on the piano glimmers with eerie life.

'Let me look at you, dear boy.'

Slim in white pants and figure-hugging white blouse, her blonde hair artfully pulled back into a careless ponytail, Marianne looks fifteen years younger than her age. She works hard at it. Andrew is used to showing off the impeccable manners she's taught him when she takes him out to dinner. He's amused when people assume she's his mother and not amused when they appear to have other ideas. Marianne's a pain in the arse sometimes and different from his mates' grans, but she never stints when he wants to upgrade his mobile or his board.

'Oh, my dear boy, you have no hair! That's the fashion, I know, and nothing can change how handsome you are, but your hair's such a lovely colour, just like your mother's when she was young. What she does to it now is unspeakable!'

Marianne scrutinises his chest, shoulders and face. 'You look weary, my dear. You don't have any burns, at least not that I can see.' She looks down at his wetsuited legs. 'You didn't get burnt, did you?'

'No.'

'I was worried sick. I don't know what possesses you to spend your university holidays fighting bush fires. I suppose your mother thinks it's fine. Sorry. I'll not go on about my daughter. She's a lost cause.'

Andrew's heart shrivels. The endless war between his grandmother and mother has no relevance to anything that matters. Marianne cultivates truthfulness. She claims that's what makes her a poet. Right now, he's turning away from any kind of truth.

He kisses the smooth cheek, careful not to smudge the make-up, strides to the French windows and stares at the sea. 'The day's not hot yet. Can we go onto the balcony?'

'If you wish, my dear. Tell me about the fires. I've been watching them on the news. Horrendous! Apocalyptic! I've written some poems about them and, since you were actually there, I'd value your comments. I want to know if my words reflect your experiences.'

Andrew squints to shield his eyes from the savage blue of the sea. He wishes he could shield his ears. He opens the windows and steps onto the shady warmth of the balcony.

Marianne follows him and arranges herself on a piece of moulded plastic, placing her leather-bound poetry journal on her lap. 'I think you're foolish putting yourself in danger, but I'm proud of your bravery. I hope the people whose homes you've saved have thanked you appropriately. So, talk to me, Andrew.'

'Can I go and get a Coke?'

'May I,' she corrects.

'May I?'

'Of course. The fridge has been stocked since you answered my text and said you were back in Sydney.'

Andrew retreats from the dazzle of the sea and serrated edges of the Norfolk pines to the sharp white interior. His eyes are drawn, as ever, to the child in the photo on the piano. Flaming red curls tumble over her shoulders. He doesn't see his mother in the child. He's never seen her natural hair colour. Nowadays, it's brown. She rejects Marianne's tastes even to the roots of her hair. The photographer had snapped her starting to run and as Andrew turns his head towards the kitchen, out of the corner of his eye, he has the impression of her red curls flaring out and crackling into life.

Sharply he veers away from the kitchen. He slides over the thick white carpet, careful not to slap his flip-flops against his heels. The lock of the front door clicks quietly behind him. He leaps down the stairs, grabs his board and, once in the street, bangs its end onto the pavement and clings to it to still his shaking. The whiteness of the apartment, the blue of the sea, the green of the Norfolk pines – none of those familiar colours is as real as the grey smoke behind the red flames shooting from the hair of the little girl running towards him. He'd ripped off his jacket and flung it over her. The heat of her body seared his chest as he sprinted and then scrambled over a smoking fallen tree to reach the truck.

Her parents appear often on social media. Bedraggled, their farm destroyed, over and over again they ask to meet and thank the unknown firey who saved their little girl's life. They also thank the doctors. He'll go and see her. Not yet. She's the brave one.

Playing Possum

My neighbour, Mr Gorman, lives in a state of constant roar, R.O.A.R. I hear him through the party wall between our two semis. Earplugs are useless. Perhaps Mrs Gorman shows more understanding and sympathy for his many grievances when he bellows. Possums and parking provoke the most violent outbursts.

No one in our street has a garage. Like several others, I sacrificed my front yard to make a car space. Luckily, I managed to save the lavender bush near the front door. Sometimes, I stay overnight at my daughter's place and mind the grandchildren. Whenever that happens, I let Mr Chan, my neighbour on the other side, park in my yard. In return, he gives me mangos from his tree. It's a perfect arrangement.

If someone parks in front of Mr Gorman's place, his fury punches through the party wall. 'Why can't that bloody moron park in front of his own bloody house?'

I can't hear the answer, if there is one.

Almost every night, the neighbourhood possums play and skitter on the corrugated-iron roof over our two semis. Mr Gorman yells to let his wife and the neighbours know that 'those bloody possums' are keeping him awake.

Mrs Gorman works in the nearby convenience store. Whenever she serves me at the cash register, we exchange polite hellos. Possums are never mentioned.

Yesterday morning, I knocked on Mr Gorman's door and asked if he could move his ute. It was blocking my exit.

'Not my fault, love. No place left on the street last night. I'll move it when I've had me brekky. You don't have any work to go to. Go home and have another cuppa.'

While I snipped dead heads off the lavender bush, furious expletives, 'that bloody witch' being the mildest, exploded into the street. Finally, Mr Gorman's ute wheezed to half-life and shuddered to the corner, backfiring phlegmy farts. I went to my volunteer job at Vinnie's and changed my normal starting time to later.

Yesterday evening, there happened to be several parking spots available in the street when Mr Gorman returned from work. Through my front window, I watched him carefully manoeuvre his ute across my exit.

I slept well last night. There was no shouting about the possums on the roof.

I'm now having a peaceful breakfast at the table by the window overlooking the street and watching the neighbourhood dogs being taken for their morning walk. Mrs Chan's pug quivers with excitement as he sniffs Mr Gorman's ute. The other dogs react with equal fascination and excess urine. Taking scissors to cut some lavender, I go outside to investigate and understand immediately why the dogs are so excited.

While I arrange the lavender in a vase on the table by the window, I see Mr Gorman come out of his front door. He takes two steps towards his ute, breaks into a shambling run, stares aghast at the tarpaulin and totters back into the house.

Through the party wall, I hear, 'Bloody mongrels and possums! Piss and shit all over my ute! I'm calling the bloody council!'

I can't hear the answer if there is one. I'm glad the possums enjoyed the mangos and maple syrup. The next time the ute blocks my exit, they'll find some more.

Finally, Mr Gorman and his stinking ute rattle off to work and I go to Vinnies. When I return home, I find a plastic bag at my front door. It's full of bruised and overripe fruit. There's an unsigned note. 'The store was throwing these out. No need to waste good mangos.'

Your Last Winter

You lie still, flat on your back, waiting for Adam to arrive. A warning twinge woke you at five o'clock and you haven't moved since. The morning light insinuates itself around and under the blind. It might be a sign of good surfing weather. He won't be late, not like the previous ones. They never allowed themselves to be pinned down.

They'd say, 'See you tomorrow, about seven thirty', or 'seven thirty give or take'.

One had said, 'Soon as I've 'ad me egg and bacon wrap and cappuccino.' He didn't last long.

The luminous hands on the bedside clock show seven fifteen. You hear the swish of the lift doors. There's nothing wrong with your hearing. Mentally, you wriggle in anticipation. His sneakers squeak on the marble floor between the lift and the front door. You feel the inrush of air from the hall as the front door swings open and you smile when he sings out,

'Hi, Rose. Are you ready for me?' He doesn't expect an answer but he likes to see you smiling when he bursts into the bedroom.

The carpet absorbs his footsteps and there he is, silhouetted in the doorway: broad shoulders, narrow hips, golden curly hair – a beautiful man.

It's an effort to speak. 'Hi, Adam. Aren't you cold? Only a T-shirt, no jacket?'

'No way. What with the heating and our bathroom shenanigans, there's plenty to keep me warm. Ready?'

'Yes.'

He grabs the bedclothes and pulls them back, leaving you exposed in your black negligee. Eileen, your niece, doesn't approve of your bed-wear. She says it's not warm enough for winter.

Adam kneels by the bed, slides one arm under your shoulders and one arm under your knees and lifts you as if you weighed no more than a doll. He carries you to the bathroom and sets you on your feet. 'Let's get this off you,' he says.

He raises the negligee slowly, gathering the silk in his huge hands so it doesn't scrape your skin. His bulk stops you from seeing yourself in the mirror. He has stood in front of it since the day you cried at your reflection.

'Do you want it standing or sitting down?' he asks. He has a wicked smile.

You respond, 'I'd like it standing today.'

He supports you with one hand and with the other turns on the taps.

I feel her trembling but I won't make her sit on the plastic chair until I sense she needs to. She's a fighter. She was a stunner too when she was young. I can still see it. She didn't have to show me the photos.

I'm glad the chamois works. A great solution. The niece brings gift-wrapped face washers. What kind of gift is that to a favourite and rich aunt? Once I couldn't help myself. Suggested flowers. Eileen said they'd die straight away from the central heating. She hasn't figured it out. Rosie now measures time in minutes. I don't use the so-called 'presents'. They made Rosie whimper when I washed her. I was polishing the BMW with a chamois one day and thought I might try one on her in the shower. Bingo! No more crying in the bathroom!

She hasn't given up the struggle yet. My other clients gave up long before they got to her stage. They wore flannelette night sacks. Rosie's nightgowns are silk – soft on her skin. I bring them home to wash by hand. I couldn't believe it when I saw the niece chucking silk things into the washing machine. She's taken to counting the nightgowns every time she visits. Trusting soul, the niece.

I finish washing Rosie just as she sags against me. I wrap her in the towel that's warm from the heat rail and carry her to the chaise lounge where I arrange her comfortably and then strip the bed and remake it. I have to watch her in case she wants to talk. She whispers and I can't hear unless I'm close to her. She opens her mouth.

'Mr Carmichael's coming tomorrow.'

'And Eileen?'

'Tomorrow.'

Of course the niece is coming tomorrow. Trying to sus out what Carmichael's up to. Can't stand it – he's the one with power of attorney, not her.

'So that means you're free to go surfing today?'

'Yes.'

'Great! I like it when you're sparking on all fours.'

'It's a long time, Adam, since I've been on all fours.'

I smile. I don't laugh. Laughter is too vigorous a response. It tires her. I suspect Carmichael smiles too. Smart lawyer, Carmichael. Keeps an eye on me and the niece. Makes sure there's no undue influence. Of course, a little gift would be nice. Rosie knows I like the Brett Whiteley.

After the mush that passes as breakfast, Adam dresses you in your surfing gear: tracksuit, fluffy slippers, warm dressing gown and watch. You love feeling his strong arms when he carries you, but going surfing requires the wheelchair. The journey to the lift and down to the garage is more tiring than usual today. Maybe you're moving into the next phase.

I lift her out of the chair and into the passenger seat of the BMW and tuck the mohair rug around her. She lets me keep my board in the garage. When she told Carmichael she wanted roof racks on the car, he organised it straight away without comment. When Eileen saw them, she went ballistic! Said it ruined the appearance of the car. It does. Said the car wasn't mine. It isn't. It's not hers either. Not yet.

You love the drive to Freshie Beach. The sky's brilliant blue and the sun's blazing through the windscreen. No need for Adam to put the heating on. It's almost the end of winter. No buds yet on the non-native trees. You long to see them. You won't see another winter, but how you're looking forward to spring! Maybe even a bit of summer.

With the disabled sticker, I can park in a no-parking area overlooking the beach. Rosie's eyesight's amazing. She can spot me among the other surfers. I get into the wetsuit beside the car. She watches me. She must have watched a lot of men in her day. And I bet they liked watching her. I don't ask her to do up the zip. She liked doing it until a month ago. Now she doesn't have the strength. I take the watch out of her dressing gown pocket and put it in her lap. She times me. Forty-five minutes. Not much, but fantastic in a working day. The niece would have a heart attack if she knew. Does Carmichael know? Maybe.

Adam trots down to the beach. His hair glints in the sun. You can always make him out from the other surfers. You suspect he adds colour to his natural blond. Good for him! He's parked at an angle so the sun's not in your face. It's very warm.

Mr Carmichael's coming tomorrow. He likes to check you have everything you need. Eileen always pops in after he's gone, in case you've changed your will and feel like telling her about it!

It's so cosy in the car. You haven't felt so warm since last summer. Adam hasn't wound the windows down. You should have asked him. Last time we came surfing, it was one of the coldest days of winter and you told him not to. You marvelled how he could go in the water. Surely a wetsuit can't be that warm!

You can't breathe very well. You'd like to push off the mohair rug, but you haven't the strength. You feel clammy. When was the last time you felt damp with heat? Oh yes. You remember. But that was passion, not sunshine. What if you're suffocating? No. That's ridiculous! Ten minutes more. Must keep awake. If you die in the car, what a mess that'd be! Eileen won't be happy with two-thirds of the estate. She'll contest the will. Mr Carmichael's reputation will be tarnished. He employed Adam and he'll be accused of not supervising him properly. You've left Adam the other third of the estate and the car and the Brett Whiteley. He reminds you of the best of the men you've loved. He's the summer of your last winter. If you suffocate, he'll be accused of negligence or worse. Thirsty. Feeling drowsy.

The tree across the road – green fuzz on it. Buds? Have you made it to spring? Are you seeing things? Ask Adam. What if…? No. He's careless, not stupid. Three more minutes. Eyelids heavy.

Three more minutes. Surf's epic. Should get back to the car. In a minute. Just one last wave.

Mother's Day

'But Mum, you can't! It's not safe. You're sixty-two years old, for heaven's sake. You've never dropped a bombshell like this before.'

Daughters Heather and Alison, one sitting on my right, the other on my left, have plotted a pincer movement. I marvel at their newfound sisterly unity. A minute ago, in premeditated collusion, sons-in-law Bob and Paul left the table to coddle their digestions in front of the television.

'What will Dad do for meals?'

So that's it! They're afraid of having him on their hands for meals, having to share him, so to speak.

'Aren't you being just a teenie bit selfish? Dad's always given you everything you've wanted.'

No, he hasn't! I keep the thought to myself. I'm not fighting that battle any more. It's long past.

'You must love your new fridge, Mum. It's fantastic with an ice-maker and everything. I wish Bob had given me a fridge like that for Mother's Day.'

'Did you ask him for one?'

Alison and Heather lean forward and raise their eyebrows at each other. Fortified by their offensive, their father joins in.

'Top of the range. As soon as you said you wanted a new one, I researched it, had a look in *Choice* and got the top of the range. I can afford it.'

'I don't remember saying I *wanted* a new one, Henry. I said we *needed* a new one.'

'Same difference. Now, Mags. We need to look at this plan of yours rationally.'

'Oh dear!' I exclaim.

'Of course we do.'

'I wasn't referring to my plan, Henry. India has just tipped her custard onto the carpet.'

Whatever possessed Alison and Bob to call the child India? Every documentary and film I've seen about India shows people living in the most appalling slums. There's the Taj Mahal, of course, but I can't equate a two-year-old with a mausoleum, no matter how dreamlike it is.

'Do you have a sponge, Mum?'

'With the cleaning stuff under the sink.'

Alison knows where the sponges are. She can clean the mess. I'm feeling a little tired. Even when I was younger, preparing Mother's Day lunch took a lot out of me. I'm not complaining. It gives me pleasure to do special things for the family. I write everyone's likes and dislikes in my recipe folder so I won't forget. Henry won't eat greens (as if I'd forget that), Alison frets about her health and is currently on a gluten-free diet and Heather's lifelong obsession with her weight has led to a recent hatred of lettuce. In spite of high cholesterol, one son-in-law devours all the cheese he can scavenge from our fridge and, in defiance of his diabetes, the other gets stuck into Henry's Scotch. India is allergic to nuts and I'm forbidden to give the baby anything. Alison prepares his purée and brings it with her. Thank heavens for Jake! At twenty-three, he loves anything I make and needs fuel for the surf and the footy field.

'Some more pavlova, Jake?' I ask.

'Best pav you've ever made, Mum.'

'You always say that.'

'Well, it's always true. They get better and better.'

He grins and my heart wobbles. I serve him two-thirds of what's left and load it with extra cream, banana slices and passionfruit. He needs the energy. He's itching to pull on his wetsuit, grab his board and meet his mates at the beach. Not for him this family discussion about my irresponsibility.

'Let's stick to the point.' Henry sounds irritated. 'It's a bit over the top, isn't it, Mags? Six weeks away. I know it's your money, but you've only just got it, after probate came through. You're still getting over your dad's death, still in mourning, not quite rational. Shouldn't you put the money on a term deposit while you think about how best to use it? Not squander it all? There's lots of things need doing around the house. The guttering needs looking at, for one thing.'

I won't rise to any of this. Yes, it is my money. Too bad if I squander some. I'd be hard-pressed to squander all of it in six weeks.

'Yes, Mum. Dad's never stinted with you. You've never had to work, even if you did insist. Helping in a shop's not a real job. So now you've got a bit of money of your own, you can contribute.'

You're right, Alison. I agreed with her in my thoughts. Your father's never stinted on the necessities. On the day you were born, I didn't want necessities. I wanted flowers. Not expensive ones. Not roses or anything extravagant from a florist's. Your father could have picked some geraniums from our backyard. It was self-centred of me. Every other woman in the maternity ward had flowers. I realised I sounded like I was whingeing when your father told me, gently, of course, that I hadn't done anything extraordinary. I'd had a baby, like all the other women in the ward. It hadn't even been a difficult labour. Only six hours. A sprint, according to Betty in the next bed. She'd had a twenty-two-hour marathon.

Henry stood out from the other fathers who came to visit the maternity ward. Red flair pants, torso-hugging pink shirt, shoulder-length hair, and sideburns – how cool I thought he looked! We'd discussed whether we ought to bring a baby into the world at all. Pollution and the Cold War weren't good for babies. Alison decided to come anyway. I didn't mention flowers at the next two births. I was lucky. Heather and Jake came even more quickly than Alison. I can't help thinking, though, daisies from the backyard would have been nice. Henry and I had been flower children after all. We'd bought a cheap package to Los Angeles for our honeymoon and, instead of using the tickets to Disneyland, took the Greyhound up to San Francisco.

'Anyway, Mum, you can't go in September. You'll miss Dad's retirement party.'

It would prove I harboured grievances if I reminded Heather that her father had missed my graduation. How churlish it would seem, especially when the children all made such an effort to be there themselves. Alison and Bob had to hire a babysitter. I paid, of course. Heather and Paul took a whole afternoon off work. Jake skipped a tutorial and brought his two surfing mates with him. What lovely boys! They actually wore white shirts and when the vice chancellor announced my name, the three of them stood up and whistled. Some of the audience laughed and I almost forgot to salute the chancellor.

How selfish it would have been to insist that Henry be there! I never insist. Henry would laugh at me for trying. He was on a business trip. Singapore or Hong Kong, I can't remember which. He goes to both so often. His secretary always goes with him. The most recent ones don't like being called secretaries. I have to remember they're PAs. Each one seems to be younger than the last, but perhaps they're all the same age and I'm getting older. Henry prefers a certain kind of woman, blonde, a bit overweight and busty. Like me. In recent years, my blondeness has been enhanced by one of the trainees in Serge's Salon. It used to be a bit of self-indulgence and I skimped on other things. For the past six months, I've paid for it out of my inheritance and Serge does it himself.

'I'm sorry I'll be missing your retirement party, Henry, but there's no need for me to be there. Ms Simmonds is organising it and I want to avoid the summer heat in Tunisia.'

Ms Simmonds is the latest thirty-five-year-old plump PA.

'What about meals?' Heather obsesses about everyone else's diet as well as her own.

'Your father's not helpless, you know.'

'No, I mean your meals. How can you go for six weeks without a healthy home-cooked meal?'

Good heavens! I'm tempted to take that remark as a compliment to my cooking! I'm the only one in the family who does more in the kitchen than heat up packaged health food dinners in the microwave and pulse strange combinations of fruit and vegetables into juices. I mustn't let vanity carry me away.

'I'll manage, I'm sure, Heather. Tunisian food is supposed to be wonderful and I'm eager to find out if it is. The sponges are under the sink, Alison. If you mop up that custard now, it won't stain the carpet too much. Your father brought it back from Hong Kong.'

'Mags, I think you should reconsider.'

These are the exact words delivered in the same exasperated tone that Henry used when I told him I'd signed up to study archaeology. 'What about dinner?' he asked. 'Will I be reduced to packages like Alison?'

'Couldn't we have dinner a little later?' I replied. 'Seven-thirty, say? Jake's rarely home before then, now he's in Year 12.'

We came to an uneasy agreement. I'd prepare dinner before I left for uni and have it ready to heat up the minute I got home. In spite of Henry's continued protests, we had dinner at seven-thirty every weeknight during the four years it took me to get my degree. It suited Jake.

As for my meals in Tunisia, I can't wait! Go to restaurants; take my time choosing from the menu – fantastic! I'll choose a different meal every night and never, not once will I have grilled chops and mashed potatoes, roast lamb and baked potatoes or crumbed fish and oven-fried potatoes. No supermarket shopping, no grease on the griller, no stacking and unstacking the dishwasher. Yippee!

'Reconsider what, Henry?' I ask. 'Oh dear. Nigel has brought up his puree and, from the smell, I think he's filled his nappy again.'

Poor little fellow. I'd throw up my puree too if it was mashed with boiled parsnip.

'Why don't you let Bob see to him, Alison,' I ask, 'while you clean the custard off the carpet?' I stand up from the table. 'Jake, have you had enough to eat?'

'Do you have another pav in the fridge?'

Heather protests. 'You're disgusting. You've already had two massive helpings.'

'Leave your brother alone. He needs the energy.'

I cringe as I hear Henry's tone in my voice. I refuse to believe that over thirty years of marriage have made me resemble my peevish husband.

'Mags, sit down. We have to thrash this out.'

'I'll sit down, Henry, when I've made the coffee. We can't talk properly with Nigel yelling and Alison on her knees.'

She's given the baby to his father and is cleaning the carpet at last.

'And Jake, isn't that your mate honking outside? Here, give me a kiss for Mother's Day.'

My six-foot-three-inch son lifts me off my feet, gives me a smack on each cheek and sets me down again. As he releases me, he booms, 'Go for it, Mum. Don't let them talk you out of it. Have a wild time in Tunisia.'

His tornado exit from the family room is a signal for Heather to stand up and Alison to stop dabbing at the carpet.

'We can't stay for coffee, Mum. I've changed Nigie twice already and he hasn't any clean clothes left. You need to talk with Dad. You know what I think. You've dropped this bombshell on him and you're being totally stubborn about it, not compromising at all.'

This is rich from the daughter who, six years ago, hysterically defended herself for leaving her adoring husband. She sobbed, 'I don't want to end up like you, Mum. I don't want to be a boring housewife waiting on my husband hand and foot.'

I was shocked. For the sake of peace, I've always acquiesced to Henry treating me like a domestic nonentity, but I didn't see myself that way. Not long after Alison moved in with the cheese scavenger, I went with Jake to Open Day at uni. There was so much choice he couldn't make up his mind. I knew straight away what I intended to do.

Napkins are flung onto the table and chairs scraped over the carpet. There's general milling around as car keys are found, baby paraphernalia collected and kisses collide.

Henry and I shuffle towards the front door behind our daughters, sons-in-law and howling grandchildren. Once again, I say thank you for my presents: a pair of crocodile-mouth oven mitts and a box of Belgian shells. Henry will eat them. I don't like milk chocolate.

After Alison's nose hits my cheek, I say, 'It'd be nice if we had Mother's Day lunch at your place next year.'

'But Mum, I don't have a table big enough for everyone.'

'The June sales are coming up. Why don't you buy one then?'

Henry and I stand in the driveway watching squirming children being strapped into car pods and listening to arguments about who has drunk the least and is fit to drive.

Henry admonishes me gently. 'I don't think that was a nice thing to say to Alison. The girl's got a toddler and a baby to think of.'

'All the more reason for her to get a family table.'

Eventually, the Rav 4 and the Mercedes roar away and Henry and I turn to face the chaos in the family room.

'Leave the dishes, Mags. You can stack them later. Come into the lounge. We need to talk.'

'Very well, Henry. Would you like a coffee?'

'Good idea. I'll check on the footy scores while you're boiling the kettle.'

Henry likes instant and I can't be bothered to make an espresso just for me. There's some red wine left, so I fill my glass. I put Henry's coffee on the small table beside his armchair and sit facing him on the couch.

'Don't you think you've had enough wine, Mags?'

'I don't have to drive anywhere, Henry.'

'Well, it'll be your headache later on. Now, tell me. Why do you want to go to Tunisia?'

Because I do. If I say it like that, Henry will accuse me of provoking an argument.

'I've studied archaeology and French for four years and Tunisia is a French-speaking country with some wonderful Roman and Punic sites.'

'And?'

'I want to see the amphitheatre in El Jem, walk where Hannibal might have trod in Carthage, see the mosaics in the Bardo Museum and bargain in French for a rug in the souk in Tunis.'

'Who with?'

'By myself.'

'A woman your age doesn't go to Tunisia by herself. It's not safe.'

'There are plenty of women researchers and archaeologists working in Tunisia.'

'That course has filled your brain with a lot of rubbish, Mags. How will you possibly manage?'

'There are guidebooks, Henry.'

No point in telling him that some of my former classmates are doing research in Dougga and I've been invited to visit the site. It's not really a lie. I'll be there for four days out of my six-week itinerary.

'Well, I've been thinking about travel and you.' He looks at me expectantly, savouring what he's about to propose.

I gulp a mouthful of wine. It goes down the wrong way. I choke at the idea of ordering roast lamb for him in French every night in Tunisia.

'What do you think about Hong Kong next weekend?'

'I know you're going to Hong Kong.'

'You do?' He rears back in his chair slopping coffee into his saucer.

'Flight Centre left a message on the phone on Friday. I'm sorry. With all the preparations for today it slipped my mind. I forgot to tell you. Your tickets are ready to pick up.'

'It was meant to be a surprise.'

It's no more of a surprise than usual. Henry doesn't tell me about his business trips until a couple of days before he wants me to pack his suitcase.

He leans towards me. 'It's a week late for Mother's Day, but you always invite the family to lunch on the day itself.'

'You mean you and I are going to Hong Kong? Together?'

'Happy Mother's Day, Mags.'

Hong Kong! Not once have I ever shown the slightest interest in going there.

'Well, I am truly surprised. A fridge and a weekend in Hong Kong – I've never had such a big Mother's Day.'

'I thought you'd like a weekend off from cooking. We can buy a silk carpet from a merchant I know. So now you can put this trip of yours into perspective and reconsider.'

Something snaps. I can't censor my words any more. 'Good!' I say. 'A new silk carpet will replace the one India's just stained. Then in September, I'll buy a handwoven wool rug in Tunis. And Hens, I've been asking you for years. I'm not going to ask any more. I'm telling you. Don't call me Mags. My name is Margaret.'

That Mother's Day conversation took place nine years ago. Henry married his PA eighteen months after my first trip to Tunisia.

Anouar and I are currently on a short visit to Sydney. At least ,we're hoping it'll be short. We left Tunisia at the start of the uprising. Anouar had to close the site in Dougga. Many of his workers have joined the protests, so we fear for them and their families. We'll go back as soon as we can. At the moment, we're staying with Jake.

It's Mother's Day next Sunday. Alison and Heather are having lunch in the homes of their respective mothers-in-law. Alison told me Henry's wife is insisting they spend the whole day with her mother in the nursing home. Jake's doing lunch for Anouar and me. He's a fabulous cook and has promised a north African feast.

The Writers' Group

I'm scared. I shouldn't have come. My friend Pam says I'm brave. She says any woman who brings up two kids by herself is brave. Rubbish! When you have no choice, that's what you do. Pam wanted me to meet her writers' group, so here I am.

I write stories in my diary. They're just for me. Pam's a real writer. She sends letters to the newspapers. She's handed out copies of the latest and reads it aloud. Everyone will have a turn to read. I'll be sixth.

The next reader's a poet. He makes his voice deep and solemn. This is his first verse.

tsunami	punches	
rams	slams	
me	to the	wall

He says it's a love poem. I don't see it that way. It's how I felt when Gary said he was in love with someone at work and was moving in with her. He'd take the kids every second weekend.

When the poet finishes, everyone stares at their copy. They must like it. They don't say anything.

The pretty young woman next to the poet has a ring through her eyebrow. I've told my daughter she can't pierce anything until she's sixteen and then she can pay for it herself.

The young woman hands out pages from her novel. It's a sex scene with lots of noise and smells and moisture. I think she's brave reading it to the group. Everyone stares at their sheets of paper.

Pam whispers to me, 'Do you think she's writing from experience?'

How would I know? Gary never used those words and never did those things with me. Nothing like that on our kitchen table! If he'd said that's what he wanted, I'd have been scared, but I'd have had a go.

I know the next man's reading a poem because it rhymes.

> The sky at dusk in Adelaide
> is orange like sweet marmalade…
> The moon's a silver sliver
> that sets my heart a-quiver!
> Yay! Ye star-pocked night –
> thou remind'st me of my dog's eyes bright!

What a funny way to talk about a dog! I didn't write like that about Blackie. His eyes aren't bright. One has a cataract. He lost the other years ago. I was taking him for a walk. It was dusk, but the sky wasn't like marmalade. Blackie was sniffing along a fence when suddenly this giant dog shoots out of nowhere and attacks him. I hit the nasty dog with my shopping bag till he let go. Pam said I was brave. Rubbish! That's what you do. He was twice as big as Blackie!

The next woman reads from her memoir. She says a teacher inspired her son and now he's a brain surgeon in a big city hospital. She goes on a bit. My son isn't keen on his teachers but he likes Mr O'Shea, his footy coach.

A few months ago, I went up to Mr O'Shea after footy practice. I said, 'Just 'cause you used to be a big rugby player and tried out for the Sea Eagles doesn't give you the right to call a kid who fumbles the ball a waste of space.'

Pam said I was brave. I don't think so. You stand up for your kids, don't you? Mr O'Shea went all red and then he grinned. He's nice-looking when he smiles. He said he'd keep my advice in mind.

Yesterday after footy practice, Mick O'Shea asked me to go to his club dinner and I'm going. I'm scared. I haven't had a date in years, but I bet it'll be fun. I'm not telling Pam.

Everyone's looking at me. It's my turn. I shake my head. I can't read the story I wrote specially for tonight. It's not exciting or poetic or sexy. It's about Blackie when he almost died. I picked him up from the footpath. He was crying and his blood soaked into my T-shirt. Someone'll probably say dogs don't cry, but he did. The group wouldn't be interested in how the kids and me, we took it in turns to nurse Blackie day and night for two weeks.

I've got a new idea for a story to write in my diary. It's about dressing up and having a lovely dinner and maybe getting a kiss in the car afterwards, before the babysitter has to go. It'll be exciting and poetic and sexy – not for the group. Just for me.

Conversations Far and Near

There've been many portraits of me. I once asked colleagues in the staff room how many portraits of themselves they'd seen. They all said 'None!' I immediately changed my mind about showing them the latest one of me. It remained in the pile of papers I'd tossed onto my desk. The conversation drifted to clever insults invented by students.

I've never felt insulted by my portraits. If my students are bored, a doodle is a mild and justified reproach. The desire to take the mickey out of me has often inspired excellent caricatures. High cheekbones, a wide mouth and frizzy blonde hair make me easy to draw. According to student sketches, my hair sticks out of my head like fusilli pasta. The pencil drawing on my desk was a different matter altogether. My hair looked chic and, from his desk at the side of the classroom, the 'artist' had drawn my face at an angle that gave it a strange elegance. When he gave me the signed drawing at the end of the lesson, it was a few seconds before I recognised myself.

I'd known he was doing something different from the rest of the class, but hadn't investigated. I didn't expect him to do what I demanded of the others. When the principal had informed me that a French boy was coming into my Year 11 French class, I'd prepared for battle. Past exchange students had been dubious assets. They addressed me in the latest teenage street slang and sneered when I didn't understand. They exuded boredom, taught my students to parrot obscenities, flirted with the girls and sniggered if the boys attempted to answer a question in French.

Jean-Luc was different. He put up his hand to answer questions like everyone else. Oh, he certainly flirted with the girls. They fought to sit near him in every lesson. He helped them do the exercises I set and made them giggle by exaggerating his French accent when he explained something in English. He was also popular with the boys. His family had a holiday house near Biarritz on the west coast of France, so he surfed. He joined the carloads of Year 11 and 12 boys who drove up Sydney's northern beaches seeking the best waves on weekends and after school, sometimes during school.

For the last lesson of his three-month stay, the girls brought (and some had even made) millefeuilles, *tartes aux citrons* and madeleines and the boys brought French pâtés and cheeses. They tried to talk me into allowing champagne and pretended surprise when I reminded them that they were minors.

There were tears and every girl lined up to give Jean-Luc a hug. A cheeky boy called out, 'Your turn next, mademoiselle,' and everyone slow-clapped me until I walked up to Jean-Luc, stood on tiptoe, put my hands on his shoulders and kissed him on both cheeks. The resulting whistles and hoots of laughter caused the geography teacher in the next room to bang on the wall. The father of one of the students, a well-known sculptor, had been asked by the class to make (for free) a small sculpture of a kangaroo and a French rooster on a surfboard. This was presented and Jean-Luc gave a speech in French and English thanking us for our welcome and hospitality. He said he lived in a big house in a village called Ferrières near Paris and everyone was invited to come and stay, 'including mademoiselle'. More hoots and whistles and banging on the wall.

He remained a presence in the class. He sent a weekly group email in English talking about his studies and repeating his invitation for everyone to visit. I based one lesson a week on a group answer in French. Some of the girls were working hard on their parents to let them go to France between the end of the HSC and the beginning of uni. The number of students intending to study French at uni jumped from five to almost the total class enrolment of twenty-four. As an experienced teacher whose students had always earned excellent HSC results, I allowed myself to take a tiny proportion of the credit for the increase!

The class of 2003 did indeed earn excellent results. Jean-Luc wouldn't start his exams for the Baccalauréat until June 2004. The group emails ended but individuals kept in touch with me and each other. It's wonderful when a teacher receives emails, postcards and letters from former students. Over the years, I've acquired a collection and enjoy reading that the Louvre or the Loire Valley or the Champagne region are just as fabulous as I'd said they were!

In January 2004, Jean-Luc sent an email addressed only to me and written in French. It was an outpouring of emotion. His father had died of a sudden heart attack. I figured out Jean-Luc must be an only child. There was no mention of siblings or relatives. His mother didn't want his friends to come to the house so he spoke to them at snatched moments on his mobile.

About halfway through, he wrote. 'Can I call you on Skype? *Maman* doesn't like me leaving the house. If you say yes, don't bother reading the rest of this. I'll repeat it anyway. It's whirling around and around in my head. I can't talk to people here. I don't want their pity and I don't want gossip. There's nothing to gossip about. Everyone in the village knows my parents didn't get on. My father wasn't unfaithful. He just worked himself to death. If you don't want to talk to me, I'll understand. You have so many students and responsibilities. What I'm doing in this avalanche of words is putting down memories of him before they fade. But it would be good to talk.'

I replied straight away.

And so began the conversations about his father. They weren't really conversations. They were monologues. The man whom Jean-Luc described was not very different from the fathers of many of my students: totally consumed by work, leaving home early and returning late, distant, distracted, always on the phone. The small child gets up early to see his father's taillights disappear in the morning gloom and fights sleep at night, watching from his window for the headlights to swing into the street and then into the garage. And when, on rare occasions, the father's full attention focuses on the child – what eagerness to please, what joy! The whole of life is squeezed into that small capsule of time.

Jean-Luc Skyped me in his father's library and I could see behind him dark floor-to-ceiling shelves lined with leather-bound books. I imagined that the books had been read or were waiting to be read by someone who enjoyed both their content and the sensual pleasure of holding them. They hadn't been bought merely for the sake of intellectual posturing.

During what became weekly monologues, always in French, I'd sip a coffee or a glass of wine.

When my glass was empty, Jean-Luc would say, 'I'm doing all the talking. Why don't you get a refill and tell me about your day?'

I'd say, 'You've seen what my days are like and the meetings I've attended were boring. What I'm reading at the moment is…'

After writing down the title and the name of the author, he'd gaze beyond my shoulder (I always sat by a window looking onto a red gum) and resume talking.

Three weeks before his first exam, philosophy, he said, 'My father wanted – he expected me to do well. I intend to fulfil his wishes. I've written a practice essay for Philo. I know I've imposed so much already, but will you read it for me?'

'I'm not a Philo teacher. I don't know the requirements of the syllabus.'

'You can tell if my argument makes sense and if it's relevant to the question.'

'What's the question?'

'Is man condemned to create illusions about himself?'

I laughed. 'I'm interested to see what you do with it.'

And so began the conversations about his studies in Philo, English, French and Italian. I wasn't a tutor, rather a sounding board. His exam results were brilliant. Vanity prevailing, I allowed myself a tiny proportion of the credit.

At this time, I was living with the head teacher of history at my school. Our colleagues anticipated a wedding announcement to be plopped into the staffroom conversation at any moment. There was an implication in the air that I was getting on. Thirty-four years old – we'd better hurry up if we wanted kids!

Darryl disapproved of my continuing conversations with Jean-Luc. 'That kid's got a crush on you,' he said. 'And he's exploiting you.'

'Isn't that what all the brightest students do? Get the best out of their teachers?'

'You're not his teacher any more.'

'I could say I'm exploiting him. He's keeping me up to date in French.'

'Adolescent street slang. You'll get a real update at Christmas.'

I shut up. The back-handed compliment – that I was capable of inspiring a student crush – was counterbalanced by the reminder of our proposed Christmas holidays.

Two of Darryl's history teacher friends and their partners were urging us to join them and rent a cottage near the World War I battlefields in the north of France. I'd been useful when we'd done this once before: none of the others spoke French. Normally eager to go to France, I was dreading the trip.

Darryl said, 'It'll be our last hurrah before we tackle the business of having a family.'

I didn't want to go to the battlefields under the grey skies of a northern hemisphere winter. The rows of graves and the name-filled memorials to hundreds of thousands of young men, many the same age as my Year 12 students, had filled me with horror the last time.

And I didn't want kids. Darryl and I got on all right, but that wasn't a basis for lifelong commitment. Every time my thoughts crept near to breaking up with him, I'd swerve away. It would so complicated – the hurt, the lack of 'good' reason, the awkwardness in the staffroom. I'd have to change schools. I didn't have the courage to start the upheaval.

My weekly conversations with Jean-Luc shone through the drabness of my personal life. After his Baccalauréat, we talked about his two-year preparation for the fiercely competitive entrance exams into a grande école, the tertiary institution of his choice. We Skyped on Sundays when Darryl played golf. Perhaps I should have felt sneaky, but I didn't. Darryl could have asked me if I was still in touch with Jean-Luc. I wouldn't have lied. So what if the boy had a crush and so what if he was exploiting me? The conversations were fun and what harm was there in that?

Suddenly everything changed. The position of head of foreign languages became available at another school. My successful application meant I'd start my new job in February. I withdrew from the group going to the north of France and told Darryl I wanted to end our relationship. He was neither surprised nor particularly regretful. I was a little hurt and wondered why I'd put off acting for so long!

Setting up in an apartment on my own and adapting to a new job took time. The school was more academic than my previous one and I was in charge of twelve staff. Plans for my next trip to France were pushed aside.

As with all ex-students, I asked Jean-Luc to call me Julia, and, like most of them, he hadn't called me anything for a while. Some ex-students never make the transition from *mademoiselle* to Julia.

One day, he spoke with unusual firmness. 'Julia, you say you love France but when was the last time you were here? You'll lose your fluency in the language. You've got three weeks' holiday coming up. I'll be twenty-one on 10 July. There'll be a big party in Ferrières. Get on a plane.'

'You think I'm losing fluency?'

He looked mildly exasperated. 'You're being coy and evading the issue. After the party, we'll go to Biarritz and we can surf.'

'You think I can surf?'

'Of course you can. You grew up in Sydney.'

'You're stereotyping me.'

'*Mes excuses, mademoiselle. Mille fois mes excuses.* A thousand pardons. So, Julia, are you coming? '

'Why not?'

He met me at Charles de Gaulle Airport. Like the last time I'd seen him face to face, but this time without prompting, I stood on tiptoe, put my hands on his shoulders and kissed him on both cheeks. He smiled, took my luggage and drove me to the home of the friends with whom I always stay when I'm in Paris.

He said, 'I hope you won't be too jet-lagged. My party's at lunchtime tomorrow. Your friends are bringing you, aren't they?'

'They might not be able to find a babysitter. Their daughter is ten. Would it be okay if she came too?'

'Of course. There'll be guests from nine months to ninety.'

The party took place in the family home in the medieval centre of the village of Ferrières, an hour's drive from Paris. The cobblestone courtyard easily held about a hundred people. The one-metre-thick stone walls kept the midday heat out of the house, so the older guests sat in the large salon, where young people took it in turns to play jazz on the grand piano. I drank water rather than wine, partly because I was still tired and partly to keep a clear head. I wanted to remember the names of people whom I met and perhaps connect them with stories that Jean-Luc had told me.

There were three groups: Jean-Luc's fellow students, employees of the family business and people from the village. I was surprised to learn that, as well as studying, Jean-Luc was running the family business, a food exporting company with several hundred employees. There were no relatives. We'd never talked about our families, but I was expecting to see an aunt or uncle and a cousin or two.

My friends' little girl, Nicole, kept close to me. As a source of Australian surf-themed T-shirts and, when she was little, cuddly marsupial toys, I'm a favourite and exotic 'aunt'.

Jean-Luc introduced me to people as 'my Australian teacher who's responsible for the excellence of my spoken and written English'.

I laughed each time and would say something like, 'If my French is good, it's because a teacher learns from her students.'

The students had congregated around a girl sprawled in a deckchair. Someone would have to pull her up from it because she was heavily pregnant. There were ludicrous suggestions for the baby's name –

Napoléon! Vercingétorix! – and jokes made about the girl's impending wedding with her laughing boyfriend.

Jean-Luc put his arm around my shoulder and said, 'This is the woman I'm going to marry when I grow up.'

Embarrassed, I laughed. Thankfully, so did Nicole, and everyone else joined in. The arrival of two men in chefs' outfits shouldering a barbecued wild boar on a wooden plank distracted attention. Jean-Luc was caught up making sure people were comfortably seated at cloth-covered trestle tables in the shade beside the house and the feasting started.

About mid-afternoon, tired from rich food and meeting so many people, I looked for somewhere to steal a few moments alone. I slumped onto a seat under a dark-leaved cherry tree in a grassy area beyond the courtyard and asked Nicole to bring me a coffee. Jean-Luc suddenly appeared and squatted down beside me.

'*Ça va?* Do you feel all right? You look a little pale. Would you like to go inside where it's cooler?'

'No, I'm fine. I'll be up again in a minute.'

'Stay as long as you like. You don't have to move from here just to be polite. This is your garden.'

I smiled.

'I meant it, you know.'

'Thank you, but I'll get up and join everyone soon.'

'No, I mean I will marry you.'

I realised my mouth had dropped open when he put a finger under my chin and gently pushed upwards. Before turmoil commandeered all of my thoughts, I glimpsed Nicole standing uncertainly in the full sunlight holding a cup and saucer. Fearing she'd turn away, I squeaked, 'Ah, my coffee!'

Jean-Luc stood up and I patted the seat beside me so Nicole would sit down. 'I'll be back,' he said. 'My mother would like to meet you.'

Nicole picked the cherries dangling around us while I gulped strong black coffee. I tried to think coherently. Marriage! He's a boy! Well, no he's not. He's a young man. From what I'd been hearing, his employees were fond of him and regarded him as a better boss than his father. An old man from the village, with gnarled workman's hands and white hair combed into furrows, addressed him as *monsieur*. Marriage! He's joking! Sometimes the humour of one culture is misunderstood by someone from a different culture. I mustn't take him seriously. He's a friend, like so many other ex-students.

Who are you kidding? I asked myself. Friend! You'd like a lot more than that, wouldn't you? How vain can you be? He's so much younger. Is that an impediment? No, don't follow that train of thought. You can't contemplate the possibility.

Jean-Luc returned amidst a swirl of children who scooped Nicole away. 'My mother's in the salon,' he said.

Mme Delavigne gave me a gracious smile, but not her hand, and gestured to a delicate chair near a small antique table. 'Will you take tea with me, Mademoiselle Leighton?' she asked.

I hate tea and I'd just had an excellent coffee, but I put on a show of restrained enthusiasm for the offered drink. Over her cream silk blouse, Madame Delavigne wore a single strand of pearls that I estimated would be worth more than my apartment in Sydney. Her clothes, elegant but old-fashioned, gave her the appearance of carefully ageing dignity.

We conversed about the weather until Jean-Luc brought a silver tray with the accoutrements necessary for tea. He set them on the table, bowed semi-mockingly to his mother, then to me and disappeared.

I enjoyed watching the ceremony that Mme Delavigne performed. If she expected me, this schoolteacher from a plebeian society in the Antipodes, to stick out my little finger, she was disappointed. I could be just as posh as Mme Delavigne, but with me it was an act. Having nothing more to say about the weather, I was silent. What topic would she turn to next?

'My son has asked you to marry him and you have refused.'

Fortunately, I'd just put my cup and saucer on the table. Otherwise,

I'd have rattled them. I had sufficient self-control not to let my mouth drop open. Mme Delavigne observed me with a strange expression on her face. I imagined what she was thinking. 'Here's this foreigner, this older woman. How could any woman possibly refuse a proposal of marriage from my fabulous son? Thank heavens she has!'

I said, 'It would not be appropriate.'

Her face relaxed. I'd said the right thing.

She said, 'It is to be expected that he'll marry someone from his own milieu, someone who'll take on the responsibilities of being the wife of a major employer in this region and the mother of his children and heirs.'

I was puzzled. Jean-Luc hadn't proposed. I hadn't refused. What had he said to his mother? How much had she guessed or thought she understood from what he'd said? I didn't see Jean-Luc's future as being what she'd described, but she and I agreed on one thing. I wasn't the right sort of person to be the wife of the scion of an old bourgeois family.

Having given one acceptable answer, I thought it prudent to say no more. We chatted politely about *Les Nocturnes*, the medieval summer festival of the village.

A few days later, Jean-Luc and I drove to his family holiday house near Biarritz. He went surfing at dawn every morning. Sometimes, I accompanied him. We spent much of our time in bed or on the living room carpet or on the divan or on the kitchen table. The sex was fabulous. No novice, Jean-Luc was inventive, playful, considerate and tender. I felt like the novice. No more waiting passively for the panting to be over. I was an energetic participant.

During the intervals, lying side by side with the sweat drying on our bodies, we talked about the same things we'd talked about on Skype: art, languages, books, history, philosophy. As soon as he finished his management studies, Jean-Luc intended to enrol in art classes. His classroom portrait of me was not a one off. He sketched me in bed, on the carpet and so on, and in the kitchen where we both enjoyed cooking, eating and making love. Actually, I did most of the cooking. While I did that or read or slept, Jean-Luc attended to company business by phone and email.

On the last day of my holiday, he drove me to Charles de Gaulle Airport. At the departure gate, he bent down, put his hands on my shoulders and kissed me on both cheeks. Tears shot up to my eyes and I tried to blink them away.

'Don't worry,' he said. 'You're the woman I'll marry.'

Until now, he'd always touched the topic of marriage lightly, like a cat patting piano keys.

What I thought was going to be a tempestuous but temporary affair has lasted more than ten years. Sometimes, Jean-Luc drops into Sydney. During school holidays, I join him wherever he is. He's expanded his company, which now has overseas subsidiaries. I've visited every country in the European Union and most of the French-speaking countries in Africa. As well as working long hours seven days a week, Jean-Luc paints. It amuses him to have his paintings hung in the various buildings where the company has offices.

He told me, 'It serves two purposes. Having my paintings there is good for my ego and saves the company money on artworks!'

If there happens to be a picture-hanging ceremony, I attend either by Skype or in person. When we're apart, we Skype every day; when we're together, the lovemaking is exciting, erotic and fun. Since he takes only a few days off at Christmas time, I stay in his apartment in Paris and make one trip to Ferrières to have tea with his mother. She and I discuss the weather in detail. It's an important topic, since the family company is based on food production.

A few days before school broke up this year, Jean-Luc said, '*Maman* has had a bad flu for several weeks. The doctor fears pneumonia. Would you spend Christmas at the house in Ferrières? You can have the whole of the second floor to yourself. I'll be busy and *Maman* will have tea with you every afternoon. The rest of the time, you can do the things you usually do. My driver will take you anywhere you want to go.'

The first afternoon when I joined Mme Delavigne in the small salon, I was shocked at how frail she looked, much older than her sixty years. Her breathlessness obliged me to carry the conversation. It was an effort for her to sit upright.

Marie-Jo, a chatty and practical woman from the village, came to look after her every day. 'It is good you are here,' Marie-Jo said at the end of the week. 'Madame makes an effort. She gets out of bed and gets dressed only for afternoon tea with you.'

Yesterday, coming downstairs after tea, I was surprised to see Jean-Luc already home from work.

He was sitting on a window seat, looking out at the cherry tree shivering in the wind. He turned and his face didn't light up the way it usually does when he sees me. 'Would you like to get married?' His tone was abrupt.

'No.' My answer was automatic.

He stood up and drew me into a trembling hug. With his lips against my hair, he said, 'My father married the boss's daughter and spent the rest of his life not living up to her expectations. I'm now living up to them for him – with the company at least. I'm not going to marry to please *Maman*, even if she is so sick. I grew up seeing marriage as emotional drudgery.'

I stood back so I could see his face. 'Then why ask me?'

'Some women think that marriage brings happiness. If that's what you want, we'll do it. Whatever makes you happy makes me happy.'

'Do you want children?' I asked.

He kissed the palm of my hand. 'We'll have as many as you want.'

'I'm past that.'

'Lots of women your age and older have children.'

'If I'd wanted children, I'd have had them in my twenties or thirties. If you want children, you'll have to choose someone else as their mother.'

'You and me, we agree: no marriage, no children. Let's get to the essential. Do I make you happy?'

'Yes.'

He held me tightly for a long time.

Today, Mme Delavigne is wearing a lot of jewellery. Is she trying to impress me? Why would she bother? The brilliant stones sink into the shrivelled skin on her neck, wrists and fingers. They make me sad.

When I sit in my usual place on the velvet chair, she says, 'Jean-Luc tells me you prefer coffee to tea. Is that correct?'

'Yes, it is.'

'I apologise for assuming our tastes, at least in beverage, are the same. It was inhospitable of me not to have asked you long ago. I've arranged for Marie-Jo to bring you some coffee. Please let me know if it is the way you like it.'

My 'thank you' sounds insincere in my ears. I'm touched but also wary. There's a barb in her apology.

The subject of the freezing weather and consequent damage to the nearby vineyards having been exhausted, Mme Delavigne looks at me and says, 'He has other women, you know.'

'Yes.'

I say no more. I'm not sure I can control my voice well enough to hide my feelings. I'm not surprised. If I'd ever allowed myself to think of such a possibility, I'd have thought it more than likely. Jean-Luc's young and vigorous. The magnetism that charmed the girls when he was in my class has intensified. When we're out together, women look at him with open invitation and at me with envy, sometimes contemptuous surprise which I assume is inspired by the age difference. We've never said we'd be faithful to one another. I'm free to have other men, but I don't. I've never met anyone as interesting, dynamic and brilliant as Jean-Luc. If there are other women, I don't want to hear about them.

Mme Delavigne gives a small nod as if in approval of my reticence. She continues, 'I'm worried about his future and the future of the company. He won't marry anyone suitable and you refuse to marry him. Why is that?'

'If he married me and was unfaithful – I know exactly where his heart is, I've heard it beating often enough – I'd stick a knife into it.'

She stares at me. I hold her gaze. A spatter of rain hits the window behind us. We both pick up our cups.

I think of the philosophy question that Jean-Luc answered as practice years ago for his Bac exam: 'Is man condemned to create illusions about himself?' I wonder which of us – Jean-Luc, his mother or I – has the strongest illusions about the long-term relationship between the three of us. Jean-Luc and I are happy. We don't think beyond tomorrow. Mme Delavigne does. I imagine she clings to the belief that Jean-Luc will eventually fulfil his family duty. He might be in his forties, fifties, sixties or even older when he finally decides to marry a mother for his children. Illusion, hope or prophecy? Who knows? Meanwhile, there's a portrait of me in Jean-Luc's office in Paris.

Emails in the Ether

17 January 2008

Dear Chris,

You wouldn't believe it. I'm in an internet café. There are lots of them in Manly. I don't want to email you from home. Your father would come and look over my shoulder to check I wasn't messing up the settings on his computer and he'd see I was writing to you. One day, he caught me writing a letter and actually said he 'forbade' me to get in touch with you. He backed down when I threatened to leave. I stopped writing letters not because of him, but because two were sent back with 'address unknown' stamped on them.

Now I've learnt how to use email and it's easier to write from an internet café. The man in charge said he'd help me when I need it, but I'm managing quite well.

I don't have any illusions about your father missing me if I left. He'd miss his meals being cooked and his clothes washed. If I sent in a robot to do the same things, he wouldn't notice the difference.

Maybe this sounds like I'm bitter, but I'm not. It's just that writing an email and sending it into the ether gives me the freedom to say almost anything. I can write things that I know annoy you. Either you will continue not to make contact or you will get so annoyed you might reply.

Do you access your emails? Are you still using this address? I suppose some mechanism in the system would tell me if the address is no longer valid.

Do you remember Naomi from next door? Her son's back from India. She's lording it over me. Her son's home and mine isn't. He arrived at the time of her birthday. I don't say 'for' her birthday. By the looks of him, I don't think he knows where he is or what day it is. At a guess, I'd say he weighs no more than forty-five kilos and he's six foot two. I'd rather you stay away and be healthy than look like him.

Are you healthy? The last time your father and I had a shouting match about you, he said you've been away so long you might be dead. I cannot, I will not believe you're anything but alive. If you read this, please answer. You don't have to write at length. Just say, 'Hello, Mum.' It would be nice to know where you're living and what you're doing but I won't insist. That's asking too much.

Be safe. Look after yourself.

Love,

Mum

24 January 2008

Dear Chris,

I'm in the internet café again. I opened my emails at home every day this week, hoping for a reply. Of course, there wasn't one. It felt so good last week to write a sort of diary entry I thought I'd do it again.

I started a diary when you were born but gave up almost straight away. I didn't like writing negative things. You and your father didn't get on from the beginning. You screamed when he picked you up. He'd shove you into my arms and you'd gurgle and drool bubbles.

How can I write this stuff? It sounds mawkish. Maybe it is. Tough! I'm just a mother yearning for her lost son. If that makes you feel bad, I'm pleased. There's not a day, not an hour goes by that I don't worry about you. I'd better not go on. I'll only get worse.

Please let me know where you are.

Be safe. Look after yourself.

Love,

Mum

31 January 2008

Dear Chris,

I wonder if we've both decided my emailing you on Thursdays is a pattern. The man at the internet café greets me like a regular customer and has given me the same computer each time.

I've been wondering what to write, what might induce you to reply. I could say your father hit me. That would get a reaction from you – well, I hope it would – but it's a lie. I have fantasies but I don't tell lies. Your father doesn't feel strongly enough about me to hit me. Oh, I'm not justifying domestic violence, but I sometimes wonder if indifference isn't a form of violence too.

Enough about your father. What are you doing? Do you have a job? A girlfriend? A wife? Am I a grandmother? Oh, how I'd love that! I'm now plunging into a fantasy of a toddler with dark curls and a dimple on one cheek like yours. I can imagine you screwing up your mouth in irritation as you read this so I won't go on. I'll ask the man to show me how to look up on the internet some of the places I guess you'd like to be.

Be safe. Look after yourself.

Love,

Mum

7 February 2008

Dear Chris,

After sending you last week's email I wondered whether to break the pattern and send you one the next day. But no. Maybe you're now opening your emails on Thursdays.

What I was going to do last Friday and have done today is attach some photos. The man in the internet café showed me how. When the idea flitted into my brain that you might have a child, I wanted little Chris or Christina to see a picture of his grandparents. I got Naomi from next door to take a photo of me and I took one of your father through the kitchen window when he was working in the garden. He's aged since you last saw him, hasn't he? It's been seven years. What really shocks me about your father's photo is how much he looks like his father at the same age. Do you remember your grandfather? At the end, he looked like an old Croatian peasant, which is exactly what he was. You know how vain your father is about having blue eyes. He thinks they make him look Anglo. They did, when he was young. Not now. I've aged too. You haven't seen me with grey hair.

I keep going over in my mind what happened during that last fight you had with your father. It didn't seem worse than any of the others. What made you storm out and never come back? Was his affair with Jenny the final straw? I've always known your father had other women. You knew it too. You didn't say anything, but I could tell. You denied knowing about Jenny – your friend's mother and my so-called best friend. Was that because you couldn't face the betrayal or thought I couldn't? Your father's women were a relief really. They turned his attention away from me and I had peace for as long as the affair lasted. I suppose that's not the sort of thing you tell a son, but since I don't know if you ever read my emails, I'll send these thoughts into the ether anyway.

You and I put up with things that I think are worse than sexual digressions. Your father yelled and sneered and put us both down. I escaped into fantasy. You accused me once of passivity. There was no point in the three of us being aggressive. He was never satisfied with anything you did. I was sad he didn't come and see your HSC paintings when they were exhibited in ArtExpress. How could he call them sissy stuff when he hadn't seen them? That was his loss. Where has his own boasted ability in maths got him? A dreary job from which he now fears being pushed into early retirement

How are you managing? Do you need any money? I save a little from my wages each month. It's on term deposit, but I can access it any time. It's surprising how the amount has grown over the years. You know you just have to say.

I'm a dreamer but one day I might open my emails and see a photo of you. Please think about it.

Be safe. Look after yourself.

Love,

Mum

10 p.m. Sunday 10 February

Dear Chris,

It's not Thursday, but I can't wait until then to email you. Instead of going straight home from the hospital, I've come to the internet café. Ahmed was just about to lock up when I arrived. I must have looked so upset he took pity on me and turned a computer back on.

This is real news, not just the begging and fantasies I usually write. Your father had a series of strokes starting at about three o'clock this morning. I suspected a heart attack, but whatever it was, I knew it was serious and dialled 000. An intensive care ambulance took us to the Royal North Shore Hospital. It didn't go over the speed limit or sound the siren. What silly thoughts to have when your father looked as if he was dying!

How I longed to see you shoulder through the plastic swing doors of the emergency department. By five o'clock this afternoon, the doctors had decided he wasn't going to die and put him in a ward. When I left the hospital at nine thirty, he was conscious but couldn't talk.

I'm sorry if you don't want to hear this, but I'm worrying more about you than him. He's got a monitor, a drip, a catheter and nurses running around looking after him. He's being well cared for. Are you?

I'm not asking you to come. I can manage. All I want is to know you're alive and well and then I can face whatever I have to.

Be safe. Look after yourself.

Love,

Mum

14 February

Dear Chris,

It's Thursday again and I'm in the internet café. I don't like using the computer at home. It's so dreary there. The café is full of people, most of them young, younger than you. I enjoy their liveliness and listening to their conversations on their mobiles. Ahmed always gives me the same computer, so I can see everyone and I'm near his desk if I need help.

I didn't really expect you to answer my last email. It would have been good if you had. Maybe you never open your emails. Writing is like chatting to you. I imagine you're sitting beside me, squinting and shaking your hair out of your eyes. Is it still long? Do you remember how your father went berserk when you put it in a ponytail? I almost burst trying not to laugh. He accused you of being a sissy, which to him is the same as being homosexual – not that he ever used that word. He preferred 'pansy' or 'fairy'. How brutal those pretty words sounded in his mouth! He should see the young man sitting next to me now. He's got multiple earrings, ropes of shell necklaces and board shorts with frangipanis on them. He's certainly no pansy according to the conversation he's having with someone called Alicia on Skype. I'm not eavesdropping; he speaks so loudly I can't help hearing.

Your poor father has gone all soft and flabby, including his tongue. It seems to be too big for his mouth and he can't speak properly. It won't be easy looking after him when he comes home. The social worker at the hospital is arranging for people to help me.

I'm not saying this to make you feel guilty about being far away. I'm beyond provoking guilt. What a waste of energy! I'm just apprehensive. Nor am I asking you to come and help me. Please send me a word and I'll be happy.

Be safe. Look after yourself.

Love,

Mum

12 June

Dear Chris,

I've given up expecting a reply. I'm writing for me now. It's like keeping a diary that a stranger might find some day by accident and read. Oh, don't worry. I'll keep sending emails on Thursdays. That's when the nurse visits, so I can come to the internet café. Ahmed gets me a coffee from the Italian place when he goes and gets his own. He and everyone else are so kind – the doctors, the nurse, the chemist, Naomi, Alicia's boyfriend and the other young people in the café – I don't feel so lonely and isolated any more. Naomi comes over for a cup of tea and a chat almost every day. Her son's gone back to India.

Your father isn't coping well. Surprisingly, I am. Oh, there's a huge amount of work involved in looking after him. He still can't do much for himself. The poor man tries to tell me what he wants, but I don't always understand. I do my best. Sometimes he goes purple and I think he'd like to hit me if he could. I hope he fantasises about it. Fantasy can give such comfort.

I'm so busy I've lost weight and feel all the better for it. I should send you a photo – not with your father. That would be too cruel. I'll get Ahmed to take one of me. I've put some colour through my hair. It's not dark brown as it was when you were little. That's too harsh for me now. I've gone light brown with streaks. Ahmed says it takes ten years off me. After I finish this email, I'll go back to the dress shop on Sydney Road and buy the top I tried on earlier. I'll wear it tonight when Ahmed and I go to the new Tunisian restaurant on the oceanfront. Naomi says she'll be happy to sit with your father.

Be safe. Look after yourself.

Love,

Mum

19 June

Dear Chris,

I'm absolutely thrilled you've 'dropped a line'. No news of what you're doing but as I've always said, the only thing I wanted was a hello. You say you're worried. It's not clear about whom. If it's about your father, what more do you want to know? I wrote in February that the doctors were warning he'd never get any better. He could have another stroke or stay in the wheelchair for years. As for me, my emails have been my personal dairy; I haven't kept anything from you.

I gather you don't like my going out with Ahmed. No, he's not a Wog. In current slang, he's a Leb, although actually he's from Morocco.

Of course I'd love you to come home but, I'm sorry, I can't send you the airfare. I've had to reduce my working hours. My savings have disappeared and most of our income goes on your father's care.

I have a mobile phone now. Ahmed gave me his old one when he upgraded. He's shown me how to use it. Send me a message when you've booked your ticket. Here's my number: 0422 879 222. I won't tell your father you're coming until you let me know the date. I look forward to seeing you when I see you.

Be safe. Look after yourself.

Love,

Mum

The Outcast of the Omar El Khayam

Nick, the tour guide, sighed. There's always one spoiler in the group. If he was lucky, he might have ten minutes of peace on the cruise boat's sundeck before the next temple visit. On each side of the *Omar El Khayam*, Lake Nasser reached out in vivid blue towards the golden mounds of sand and pyramid-shaped hills of the desert.

It was a good group, one of his best in terms of interest in Egyptology and cheerfulness in the face of minor discomforts and upset stomachs. He hadn't picked Beatrice straight away as the spoiler. A podgy little French woman, she had broken the ice at the first meeting of the group in the hotel restaurant in Cairo.

'*Bonjour*. I am Béatrice. Let me read your name. Ah, Jim. I am pleased to meet you. You are excited too? This trip, it will be wonderful. The agency, they tell me we have *un guide fantastique*. You are Charles? Your drink is nice? It is *karkaday*, a hibiscus drink. I remember. I am born here. My family leaves when I am small. Ah, bonjour. The label on your pretty blouse says Margaret. You are pretty too. When I was little, my mother and my aunts, they teach me the belly dance. Perhaps we find a place where we can dance.'

Nick observed each person brighten as Beatrice's accent made his or her name sound unfamiliar and exotic. Before meeting her, Jim (pronounced 'Jeem'), had appeared morose and introverted, Charles ('Sharrl') irascible and Margaret, prim. Maybe 'Marguerite' would eventually laugh at his silly jokes. He wouldn't try any blue ones with her, not to begin with at least. The worst he thought of Beatrice was that he'd probably get sick of her chatter. He could tune out when she irritated him.

Last night, however, as the *Omar El Khayam* set sail from Aswan to Luxor, there had been a premonition of trouble. Beatrice chose Scotch as an aperitif. Nick was explaining Ramses the Great's battle tactics to Charles when a harsh voice crackled near the bar.

'*Hé! Garçon.* I ask for another drink. You forget me last time. You serve the others. You forget me again.'

Nick wondered how many 'last times' there'd been. Did he have a drunk on his hands? Well, he'd dealt with drunks before. Maybe she'd be the gentle kind and just fall asleep. Maybe he'd have to sling her arm around his neck and drag her to her cabin every now and then.

The next afternoon, he was leaning against the boat's railing, looking at the treeless shore, when a voice called from the other side of the sundeck.

'*Hé*, Nicolas!'

Not recognising his name, he failed to respond.

'*Hé*, it is not good you ignore me.' The voice came nearer. 'Have a Scotch with me. I offer it to you. How do you say in Australian? – I shout.'

'No thanks, Beatrice. I don't drink when I work.' He knew he sounded prissy

'But you do not work now. All your little tourists are in their cabins.'

'We're meeting on the lower deck in a few minutes. We're about to visit the Roman shrine of Maharakka.'

He might as well be saying Mahabaliporum for all the name meant to Beatrice.

'I do not go. We see a temple yesterday and the day before. I stay and rest my eyes from temples.' Beatrice turned and made a careful straight line to the bar.

Thank Christ for that! Nick thought, with what he knew was only temporary relief.

Three hours later when the group returned to the *Omar El Khayam*, white-coated stewards handed each person a hot hand towel and a sherry glass of fruit juice. Beatrice, whisky glass in hand, prowled un-steadily on their periphery, scattering slurred greetings.

The group members tossed their towels into a plastic bucket, handed their empty glasses to the stewards, dodged around Beatrice and fled to their cabins.

Beatrice skewered Nick with red-eyed determination. 'You drink with me now. Your work, it is over. I offer.'

Socialising with the clients was part of his work. Maybe this was the time to socialise with Beatrice. There was no point in waiting for her to be sober and more coherent. When would that be?

'Thanks, Beatrice. It's hot work visiting a temple. A Stella'd be good.'

She pouted as if beer was not a proper drink, but ushered him to the sundeck with a gesture of her beautiful hand. She marched to the bar and demanded a Scotch and a Stella. The barman looked at Nick to confirm the order, which he did with a small nod.

They sat at a table from where they could see the sunset turning the lake coppery blue. Beatrice lit a cigarette and fidgeted, picking non-existent bits of fluff off her yellow T-shirt, smoothing her crumpled Capri pants and twisting around to look for the barman. Just as she leaned halfway off her chair and opened her mouth to call for him, he arrived and set the drinks on the table without looking at either of them.

Nick raised his glass and said, 'Cheers.' Beatrice said, '*Santé*', and gulped mouthfuls of Scotch as if it was water. He marvelled at the trans-formation. From a twitching, crumpled, ageing woman, she relaxed and sat back comfortably in her chair, one fine-boned hand dangling ele-gantly from the armrest, the other affectionately holding her glass to her chest. Once again, she became the charming chirrupy woman of the first group meeting, regaling Nick with stories of a joyful childhood in Cairo in a household tumbling with children, aunts, uncles and cousins. She looked forward to tasting *sahlab* again and other favourite desserts.

By the time Nick finished his beer, she had downed three Scotches. Her voice grew louder and tourists at other tables were pretending not to listen. One grey-haired woman gathered up her glasses, Perrier water and book and moved away.

For the next two days of the cruise, Nick managed to keep Beatrice relatively calm by having a beer with her every time the group returned from a trip on shore. He observed her increasingly aggressive attempts in French, English and Arabic to talk to anyone within far-flung earshot. Passengers scattered when she came on deck and the barmen, stewards and crewmembers were warily polite and avoided eye contact with her.

Each member of his Australian group claimed a favourite spot on the sundeck. Jim read in an armchair in the shade. Margaret shed her primness with her clothes and toasted herself by the pool. Charles paced from one end of the boat to the other, taking pictures and twiddling with complicated photographic paraphernalia. Beatrice dragged a table and chair to the bar, sat on the table and used the chair as a footstool. Under the expressionless gaze of the barman, she spread her book, postcards, pen, drink, cigarettes, lighter and ashtray over one corner of the bar. The German and French groups gave the Australians a wide berth. Nick knew from other trips that each nationality would keep to itself. The French, he noted, were uneasy about the French-speaking drunk even though she did not belong to their group.

Having identified Beatrice as the spoiler, he'd looked up her file on his laptop. Her daughter lived in Paris. He entered her number into his mobile. If Beatrice became ill or out of control, he would phone. He wondered how much justification, persuasion and diplomacy he'd need if he said Beatrice had to return to Paris.

On the last night of the cruise, the entertainment captain of the *Omar El Khayam* insisted that all passengers attend a party in one of the lounges and encouraged them to hire Egyptian outfits from the boat's collection.

Jim slid towards Nick in his curly-toed babouches.

'What do you call this thing again?' he asked, touching his sleeve.

'A *gallabiyah*.'

'Feels like a bloody dress.'

'It's much cooler in summer than trousers.'

'If you say so, mate.'

Margaret giggled. 'I keep forgetting to hold my stomach in. This costume is so revealing.'

Less revealing and more erotic than the bikini you wear by the pool, Nick thought.

'*Hé*, Marguerite, you have the tummy of a dancer. You must learn to use your muscles.'

Beatrice tugged at the bottom of her T-shirt and Nick feared a demonstration. The delivery of a bright red cocktail to one of the Germans distracted her. Half aggressively, half playfully, she slapped the steward on the arm and demanded to know the ingredients. She ordered the same with gin. In spite of dreading what she would do next, Nick admired her capacity for drinking huge quantities of Scotch without falling over. Gin was a new development.

She drank the red cocktail as if it were a *karkaday* and then disappeared. Nick slipped away from the forced gaiety of the party and strolled to the bow of the boat. Stars glittered in the desert sky like diamonds tossed over black velvet by an ancient croupier god. Voices, one loud and harsh, arose from the lower deck. He leaned over the rail and saw three crew members, their cigarettes twinkling like fireflies, lounging on piles of coiled rope. Beatrice flicked a butt over the side of the boat. Its end slashed a red arc against the black water. She staggered over to a young sailor, slapped him on the shoulder and demanded another cigarette. He slid off the pile of rope and backed out of sight. The other two shifted uneasily and smiled, their teeth gleaming white in their night-darkened faces. One took a cigarette from behind his ear and gave it to her.

'*Donne-moi du feu,*' she said and, even from the deck above, Nick could hear the pull in her throat as she leaned over the lighted match and dragged back the smoke.

Her cigarette dangling from her mouth, she gestured to the men to come and stand on either side of her. With her hands on their shoulders, she hoisted herself onto the canvas cover of the life raft and then sat swinging her bare feet between the heads of the grinning men.

Nick turned round and tried to concentrate on the arched bow of the silver crescent moon. He wished there was someone he could talk to. Margaret was the only member of the group who listened to Beatrice's meanderings and showed neither disapproval nor distaste. Jim gave Nick sympathetic looks when Beatrice raucously ordered him a Stella and Charles once helped him drag her to her cabin and lift her onto the bed. No, Nick thought. It's unfair. They're on holiday. He couldn't take advantage of their goodwill.

Suddenly shouts in Arabic erupted from the lower deck. Nick looked down. Beatrice was perched on the railing of the *Omar El Khayam*. She slapped at the restraining hands of the crewmen and, unlikely as it was for someone as drunk and unfit as she, almost succeeded in standing up. Nick raced to the stairwell and leapt down the steps. By the time he reached the lower deck, the crewmen had manhandled Beatrice off the railing and were standing on either side of her, each holding an arm, like policemen who'd apprehended a suspect.

Nick spoke to them in Arabic. 'Thank you. You can let her go. I'll handle this.'

Their faces blank, the men dropped their hands and vanished into the shadows.

'Beatrice, come with me.'

She stood facing him, swaying.

'Come on.' He did not take her arm. She'd have to manage. 'Now, Beatrice.' He turned sideways and gestured for her to go ahead of him.

She slid one foot forward and stopped.

'Come on. Don't keep me waiting.'

She slid the other foot up to the first.

'I don't have all night.'

'Nicolas, *chéri*.' She stretched her hands towards him in a gesture reminiscent of Edith Piaf at her most dramatic.

He moved away from her and heard the slither of her feet. Little by little, he walked and she shuffled towards her cabin.

At the door, he held out his hand and said, 'The key, please.'

She fumbled in her pants' pocket and pulled out the key with a little cry of triumph. Her hand swung over his. She aimed again and placed the key carefully on his palm.

He opened the door, stood back to let her pass and said, 'Inside and sit down.'

She plopped onto the bed and fell backwards so she was spreadeagled in front of him like a weary and repugnant whore. She looked up at his face, trying to focus with wide eyes, and then jerked herself into a sitting position.

He left the door open and took his mobile out of his shirt pocket. 'Beatrice, this can't continue.'

Dimples rippled over her chin and she put both hands on her heart as if it was hurting.

He softened the tone of his voice. 'I'm going to phone your daughter. I'll arrange with her for you to fly back to Paris.'

She straightened her back, drew her knees together, put one bare foot in front of the other on the floor and crossed her long elegant hands in her lap. Tears flowed down her cheeks. She watched his face throughout the conversation. As he talked, he smelt the tobacco and alcohol on her body.

Finally, he closed his mobile, put it in his pocket and said, 'Get some sleep now, Beatrice. I'll make arrangements in the morning and let you know.'

Beatrice spoke slowly, but the words weren't slurred. 'She was surprised?'

'Er. No.'

'She was angry?'

'No. Get some sleep. I need to get some too.'

'Thank you, Nicolas. You are *gentil* – kind. A gentleman. You have been patient with me, but you tell a lie. Yes, she was surprised. You waited longer to phone her than any tour guide I have ever had. Yes, she was angry. She must take time from her work to meet me at Charles de Gaulle. She is happy while I am away. Watch out.'

A faint smile deepened the lines around her mouth. 'Do not let her book me on one of your trips again.' She stood up and walked firmly towards him.

Before he had time to react, she put her hand lightly on his chest and, in a fog of gin, rose on tiptoe and kissed him on both cheeks. *Je vous remercie de tout mon cœur.* My whole heart thanks you.'

He had done what had to be done. Why then, did he feel he'd betrayed her?

The Dreaded Visit

Florence lay in bed waiting for the alarm. She lay flat on her back. By not moving, she retained the illusion of youthfulness. The alarm was set for six a.m. That gave her plenty of time to get ready for the dreaded flight to Melbourne.

The light seeping between the slats of the cream plantation shutters caressed the two children in the black and white photo on the chest of drawers. Framed in antique silver, a little girl and an older girl, both with big bows on top of their heads, held hands and smiled, squinting into the sun. The little girl was slim, her smile cheeky and toothless. The older girl was plump. Her uncertain smile gave the impression of anxious motherliness.

The increasing light traced the contours of the objects in the room. The golden oak of the chest of drawers glowed. The slender legs of an antique chaise lounge tip-toed beneath the window on dainty porcelain wheels. A watercolour of the Champs-Elysées on a summer day added its sun to the gaiety of the yellow gerberas in a crystal bowl.

So slowly as to retain the semblance of stillness, Florence turned her head towards the clock. Ten to six. Momentarily, she wished for the reflexes she'd had in her seventies. With stubborn self-discipline, she undertook the process of getting up: roll slowly onto her side, push back the bedclothes, inch her legs towards the edge of the bed, brace both hands against the mattress and heave herself into a sitting position. That much accomplished, she reached for her dressing gown and pulled it around her shoulders. Which body parts would torment her today?

Florence remembered with pleasure, rather than regret, the way she used to get up: hit the alarm, fling off the bedclothes, swing her legs onto the floor and bounce onto her feet. She hadn't yet succumbed to wearing one of those shapeless dressing gowns that other eighty-somethings referred to as 'woolly' and 'comfy'. Hers was certainly comfortable and of fine wool, its cost and style reminiscent of the days when waking up beside an exciting man entailed instant attention to her appearance.

It was a struggle still to dress smartly, but she was damned if she was going to wear lace-up shoes, ribbed stockings and the sort of baggy garment featuring cable knitting and hankie-infested pockets that many of her contemporaries referred to as a 'cardie'. Florence banned 'woolly', 'comfy'. 'hankie' and 'cardie' from her vocabulary and her wardrobe.

In her youth, neither pretty nor beautiful, she'd cultivated a sophistication and stylishness that, with her wit and vivacity, attracted men who were happy to spend money and energy on giving her a good time. She owed the continuing struggle for elegance to the memory of evenings spent on games of seduction with gallant and dynamic men.

Getting out of bed having been accomplished, Florence grimly contemplated her reflection and the day ahead in the bathroom mirror. Visiting her old friend was a chore made the more onerous by having to fly to Melbourne. She'd always travelled well. In her youth – before she'd turned eighty – the gruelling twenty-four-hour flight to Europe had been a pleasure if only in the anticipation of the joys to come. Today's trip to Melbourne would be gruelling, full stop.

First there was the drive to the airport. How lucky she was she could still drive a car! Some of her friends drove only their motorised wheelchairs! Admittedly, she no longer drove the snappy red sports cars that used to attract the attention of the traffic police, but happily her current Alfa could not be described as 'comfy'. Its luxurious interior had too much panache. She enjoyed feeling the car's power beneath her. Her libido still lurked, elusive but identifiable, under the loose flesh and layers of years. Nowadays, she was amused to think, it was satisfied by memories of passionate affairs, the throb of her car and meetings with the men in their fifties who looked after her financial, medical and legal affairs. Each one smiled whenever she addressed him as 'my dear young man'.

Given her age, affluence and first-class ticket, Florence could have taken a limousine to the airport and asked for a wheelchair, but she had no intention of displaying such evidence of frailty until coming face to face with old age some time in her nineties.

The flight itself was a hiatus between dazzling Sydney and dreary Melbourne. The seasons of her Melbourne childhood were dressed in greys and browns – grey drizzle, grim skies and bone-chilling cold in winter; dead brown grass, dust, flies and stifling heat in summer. Old acquaintances, whom she didn't particularly like, whom she'd never liked, insisted she keep in touch. She did so partly out of a sense of duty to the hopeful children they'd been before hunkering down in red-brick suburbs. She felt compassion for those who were frittering away the ends of quiet lives in the querulousness of nursing homes.

Betty was one of those. Their acquaintance dated back to when their families lived in the same street in Melbourne. Nine-year-old Betty was given the responsibility of taking six-year-old Florence to and from school. Betty liked the importance of playing mother and on the first day insisted Florence hold her hand. Florence twisted out of her grasp and skipped ahead. Betty was too old to skip. Released from school that afternoon, Florence tore along, zigzagging up and down the grassy embankment between the footpath and the railway line. Slipping on some pine needles, she tumbled and rolled down the slope. What fun! She ran up the embankment and rolled down again.

In imitation of her mother, Betty put her hands on her hips and yelled, 'Florence! Stop that! They can see your bloomers.'

At the bottom of the slope, Florence jumped up and looked around. 'Who? There's no one here.'

'You have grass all over you. You'll get into trouble.'

'I don't care.'

Over the next few days, Betty walked primly along the footpath while Florence, becoming bolder, ran along the railway line before circling back and rolling down the slope. On Friday afternoon, she was just about to yell, 'Watch me!' from the top of the embankment, when she saw Betty talking to a man. He was wearing a hat and coat. Florence thought he must be hot. She was hot in her summer dress and petticoats. The man opened his coat. Betty was looking up at his face and smiling. Florence squatted down to watch. He put his hand inside his coat. Florence picked up a handful of pebbles from the railway tracks and let them dribble down the slope. Neither Betty nor the man noticed. Florence picked up another handful of pebbles. Betty reached towards the man. Florence threw the pebbles. The man tilted his head. Florence couldn't see his face under the brim of his hat.

'Hello,' he said. 'Come and see what I've got.'

He had a funny voice, like a whisper except she could hear him clearly. She threw some more pebbles.

'Hey!' He shouted. He closed his coat and stepped onto the beginning of the slope.

Florence looked down, her heart pounding. 'My daddy's a policeman,' she called.

The man hesitated and then, buttoning his coat, hurried off.

Florence raced down the slope and jerked to a stop in front of Betty who was looking cross.

'What did you say that for?' Betty demanded. 'I'll tell your mother and you'll get into trouble for telling lies.'

'My mother says never speak to a strange man.'

'He wasn't strange. He was nice. He was going to give us lollies.'

Betty told her mother about Florence's lie and got into trouble for talking to a stranger. She wasn't allowed any lollies for a whole fortnight.

Florence's mother said, 'Good girl. Sometimes a fib can make you safe, but you mustn't ever tell lies to Daddy and me.'

From then on, either Florence's mother or Betty's walked with the girls to school. Florence couldn't roll down the slope any more, but she was glad not to see the man again. Remembering him gave her the creeps.

Florence never lost the sense of having taken responsibility for Betty's safety. Looking back on the incident, she didn't attribute her six-year-old self with insight or understanding. Quite simply, she hadn't liked the man's voice.

Years later, when Betty gave her small children a plate of liquorice allsorts to offer to guests, she always said, 'You don't have to offer any to Auntie Florence. She doesn't like sweets.'

Florence wondered if Betty remembered the origin of that erroneous belief.

In contrast to Betty, the friends who'd lived the fast life, full of tumultuous love affairs, venomous hatreds and searing emotional crashes, were dead or suffering dementia or helpless in the hands of inheritance hungry children. Florence's friend, Liz, had been dumped in a dismal nursing home by her daughter and son-in-law. In spiteful disapproval of what they regarded as her morally lax youth, they'd chosen the cheapest institution available and waited, while the old hag tottered towards death, for the inheritance that their imaginations inflated to dizzying millions. Having witnessed Liz's will, Florence knew it to be so complicated that a lather of lawyers would soon deplete its few hundred thousand dollars, leaving the dregs to be divvied up between a dozen charities for derelict dogs and donkeys.

Mercifully, Florence had no children and she was damned if she'd ever go into an institution. When she could no longer manage on her own, she'd instruct her young legal man to employ a companion/carer whose salary would be generous and living quarters sumptuous. The terms of the companion's contract would state that any attempt to influence Florence to change her will would precipitate instant dismissal. With Liz as a warning and role model, Florence was leaving everything to two charities, one for humans, one for animals.

During their last weekly phone conversation, Liz had said, 'You're off to Melbourne again! I don't know why you bother. Betty will hardly know you're there. "Betty the Bland" I call her.'

'You call her that every time we talk about her,' Florence said.

'Well she is. You think it. You're just squeamish about saying it out loud.'

Liz was right. Florence thought a lot of things that she didn't say out loud. Betty the Bland, sixty years the wife and chattel of George Bradley, had been widowed too late to enjoy her freedom. Florence wondered if Betty had ever craved enjoyment or lusted after freedom. A brief romance with George and a long separation during World War II were the great dramas of Betty's life.

Every time Florence visited her, Betty chattered on. 'Thank you for bringing fruit cake. Fancy you remembering, specially when you don't like sweet things. It was George's favourite too. I used to make fruit cake for him during the war. I'd wrap it in lots of brown paper, put it in a soldier's cake tin and mail it. He'd write and say how good it was. He said the other Rats were jealous. Their cakes weren't as nice as his. He was a Rat of Tobruk, you know.'

Florence always replied, 'Yes, I remember.'

As soon as George had been demobbed, he'd gone into an office. No trauma counselling or rehabilitation for him! There he stayed until retirement.

After his death, Betty told Florence, 'Every morning I used to wrap his sandwiches in greaseproof paper and put them in his old army kit-bag with his newspaper, minus the crossword. He used to tear that out for me. He'd go off and catch his tram. I'd clear the breakfast things and then came the really good part of the day. I'd make a cup of instant coffee, light my first cigarette and do the crossword.'

Florence contrasted the tempestuousness of her own relationships with the dullness of Betty's marital routines. Had Betty found them dull? Florence suspected not.

Betty and George had been lucky with their children. The boy and girl had been only mildly rebellious during adolescence, had settled into their suburban mortgages in early adulthood and soon afterwards provided grandchildren for George and Betty to put in frames on the living room walls. When the grandchildren were little, they were brought to lunch every Sunday. When they were adolescents, they were brought for presents on the Sunday of the week of their birthdays. Florence dutifully attended family celebrations.

At her fiftieth birthday party, in spite of the impatience of the smallest grandchildren for the candles to be lit on the cake, Betty took a long time to open Florence's present. She untied the bow and smoothed the ribbon, slit the sticky tape with a vegetable knife, unfolded the sheets of tissue one by one and lifted the shawl so its silken folds shimmered onto her lap. Ignoring the escalating clamour for cake, she draped the shawl gently over its box and put it out of small hands' reach on top of the piano. For the rest of the afternoon, she kept sidling up to it and stroking the silk with her fingertips.

When Florence's taxi arrived, Betty walked down the front path with her and asked, 'You bought the scarf in Paris?'

'Yes. In the Marais.'

'The Mar-Ray. I have to remember. Mrs Phelps next door will ask. Is it a posh part of the city?'

'It's full of trendy shops.'

'French fashion like in the magazines? Ooh, she'll be so jealous.'

'It has lots of exciting young designers. It's also the Jewish and gay district.'

Betty's face closed like a flower drawing in its petals at dusk. 'It's a pretty scarf. I almost forgot to say thank you.'

Florence never saw her wear it.

Safely installed in a nursing home after George's 'departure to the other side', Betty had resumed the crosswords, true romances, television serials and knitting that his retirement had interrupted. She expected Florence's visit at regular intervals and had no concept of the effort that ended in her friend's graceful stroll into her room.

At Sydney airport, a young woman in an ill-fitting black uniform made Florence move away from the other passengers and waved an electronic wand around her. What terrorist group, Florence wondered, would recruit a middle-class female octogenarian? She'd heard of young people being suicide bombers. Older people were too aware of the preciousness of the time left to them to indulge in such nonsense. She knew how silly it was to feel glad that no explosive material had been detected. She felt the same irrational gladness when a random breath test didn't react to the pharmaceuticals with which she was riddled and registered no alcohol because she hadn't had any. She was looking forward to a glass of champagne when she got home. She'd opened the bottle last night to fortify herself for today's visit.

An uneventful flight brought her to the uneventful city. A biting cold wind whipped out of the grey sky. Drought-dead brown grass surrounded square red-brick houses. The morose taxi driver brightened only when she paid a big tip and asked him to come back for her at three thirty.

Florence had doused herself with French perfume so, as she crossed the communal lounge room of the Yellow Roses Retirement Home, the fragrance slugged it out with the fustiness of old age wrapped in woollies. Judgemental eyes scrutinised her Italian leather shoes, tailored dress and chic white hair. She'd be condemned for overdoing the perfume.

Betty's room had the same floor area as a nun's cell. Its size was the only way it resembled the cells that Florence had seen in medieval convents in Italy and France. Although their stone walls made them freezing in winter, their high ceilings, tall windows and stark furnishings gave them a spirituality that was totally alien from Betty's lair. A low ceiling spackled with soundproofing material, brick walls painted cream, a small sash window covered by brown curtains, a sturdy carpet with brown swirls – into this decor Betty had stuffed bed, armchair, chest of drawers, walker, television cabinet, card table and an upright chair.

'Who's that? Is that you, Florence? Good of you to come.'

This greeting having consumed all of Betty's energy, she remained propped up by pillows on her bed. A picture of Mme Récamier reclining on her chaise longue flitted through Florence's mind. The contrast was ludicrous. Besides, Betty had never heard of Mme Récamier. She was wearing her good dress. The shiny black material emphasised the boniness of her once plump body. Her legs, two long sausages in brown stockings, were linked to two short sausages zipped into soft pink slippers.

Florence bent to kiss her and then brought the upright chair to the side of the bed. Red lipstick made Betty's mouth look like a newly inflicted gash. Her eyebrows were furry grey caterpillars. The tortoiseshell frames of her glasses dominated her shrunken face. Every time she moved her head, Florence saw that her thin hair, flattened by the pillow, was sticking to her scalp.

More distressed by Betty's appearance than she had been during her last visit, Florence gazed around the room. Flat surfaces were covered with medications, tissues and toiletries. Blown glass animals with smiley faces stood on the cloth-covered chest of drawers. Betty having fallen into a doze, Florence stood up, went over to the chest and touched the cloth with her fingertips. It was the shawl she'd given Betty for her fiftieth birthday.

A quavering voice rose from the bed. 'I found it at the back of George's wardrobe after he died. A funny thing to have among all his old stuff. Don't know where he got it from.'

Florence returned to the chair and sat down heavily. She didn't know what upset her more, Betty's wandering memory or her own speculations about what George had done with the shawl.

The quaver resumed. 'Cup of tea?'

'Of course.' Florence stood up again and steadied herself on the back of the chair. 'Would you like a slice of fruitcake?'

'Yes, please.'

Florence went down the hallway to the communal kitchenette where she opened all the cupboards in the hope of finding crockery. She took out two saucers that would have to do as plates and two Styrofoam cups. She boiled the jug and made No Frills tea for Betty and instant coffee for herself. The horrible coffee would sustain her until three thirty, in the same way as horrible sherry had sustained her in the past.

At the many family celebrations that Florence had attended in the home of Betty and George, the men drank beer, the women non-alcoholic punch, the older children Coke and the small children cordial. Once, made desperate by flaccid fruit in flat ginger beer, Florence had fossicked through the kitchen cupboards and found some cheap sherry among the sugars and dried fruits. It was an ingredient for Christmas cake. She poured a little into her punch cup and did so at subsequent events. She replaced each empty bottle with a reasonably priced one.

At Betty's fiftieth birthday party, as Florence was reaching up to put the sherry bottle away, George came up behind her and smacked her on the bottom. 'Taking a nip? Naughty, naughty. But then you always were.' He rubbed her bottom with a circular motion.

She removed his hand and stepped away from him.

'Being proper, are you? Starting to feel your age, are you? You used to spread it around. Don't I have enough money for you?'

'You don't have enough of anything, George.'

Florence spilt the brown contents of her punch glass onto his cream-coloured trousers as she swept past him and entered the lounge room, where the children were demolishing the cake.

In the kitchenette of the Yellow Roses Retirement Home, she cut slices from the fruit cake she'd bought in a gourmet shop in Sydney and put the coffee, tea and saucers on a tin tray. She sighed. What had George done with the shawl? Had he hidden it after Betty's party? If so, how cruel! Had he used it as a sexual fetish? Florence shuddered. Perhaps Betty's forgetfulness about the shawl was a remnant of her sense of self-preservation. Only once had she ever let slip that George was less than the perfect husband.

They'd gone on an eight-day cruise to the Pacific islands – a fiftieth wedding anniversary present from their children and grandchildren.

Betty said afterwards, 'It was such a pity. George didn't enjoy it. He said Nouméa and the other ports stank and he hated the food on the ship. He said it wasn't cooked properly. His lamb chops were always pink. I loved the fish. There were so many different types to choose from. On our anniversary, there was a cake and the ship gave us real French champagne. It was wonderful. I've never had it before. You like champagne, don't you?'

Florence opened her mouth to reply, but Betty surged on.

'After my second glass, George leaned over to me. I thought he was going to kiss my ear. He used to do that when we were young. I'd forgotten. But he didn't do that at all. He hissed. He really did. He hissed in my ear. He said I mustn't drink any more. It was an overpriced fizzy drink and was making me silly. He said only trollops drink champagne. Some of the people at the table heard him. They might have thought he knew women like that. I went really mad at him when we got back to the cabin, I can tell you.'

What did Betty think about all day in the Yellow Roses Retirement Home? Florence suspected that her mind was blank. She lay on her bed, the newspaper unopened beside her, the television silent. It wasn't that she was losing her faculties. She was just wearing out. To Florence's surprise, occasional remarks rose from the bed like bubbles through murky water.

'After he stopped working, George didn't tear the crossword out of the paper for me.'

'I'm always clean. You get grass on your dress and you never get into trouble.'

'Fruit cake batter's heavy to stir. If I stop making them, you won't bring any more of that nice sherry.'

'I wanted to dance on the ship, but George doesn't like dancing. You like dancing, don't you?'

'Yes,' Florence replied.

'Are you going to Paris this year?'

'Yes.'

During the long silences between the remarks, Florence chatted about the television soaps she'd deliberately watched the day before.

Betty appeared not to be listening. Occasionally, however, something would make her spark up and she'd ask a pertinent question. 'What did Schantelle-Rhys say to her mother's teenage boyfriend?'

By three fifteen, Florence felt weariness seeping out of the walls and into her veins. She roused herself and returned the saucers and cups to the kitchen.

When she picked up her handbag, Betty asked, as she did at the end of each visit, 'How long will it take you to get home?'

'The flight's an hour and a quarter but it takes longer than that to get to the airport and then I'll be in peak-hour traffic in Sydney. If I'm lucky, I'll be home by seven thirty.'

'Good heavens! What a long time! Thank you for coming and thank you for the fruit cake. It was nice of you to make it. I know you don't like sweet things.'

On the way to the airport, the taxi driver was less morose than earlier, probably in anticipation of another big tip. A delayed flight, another dusting with an anti-terrorist wand – the normal inconveniences of travelling added to Florence's weariness. At Sydney, the parking attendant's admiration of the Alfa was pleasing. Florence's spirits rose. She looked forward to a glass of Moët when she got home. Two perhaps.

The next morning, she dozed in bed until the telephone jarred her awake. Its ringing stopped before she had time to roll onto her side and pick up the receiver. The voice on the message machine asked her to phone the Yellow Roses Retirement Home at this number. Florence didn't think she'd left anything behind, but she might have. Perhaps Betty had had a fall. She'd had several falls in recent years, but never before had Florence been called straight away. She heaved herself into a sitting position and pulled her dressing gown around her shoulders. She reached for the receiver. The shaking of her hand had nothing to do with her age. The phone rang again. She snatched her hand away. Her heart thumped.

She pushed the answer button. 'Florence McKenzie.'

'Hi. It's Liz. Well, you could've saved yourself the trouble and not gone to Melbourne at all.'

'I beg your pardon.'

'Didn't they call you?'

'Who?'

'Yellow Roses.'

'There's a message to ring them.'

'Well, I'll tell you the news and save you the bother. Betty died last night.'

Florence could think of nothing to say. Her bones felt brittle with cold.

Liz said, 'Hello. Hello. Are you still there?'

'Yes. What time did she die?'

'I'll quote what the woman said. I couldn't forget it.' Liz rounded her vowels and hoisted the pitch of her voice. "'Mrs Bradley died peacefully in her sleep at five o'clock yesterday afternoon. According to the other residents, she'd waited for the visit of her friend from Sydney before allowing herself to die.'"

Liz resumed her normal voice. 'A lot of idiots, those other inmates. People don't decide when they're going to die.'

Oh yes they do, Florence thought. She was too stunned to argue. 'When's the funeral?' she asked.

'Don't tell me you're going! Whatever for?'

'I have a duty towards her.'

'At our age, we don't have duties. What did she ever do for you?'

She walked beside me all my life, Florence thought.

After calling Betty's son and daughter, Florence had a shower, got dressed, put on her make-up and went to sit on the balcony. She gazed past the surfers and sailboats towards the horizon. It was a warm day, but she draped around her neck a silk shawl that she'd bought in the Marais the same day that she'd bought Betty's fiftieth birthday present. It comforted her. She didn't cry.

At three o'clock, she dialled a mobile number which, like all the numbers that were important to her, she knew by heart.

When the cheerful voice answered, she said, 'Hello, James, my dear young man. This is Florence McKenzie. How are you? … I'm pleased to hear it. I'd like you to put your legal mind to work for me, please. Could you advertise for a companion according to the terms we agreed on? I'd like him or her, preferably him, to be well used to my ways by the time I go to Paris in July. I'm about to phone the travel agent. In the meantime, could you employ someone temporarily for next Monday? I need a companion to go with me to Melbourne for a funeral. And also, I want to change my will.'

'Again?'

'No need to be facetious, young man. I worked hard for my money and I want it to be carefully spent.'

'Sorry.'

'Would you have someone in your office prepare me an annotated list of charities that look after abused women? Not necessarily physical abuse. Neglect, psychological abuse, imprisonment – that sort of thing.'

'I'll get onto it right away.'

'You're a darling – as well as efficient.'

After calling her travel agent, Florence opened the balcony bar fridge and poured some champagne. The afternoon had become hot and she removed her shawl before settling on the cushions of the cane lounge.

A strange mixture of liberation and loneliness hovered in her head and she wondered if that's what a new widow would feel after more than fifty years of marriage to an unloving husband. No more lack of understanding, no more talking without communication. She thought about her long walk with Betty. She didn't envy anything about Betty's life, but she admired her decision about when to leave it.

May I follow her with the same dignity and strength, she thought. May I die on the day I choose – here or in Paris.

She touched the soft folds of the shawl beside her.

Not this year, I hope.

Big Words

Trevor and me, we have a corner shop. It's cold in here today. We're waiting for the glazier. The door's smashed.

You see, one afternoon two months ago, we get this new customer. She comes in just before the schoolkid rush. Trevor watches her. He watches everyone. He loves catching shoplifters.

He blasts a whisper at me. 'Take a look at this one. Room in that bag for all the tinned spaghetti we got.'

I wish he'd keep his voice down. I don't think this white-haired lady eats tinned spaghetti. She's wearing a lovely dress with a scalloped hem and has a smart handbag. A capacious handbag.

(I love big words. I get them from the crosswords. Trevor doesn't like me using them. He says I sound up myself.)

The lady dawdles along the shelves murmuring. Every now and then, she stops and looks at her feet. Her elegant shoes must be hurting.

Eventually, she wanders to the counter. 'Aha. Smarties! There they are! For my grandson, Matthew Brown. He's addicted to them.'

She pronounces his name as if he's a celebrity. It sounds familiar but I can't think why.

After that, the lady buys Smarties every school day afternoon.

She gets upset one afternoon when we're out of stock. 'What am I going to do? School will be out soon and Matthew needs Smarties to concentrate.'

Trevor sniggers. 'Concentrate?'

'Yes. He's a spelling bee champion. We practise every afternoon. He has an extraordinary vocabulary.'

Mystery solved. I've heard his name on the radio. I listen to the spelling competitions when Trevor's at the pub.

'Here,' I say. 'Take some M&Ms. Apologise for me and tell him we'll have Smarties tomorrow.'

Trevor snorts while the lady dithers out the door. She always holds it open for a long time, murmuring at her feet.

'Apologise!' he expostulates. (I've just learnt that word.) 'Use what few brains you have, woman. There's no one to apologise to. The old chook lives in la la land. Where's this genius grandson? She's made 'im up. She's the Smartie junkie.'

Trevor doesn't like being wrong, so I never contradict him.

After that, the lady tells us a lot about Matthew. There's a cabinet full of trophies. I imagine a scrawny little boy with glasses. He gets bullied at school.

Trevor and me, we're both wrong. Yesterday, the lady comes in with a six-foot hulk. Spiked hair, nose stud, braces glistening on his teeth – Matthew probably terrorises his opponents into…unintelligibility. (I've never used that word before.)

The lady introduces him. Politely he says hello. She pays for the Smarties. He rips open the packet and tips a stream down his gullet like a man slamming down a beer. He hitches up his pants, shambles to the door, jerks it open and waits benignly while his grandmother makes her usual dithering exit.

'Stupid old chook.' Trevor does a whisper blast. 'Wobbly and gaga.'

The door crashes back against the wall. The glass rattles in its frame.

'Wotcha say?' Matthew storms up to Trevor. Spikes, stud and braces glitter. His left hand secures his pants; his right hand flexes.

Trevor flattens himself against the spaghetti. Matthew towers over him. Trevor swivels his head, dodging flecks of spittle.

'My gran is no dotard.' He looks at me. 'I gave her a virtual silky terrier after her last one died. She talks to him. He's an intelligent interlocutor.'

He swings back to Trevor. 'Not like you, you piece of…' Matthew spells the words slowly like in the competitions. 'E.X.C.R.E.M.E.N.T, synonym, S.H.I.T.'

Trevor shrinks back. Spaghetti tumbles.

Matthew nods to me and leaps into the street, slamming the door behind him. Through the shattered glass I see him, pants descending, swagger to his grandmother's side. She reaches up and pats his spikes and they saunter away. A gust of wind, or a little dog dancing around her feet, ruffles the scallops of her skirt.

Trevor and me, we're expecting a new grandson. I won't use childish words when I babysit. I'll use big ones and hope he'll grow up to be chivalrous, articulate and perspicacious – just like Matthew.

Just Another Saturday

Droplets sparkled in the morning sun on the drab brown feathers of the little birds playing in the birdbath. Carolyn turned her back on them. It was going to be just another Saturday.

She counted the pile of essays that had to be marked. It was a delaying tactic and was rewarded by a surprise – only twenty-three essays. Two missing. That meant twenty, maybe thirty minutes less time spent on the attempts of her HSC students to relate Juliet Capulet's problems to their own. There'd be less time mentally and physically scrunched at this garden table, ignoring the birds and Peter's beautifully tended flowers and vegetables. The small surprise and associated pleasure energised her to pick up her red pen.

A squawk and responding shrills announced the arrival of the bully cockatoo. Carolyn sighed and got up to chase him away and make a coffee. Peter had gone on his usual Saturday walk. He didn't have to spend as much time on marking as she did. He marked maths assignments while watching the news.

He'd brought her tea in bed this morning, as he'd done every Saturday for the past thirty-eight years. He'd plopped some sugar in and apologised, as always, for slopping tea into the saucer. She hated sugar in tea and coffee. After the first six months of marriage, she stopped telling him so. She'd told herself how lucky she was to have such a kind, if absent-minded husband.

The hiss of the espresso pot startled her. Peter disliked coffee. She'd make his tea when he returned from his walk. Comfortable routines and small considerations towards one another characterised their marriage. Wasn't he bored? She was. After Sundays spent watching him putter in the garden, helping him prepare and freeze the weekday lunches that they'd take to their respective schools and acquiescing in his choice of science documentaries, she burst joyfully into her classroom on Monday mornings.

Oh, the excitement of it! The yelling of the students as they surged towards their desks, their aggression, their easily toppled self-confidence – what strategy would she deploy to calm them this time? An old one or something new?

She wondered if the disappearance of Emily, their shy awkward daughter, was what aroused such depth of affection for her students. That's what the school counsellor would probably say. Fifteen years ago, Carolyn had sought and then followed the counsellor's advice. She'd tried to hide her dismay and worst premonitions when Emily brought her fiancé to dinner one Saturday night. He was a divorced supermarket manager with two sons who were closer to Emily's age than she was to his. Peter had repressed his feelings too. In that way, they presented a united front.

Emily had seen through them. 'So what if he's older! That makes him more mature. He values me for who I am and doesn't care that I'm not pretty. He doesn't want a silly woman who flutters over the sort of bouquet she'll have at her wedding or how many flower girls there'll be. He's been through all that. You're both looking po-faced and disapproving. Well, you won't have to put up with us. We're leaving Sydney. Brian's been transferred to Perth. His boys live there with their mother.'

Carolyn had never felt so helpless. From a placid, contented baby, Emily had grown into an earnest little girl. As a teenager, she'd been quietly hostile towards Carolyn and charming towards Peter when she wanted something. At university, she'd studied and exercised obsessively, earning brilliant marks and maintaining a slender figure that bordered on the skinny. Carolyn ached at the thought that the fiancé didn't find her pretty. She wasn't conventionally so, but intelligence and an occasional spark of sharp wit lit up her face and gave it a shining beauty. Carolyn feared she was being just a self-delusional mother. Peter's only comment, in private of course, was that the man had a steady income and could provide a good home.

With their only daughter far away and discouraging visits, emails and phone calls, Carolyn was always delighted to dive into the maelstrom of school. The Monday morning staffroom conversations were fun too, full of things she and Peter knew nothing about

'Didja see that goal? Almost as good as Thierry Henry in the quarter final against Brazil in 2006.'

'Greg and I went to another auction. Sixty people! The bidding was out of our range in thirty seconds! I don't know how much longer we can live with his parents. They're nice but…'

'That's the fourth one I've met on that site and every one of them looked older than his photo. Do all men post photos from when they were ten years younger?'

Hot coffee spurting from the pot brought Carolyn back to the present. She poured the coffee into her mug, smiling at the fact that she wasn't adding sugar. Dear Peter. He'd adored Emily from the moment she was born. Carolyn had wanted more children. A whole netball or cricket team would have been fine.

Peter said, 'One child's all we can afford. We're on teachers' salaries. If you stopped work, we'd be struggling.'

Why hadn't she insisted? Other teaching couples had more than one child. What was wrong with struggling? She could have 'forgotten' to take the pill and coped with the consequences. Cowardice? Deception rather, and trickery. That's not the way they behaved with one another. Acquiescing, Carolyn applied for a position as head of department and ever afterwards earned more money than Peter, who never aspired to promotion and the accompanying increase in administration and people management.

Back she traipsed to the garden table. There was one essay at least to look forward to – that of the boy who'd said in class, 'Juliet was how old? Thirteen? That's jail bait!'

Two and a quarter hours later – coffee drunk, eleven out of twenty-three essays marked, sun blazing on the bird bath, birds gone. Carolyn stretched. 'Bugger it! I'm going for a bloody walk. Head for the shops. A gelato. Give myself a treat.'

She never swore in front of Peter. Years ago, she'd tried to explain that if it was good enough for Shakespeare's characters, it should be good enough for her. He'd replied gently, 'I don't see the relevance and I don't like it.'

Carolyn strode across the park. A brisk pace partly alleviated her guilt about leaving her marking. Besides, it was a form of exercise. As she approached the café next to the gelato bar, she saw Peter. He was sitting with a woman at a table by the window. She saw his face and the woman's back. They were holding hands. Carolyn jolted to a halt. Perhaps attracted by the sudden movement, Peter turned his head towards the window. He was smiling. He saw Carolyn and the speed with which his smile changed to an O was almost comical. So this was how he spent his Saturdays! She rushed past the gelato bar and two other shops and wheeled around the corner. On the footpath ahead, a small real estate board announced an open house. The agent was taking names and phone numbers of people lining up to inspect it. Without having any idea why, Carolyn gave Peter's name and mobile number. The agent wrote her name as 'Peta'.

Once inside, Carolyn shuffled along with the crowd. Even if he'd come after her, Peter wouldn't look for her here and she could linger in one of the upstairs rooms and think. Her heart pounded as she climbed the stairs. Physical exertion or emotion? She stood in front of a bookcase catching her breath and trying to identify what she felt. Anger? No. A sense of betrayal? No. Jealousy? No. Why wasn't she feeling any of those things? Weren't they what she was supposed to feel?

Firstly, there was disbelief. Peter was sixty-five. He could have retired years ago. He was a nice man, kind, a good teacher, much loved by his smarter students, some of whom had won scholarships because of him. That was all very well, but hardly made him an interesting romantic prospect. He looked like any other reasonably fit sixty-five-year-old —

fairly slim, grey hair, glasses, sagging flesh. Had the woman seen the sagging flesh? Carolyn's thoughts flashed to her. She'd only seen her back. A grey jumper stretched over bulging fat. Orange-streaked hair. Perhaps one of Peter's school colleagues. What a strange couple!

As for Peter's expression when he saw her, Carolyn wasn't sure how to interpret it. He looked surprised, certainly, but had there been an element of guilt?

A small child bumped into her legs and the parents apologised profusely. She must look like a bewildered pathetic old woman. She gazed around the small room. Within reaching distance of an antique bookcase there was a leather armchair and a dainty inlaid table only big enough to hold a book, a glass of wine and a dish of olives. The books were almost exclusively to do with Italy: travellers' tales, guide books, Renaissance art and sculpture, cookery, Italian–English dictionaries and what appeared to be novels written in Italian. It was a lovely peaceful room. Now, however, prospective purchasers were storming through it, impatient to find the more important bedrooms.

Carolyn shook her head as if to shake some sense into herself. The open house would soon be over. She looked out of the window onto the street. Peter wasn't lurking there. Why should he be? First, he'd have to get rid of the woman and then, surely, he'd go home and prepare his story. Carolyn headed for the stairs. She clung to the rail. Wouldn't that be dramatic, a wife falling down the stairs after finding her husband with someone else? Almost in flagrante delicto – isn't that what the Italians called it? Carolyn giggled and covered her mouth with her hand. She was surprised at herself.

In the street, she looked both ways in case Peter suddenly materialised. She walked slowly and took the long way home, avoiding the café and park. The more slowly she walked, the more light-hearted she felt. If Peter said he was going to leave her, she wouldn't try to stop him. No way. She'd be free. She stopped suddenly in the middle of the footpath. That's it! That's what she felt – a longing for freedom. Never, not once had she considered leaving Peter. They got along all right. He'd be terribly hurt and wouldn't understand. But now, now! Had she been even ten years younger, she would have skipped to the corner. She giggled again. She'd probably fall over and need a hip replacement. And why shouldn't she skip? Other women her age went to a gym. That's what she'd do when she was alone: she'd sign up to a gym! And what else? By the time she turned the corner into her street, she'd fantasised about retiring: she'd cashed in her superannuation, learnt Italian, rented a cottage in Tuscany, met an exciting man on line and was going with him to see a World Cup game in Milan.

And there he was – not an exciting man, indeed a very ordinary one who was about to be knifed in the stomach by his apoplectic wife. Peter was opening the front door of their family home and ushering the woman ahead of him. What fat legs she had! And yet her ankles… Carolyn gave a little shriek. She recognised the ankles. The woman turned and looked at her. Carolyn slapped a smile on her face as she did when confronted with a difficult student at school.

'Look who's here, my dear!' Peter positively crowed. 'It's Emily, she's moving back home. Isn't that wonderful?'

As she hugged the rolls of fat that blanketed her skinny daughter, Carolyn thought it certainly was wonderful. She'd had a whiff of freedom. It smelt delicious. With Emily to look after, Peter wouldn't be lonely. He mightn't even notice that Carolyn had gone.

During the HSC English Exam

The woman makes my flesh crawl. I recognise the smell and can't believe my nose! That smell, right in the middle of my HSC English exam! Nicotine saturated her body when I was in Year 8. There was an underlying smell that I couldn't identify then and still can't. It isn't unpleasant or dirty, just distinctive. Maybe she has a favourite food that comes through her pores. She's certainly not a drinker. She doesn't have that nauseating combination of nicotine and alcohol like Dad. I wish she'd go and stand beside someone else. I look at her feet. She's wearing worn out shoes deformed by her bunions. I glance sideways. A faded dress hangs from her scrawny shoulders like a sack on strings – just like when she taught me in Year 8. She never wore new clothes or shoes then. Perhaps she kept new things for good. She certainly didn't try to dress nicely for work. Her attitude seemed to be, 'Why bother in a girls' school?'

Big mistake. The moment she entered the classroom for the first history lesson of the year, the girls in 8 Blue decided they weren't going to like her. And that was before they got a whiff of her! I talk about the class as if I wasn't part of it. And in a way I wasn't. My hair was frizzy, I had puppy fat and pimples and my brother was too young to be interesting. Because I was quiet, I was condemned as a nerd. Occasionally, I did something naughty or outrageous to show I wasn't totally boring. Miss Grimshaw's appearance signalled a dreary year in history. Nonetheless, hoping there might be a clash between her appearance and interesting things she might talk about, I delayed judgement.

She's moved away, thank goodness. She won't speak to me during the exam unless I want an extra writing booklet. I'll make my writing small so I won't need one. There are seven supervisors and it would be just my luck for her to be the one to respond to my hand being up. If I keep my head down, perhaps she won't recognise me.

I've changed a lot since Year 8. Being a nerd isn't so bad now and the students in Year 12, boys and girls, don't seem to mind. I help some of them with English and history and they like to tease me because I give as good as I get. I've learnt that from dealing with Dad. Not that he teases me. He yells. Mum doesn't respond. Sometimes, I can't stand his abuse and her silence any longer and I shout back. The other day, he lashed out to hit me but was so drunk he toppled over, fell on the floor and remained still. Mum panicked, thinking he'd hurt himself, but he'd just passed out.

There are two big physical changes that hopefully will keep Miss Grimshaw from recognising me. My hair stopped being frizzy when I had it cut, and I've lost weight. I've got a shape. No thanks to sport or dieting or anything like that. I got the mumps last Christmas holidays and couldn't eat. When I went back to school, my clothes were hanging off me, just like Miss Grimshaw's.

Damn! Here I am mentally blathering while I should be concentrating on this exam. Two-thirds of the way through. So far so good. Mustn't be distracted now. Drat the woman!

I used to think of her as poor Miss Grimshaw. Her smell, her clothes – those faults were just the beginning. At lunchtime one day, I was sitting with a group of girls who were egging each other on to mimic her.

'Actually, the Tudors were a bloodthirsty bunch.'

They used a quavering falsetto. I said she had a grinding voice, so why not call her Grinding Grimshanks? They squealed with glee and for the rest of that lunchtime I was part of the in-crowd. When the bell rang for afternoon classes, I became a nerd again and, after that, kept my thoughts about her to myself. Grimshanks was one of the kinder names they called her and their relentless sneering bored me.

What irritated me most about Miss Grimshaw was her repetition and drawn-out pronunciation of the word 'actually'.

'They act-ually plucked the guts out of traitors while they were still alive.'

'There were act-ually witnesses present in the bedroom on the king's wedding night.'

If I blocked out the 'act-uallys', what she told us about Tudor history was fascinating. She was a great storyteller, much better than Miss Barnes had been in Year 7. Miss Barnes had made the pharaohs dull, but I was riveted when Miss Grimshaw said, 'Old Henry act-ually showed kindness to Anne Boleyn by employing a French swordsman.' In contrast, Miss Barnes was both glamorous and popular. Girls cried when they heard she wasn't going to be our teacher in Year 8. She was young and engaged and kept changing her hairstyle. She made us learn pages of stuff for our tests. I can still recite lists of dates about the pharaohs and their dynasties. Our class in Year 7 always got better marks than Miss Grimshaw's.

Marks – I must pull myself together and earn some. Stick to the plan: hard work, good results, scholarship and various jobs to support me through uni. Forget about Miss Grimshaw and what happened to her. Look at the question paper.

Section III
15 marks
Attempt Question 3
Allow about 40 minutes for this section
Compose a creative piece that captures the significance of
remembered places to the experience of belonging.

Ha! Miss Grimshaw and I could both write copiously on that question. The last time I saw her, she was doing yard duty at lunchtime. It was early December. I was in 8 Blue and about to transfer to a public high school. Miss Grimshaw didn't belong in that ladies' college in Neutral Bay and neither did I.

If any of the girls from that 8 Blue class had Miss Grimshaw as a supervisor for this English exam, they'd probably make their parents phone the school and protest, even put in a misadventure appeal. Mum did supervision at my school when she had to take any work that was going. She isn't supervising this year. There's a rule that you can't supervise if a close relative is doing the HSC. The parents of 8 Blue would probably argue that the same rule should apply to a former teacher.

Poor Miss Grimshaw. Is working as a supervisor the consequence of what those parents did four years ago? Couldn't she get another teaching job? Instead of being in a nineteenth-century hall, its wood panelling covered with portraits of past headmistresses and illustrious 'old girls', Miss Grimshaw and I (and 107 exam candidates) are in a gym that can only be described as functional. Oh, and it's clean.

Miss Grimshaw's here because she was fired. I'm here because Dad was retrenched. His payout covered one year's mortgage payments and school fees. Mum started doing office jobs here and there. One of her employers offered Dad some shifts driving a taxi. He refused, saying he was overqualified. I hated going home from school. Mum was either at work or picking up Jack from kindy and Dad was lying on the couch staring morosely at the TV. He started to smell like Miss Grimshaw. Snapping back at Mum's nagging, he said he'd give up the cigarettes when he got a job.

Then there was another smell and the yelling started. The first time was when Mum poured half a bottle of whisky down the sink. They fought all night. I trembled in my bed. Next morning, when I went to wake Jack and start getting him ready for kindy, I saw he'd wet his bed. I stripped off the sheets and put them in the washing machine so Mum wouldn't know, but she saw the wet patch on the under blanket. After that, I never heard her fight back again.

Since home was horrible, I hovered more clingingly to the fringes of the various groups in 8 Blue. I refused invitations to birthday parties, because I couldn't ask Mum to buy me nice clothes (thank goodness for a school uniform!) and the invitations stopped. I became more silent and inconspicuous. The girls talked freely in front of me as though they forgot I was there.

In November, we had exams; 8 Blue was in a panic about history.

'She hasn't given us any notes to study from.'

'She didn't follow the textbook or cover all the topics.'

'She didn't give us homework.'

'All she ever did was grind on about how Henry was hoisted onto his horse. What's that got to do with history?'

'She didn't make us learn any dates.'

'Miss Barnes's class is way ahead of us.'

I didn't care very much. Once I'd overcome the clothes, the voice, the smell and the 'act-uallys', I'd enjoyed the lessons. What difference would marks make to what was happening in my life? I was going to leave the school anyway. The next school would probably be awful. At home, Dad was usually comatose and Mum was exhausted from going to work, organising the sale of the house and getting rid of furniture that wouldn't fit into the rented unit. Jack had nightmares at least twice a week. His screams woke me up and I'd try to get to him before he woke Mum. She and I always arrived at his bedside together. Dad never woke up, not even when the screaming made next door's Doberman howl.

I'm spending so much exam time thinking about the past, maybe I can actually (that damn word!) shape my thoughts into a 'creative piece'. To the English markers, I'll be a number and they won't know whether I'm writing truth or fiction.

Predictably, 8 Blue got lower marks in the history exam than Miss Barnes's class and the nastiness escalated.

'My father says he's going to see the principal.'

'My mother's already made an appointment. She met Grimshanks at parent-teacher night and says she's not fit to be in a school like this.'

A week before the end of the school year, a gossip group gathered in the toilets.

'Hey! Everyone. Have you heard?'

'Heard what?'

'I'm not supposed to tell. It's a secret. You mustn't tell.'

'Ooh, no. We won't tell.'

'My uncle's on the board of governors and he told Dad…'

'What?'

'Grimshanks has been fired.'

'No!'

'Wow!'

'Nasty old bitch.'

They squealed at the bad word and scurried outside to continue gloating. I was about to tag along when a notorious Year 11 girl came into the toilet area. I started scrutinising a pimple in the mirror over the washbasin. The girl always left her big folder on top of the lockers when she went into a cubicle and younger girls liked to peek at the magazines she kept in it. On that day, as soon as she closed the cubicle door, I turned on a splashy tap, opened the folder, flipped through a magazine, tore out a page and stuffed it into my blazer pocket.

The first lesson after lunch was maths. During the shuffle of opening books, I took the page out of my pocket, folded it as small as I could and flicked it onto the desk of the girl behind me. A moment later I heard an intake of breath and then a giggle. Soon muffled giggles bubbled up all over the room.

'What's going on?' Mrs Travers's voice thundered.

In the silence, a giggle was converted ineptly into a hiccup.

'Sophie Wilkinson, what's that on your desk?'

'Nothing, Mrs Travers.'

'Bring it to me.'

A scarlet-faced Sophie crumpled the paper. For a moment, I thought she was going to put it in her mouth and swallow it.

'This minute!'

The sound of Sophie's chair scraping on the floor made my heart race. Mrs Travers plucked the paper from Sophie's shaking fingers and smoothed it on the teacher's desk. 'Is it yours, Sophie?'

'No, Mrs Travers.'

'Whose is it?'

'I don't know.'

'The whole class will do extra homework tonight unless the person who brought this…this into the class owns up now.'

I put up my hand.

'Yes. Elizabeth. You have something to say?'

'It's mine, Mrs Travers.'

Her mouth dropped open. 'Yours? Yours, Elizabeth?'

I nodded, my heart hammering.

'I…I'm…I'm going to write a note and you will take it with this… this…page and stand outside Mrs James's office until she's ready to deal with you.'

With a show of bravado to impress the class, I took the folded note and magazine page from Mrs Travers's thumb and forefinger and bounced out of the room. I then slunk along the corridor and handed over accusation and evidence to the principal's secretary. It seemed like hours before she opened the heavy oak door and signalled for me to enter the office.

Mrs James was sitting at her desk with the two sheets of paper in front of her. 'Sit down, Elizabeth. Mrs Travers has written that you confessed to circulating this page in your maths class. Did you?'

'Yes, Mrs James.'

'Why?'

'I wanted to see you.'

'I don't understand.'

'You told us at assembly that any girl can make an appointment to see you, but I couldn't.'

'Why not?'

'They'd call me a scab.'

'Who?'

'Please. Can't I say what I came here for? You can punish me after.'

'Go ahead.'

'They say Miss Grimshaw's been fired because she's a rotten teacher. That's not fair. She makes history really interesting. I know 8 Blue got bad marks in the exam, but marks aren't everything, are they? They're just for dates and things you can learn from books. Miss Grimshaw tells us stories about real people. That's what she says history is, actually.'

Mrs James's mouth wobbled. 'You sent a picture of a naked man around your maths class so you could come and tell me this?'

'Yes, Mrs James.'

She looked at me appraisingly. 'You are to write a letter to one of the Tudor monarchs requesting clemency. Do you know what clemency means?'

'Miss Grimshaw told us.'

'Your crime was subversion. Do you know what that means?'

'Miss Grimshaw told us.'

'Bring me the letter at eight thirty tomorrow morning. You seem to have heard gossip, Elizabeth, and I am going to tell you fact. It's true Miss Grimshaw's leaving the school, but she wasn't fired, she's retiring. She has some exciting plans.'

The girls were agog to know what Mrs James had done to me. I whined about having to write a silly historical letter when we hadn't been taught any history.

Yes, I have it sorted in my mind, now. I'll do a creative piece on the significance of places: principal's office, classroom, toilets. I'll rejig the letter I wrote to Elizabeth I. I'd visualised her as Mrs James in wig, ruff and lead face powder.

I delivered the letter on the second last day of the school year. The buzz in the toilets was about the present each girl was going to give her favourite teacher. There was talk of Royal Doulton china, Waterford crystal and for Miss Barnes, even though she wasn't our teacher, funky jewellery. That evening, I didn't ask Mum for money but she'd foreseen my dilemma. She suggested I write to each of my teachers thanking them for teaching me. She had bought some apples and explained the American tradition of giving an apple to the teacher.

The next day, I arrived early and put an apple and a letter on the big desk in the classroom of each of my teachers, including Miss Grimshaw.

That lunchtime, there was another thrilled gossip session in the toilets.

'Did you see Grimshanks? She spat and spat!'

'Eeew!'

Sophie looked meaningfully at the rubbish bin. 'And guess what?'

'What?'

'The apple had a worm in it.'

'Eeew!' They gloated with disgust.

I crept into a cubicle and leant against the wall, shaking. My apple. Miss Grimshaw had eaten my apple and there was a worm in it. I'd added to the horrible things that were being done to her.

I realise now that Miss Grimshaw didn't retire, just as my father wasn't retrenched. Retirement and retrenchment are gauzy words placed over knife wounds.

Yes. I'm ready to write. Twenty-five minutes left in this exam. I can do it. I'm a fast writer.

Done! Just. Get out of here. Quickly.

'Elizabeth.'

The voice grinds me to a halt.

'Oh, hello, Miss Grimshaw.'

'I'm so glad to have this opportunity to speak to you. I still have the thank you letter you wrote at the end of Year 8.'

'Really?' I cringe at my Year 8 childishness.

'Yes. I was touched. What an imaginative way to write a letter, casting me in the role of Mary Queen of Scots. The background was historically accurate. There can be no greater tribute to a history teacher. As for the apple…'

'I'm so sorry.'

'Whatever for?'

'The worm.'

'Oh, that wasn't in your apple. I eat five or six apples a day. You'd obviously guessed they're my favourite fruit. I like to think they counteract the smell of cigarettes. The apple and the letter gave me joy on an otherwise ghastly day. Thank you.'

'That's okay.'

'Are you taking history for your HSC?'

'Modern and ancient.'

'Good. With the money I earn supervising, I intend to pay a uni student to do some research for me. I did my PhD after leaving that school and now I'm writing a book on Lady Jane Grey. You wouldn't be interested in a very short research job, would you?

'Act-ually, Miss Grimshaw, I would.'

Noisy Neighbours

My new neighbours have a wild sex life. You wouldn't think it by looking at them. With their grey hair and drab clothes, they're not the sort of people you'd expect at Potts Point. How do I know about their sex life? Well, I hear everything. Not that I listen. When the owner divided this old mansion into flats, he did it on the cheap. The walls are plasterboard.

Well, do they go at it! Morning and night and not just in the bedroom. My bathroom's next to theirs and I hear them when I'm getting ready for work. She does all the talking. He never says anything. He's saving his breath.

'Ooooh,' she moans. 'Do you like that? No, I won't stop. You want more? Turn over. I'll give you more.'

Wouldn't I like someone, a hunk, not an old guy, to say that to me!

Then he takes over and she coos, 'Don't, George! Stop it! Oh, you are bad. No more now. I'm in a hurry.'

Would I object if a hunk made me late by doing what he's doing? I don't think so.

And I wouldn't be squeamish either.

'Don't do that, George. Get your face out of there. It's disgusting!'

He's pretty vigorous by the sound of things. I've heard china smashing and books tumbling off shelves. She groans and laughs.

We say hello when we meet near the letter boxes. You wouldn't think he had it in him. He's round-shouldered and shuffles when he walks. He's probably exhausted. Her lumpy body and pudding face make you wonder what turns him on. Something does!

The thunderstorm last night really set them off. There was banging and crashing all over the place. We're in for another storm tonight. They won't have any china left. More joy to them! Yep, there's the lightning. And there go my lights. Are they off next door too? The lights, I mean. I'd better ask George and What's-her-name before they get started.

'Oh, hello.' She answers the door in her dressing gown. Pink chenille and fluffy slippers – hardly lust-provoking.

'Oh,' she trills, 'George, come here!'

What's his dressing gown like? Green tartan, I bet. I can't see. Their flat is dark. That's it! They can't see one another.

'Storms excite him,' she simpers.

I've noticed.

'If I'm not careful,' she says, 'he'll slip out and slink down the stairs.'

Playing hide and seek also turns them on?

'He's always lived in a house with a garden. He gets all worked up when he's confined.'

I don't want to hear any more.

'He's kept his habits. In the morning, he still rolls over so I can stroke his stomach.'

Too much information.

'He's old now, so he sometimes misses when he jumps on the furniture.'

She has to be kidding.

'The worst is when he drinks from the toilet.'

What!

'Have you ever known a cat to do that?'

Awards and Publications

'Last Day of Term', published in *fourW thirty New Writing Pearl*, four-Wpress, 2019.

'The Exam Supervisor, the Accountant, his PA and the Wild Young Man', shortlisted, FAW Marjorie Barnard Short Story Award 2019.

'Your Last Winter', published in *In the Depths of Winter*, Better Read Than Dead Winter Writing Competition 2018.

'Conversations, Commotion and Silence', Third Place, 2018 Trudy Graham-Julie Lewis Literary Award for Prose.

'An Artist and his Models', First Prize, FAW Eastwood/Hills Branch, 2018 Literary Competition, Short Story Section.

'A Gentleman and a Scholar', First Place, Stringybark, Dog Eat Dog Short Story Award 2017, published in *A Gentleman and a Scholar*, edited by David Vernon, 2017.

'Just Another Saturday', Commended, Peter Cowan 2017 Trudy Graham/Julie Lewis Award.

'Goodbye Atlanta GA', Commended, Peter Cowan 600 Word Short Story Competition 2017.

'Big Words', Highly Commended, FAW Eastwood/Hills Branch, Pauline Walsh Award for Short Story 2016.

'Playing Possum', Highly Commended, Peter Cowan 600 Word Short Story Competition 2016.

'Children's Hands', published in *Non Posso*, edited by David Vernon, 2015, First Prize, FAW Manly Peninsula Short Story Competition, 2009.

'The Writers' Group', Highly Commended, Hervey Bay Arts Council Adult Writing Competition 2015.

'Lemon Meringue Pie', Shortlisted, Albury City Short Story Award 2012.

'The Outcast of the *Omar El Khayam*', Commended, FAW Manly Peninsula Short Story Competition, 2012.

'Mirrors', Highly Commended, Society of Women Writers Tasmania Short Story Competition 2012.

'Mother's Day', Second Prize, FAW Manly Peninsula Short Story Competition, 2011.

'Emails in the Ether', Second Prize, FAW Manly Peninsula Short Story Competition, 2010, published in *Signatures*, Winter 2011.

'Guilt', Worthy of Mention, FAW Great Lakes Short Story Competition 2009.

'Anzac Assembly', Second Prize, *Positive Words Magazine* Short Story Competition 2009, published in *Positive Words Magazine*, August 2009.

'Noisy Neighbours', Third Prize, NSW Writers' Centre 2008 Inner City Life Competition, published in the *Village Voice Drummoyne*, Summer Edition 2008.

Acknowledgements

These stories were written over the course of my membership of the Open Genre Writers' Group at Writing NSW since 2005. I thank all members of that group for their helpful, challenging and inspiring advice. I particularly want to thank members who encouraged me at the beginning and those who have done so for many years: Pascal Adolphe, Brian Bell, Charles Cox (deceased), Sam Fahmy, Zita Fogarty, Sydney Srinivas, Lucie Stevens, Alita Tanswell, Louise Wildman, Suzanne Wohlthat and Aleit Woodward.

I also thank more recent members for their constructive critism and insights: Lorraine Bower, Matan Elul, Helen Grant, Josh Hindle, Jack Peck, Tara Wesson, Robert Yates and Zoe Karpin.

I am grateful to members of the Waratahs writers' group for their thoughtful criticism, support and mentorship: Cindy Davies, Jacques Horringa, Felicity Pulman, Vivien Wilson, Beatrice Yell and Margaret Zanardo.

To my friends Jeannette and John Baird, Chantal Gilroy and Adrian Slater, who've actively supported all my writing endeavours – *merci!*